The Chinaman Pacific & Frisco R.R. Co.

SHORT STORIES BY FRANK CHIN

The Chinaman Pacific & Frisco R.R. Co.

COFFEE HOUSE PRESS : : MINNEAPOLIS : : 1988

Acknowledgments: "Railroad Standard Time" (© 1978 by Frank Chin) first appeared in *City Lights Journal.* "The Eat and Run Midnight People" (© 1976 by Frank Chin) first appeared in a different form in *Chouteau Review.* "The Chinatown Kid" (© 1973 by Frank Chin) first appeared in *Cutting Edges.* "Yes, Young Daddy" (© 1971, 1972 by Frank Chin) first appeared in *Panache.* "Give the Enemy Sweet Sissies and Women to Infatuate Him, and Jades and Silks to Blind Him with Greed," (© 1970 by Frank Chin) first appeared with a different title and in a different form in *Carolina Quarterly.* "A Chinese Lady Dies" (© 1970 by Frank Chin) first appeared under a different title and in a different form in 19 *Necromancers from Now.* The author thanks the editors of the above publications.

This project is supported in part by The National Endowment for the Arts, a federal agency; Star Tribune/Cowles Media Company; and United Arts. The publisher also thanks Minnesota Center for Book Arts, where Coffee House has been a Visiting Press since 1985.

Coffee House Press books are available to bookstores through our primary distributor: Consortium Book Sales and Distribution, 213 East Fourth Street, Saint Paul, Minnesota 55101. Our books are also available through all major library distributors and jobbers, and through most small press distributors, including Bookpeople, Bookslinger, Inland, Pacific Pipeline, and Small Press Distribution. For personal orders, catalogs or other information, write to: Coffee House Press, Post Office Box 10870, Minneapolis, Minnesota 55458.

Library of Congress Cataloging in Publication Data
Chin, Frank, 1940-
    The Chinaman Pacific and Frisco R.R. Co.: stories / by Frank Chin.
      p. cm.
    ISBN 0-918273-44-7 (ALK. PAPER) : $9.95
    1. Chinese Americans — Fiction. I. Title.
PS3553.H4897C49 1988
813'.54 — DC19   88-30326   CIP

CONTENTS

Railroad Standard Time

"This was your grandfather's," Ma said. I was twelve, maybe fourteen years old when Grandma died. Ma put it on the table. The big railroad watch, Elgin. Nineteen-jewel movement. American made. Lever set. Stem wound. Glass facecover. Railroad standard all the way. It ticked on the table between stacks of dirty dishes and cold food. She brought me in here to the kitchen, always to the kitchen to loose her thrills and secrets, as if the sound of running water and breathing the warm soggy ghosts of stale food, floating grease, old spices, ever comforted her, as if the kitchen was a paradise for conspiracy, sanctuary for us *juk sing* Chinamen from the royalty of pure-talking China-born Chinese, old, mourning, and belching in the other rooms of my dead grandmother's last house. Here, private, to say in Chinese, "This was your grandfather's," as if now that her mother had died and she'd been up all night long, not weeping, tough and lank, making coffee and tea and little foods for the brokenhearted family in her mother's kitchen, Chinese would be easier for me to understand. As if my mother would say all the important things of the soul and blood to her son, me, only in Chinese from now on. Very few people spoke the language at me the way she did. She chanted a spell up over me that conjured the meaning of what she was saying in the shape of old memories come to call. Words I'd never heard before set me at play in familiar scenes new to me, and ancient.

She lay the watch on the table, eased it slowly off her fingertips down to the tabletop without a sound. She didn't touch me, but put it down and held her hands in front of her like a bridesmaid holding an invisible bouquet and stared at the watch. As if it were talking to her, she looked hard at it, made faces at it, and did not move or answer the voices of the old, calling her from other rooms, until I picked it up.

A two-driver, high stepping locomotive ahead of a coal tender and baggage car, on double track between two semaphores showing a stop signal was engraved on the back.

"Your grandfather collected railroad watches, Ma said. "This one is the best." I held it in one hand and then the other, hefted it, felt out the meaning of "the best," words that rang of meat and vegetables, oils, things we touched, smelled, squeezed, washed, and ate, and I turned the big cased thing over several times. "Grandma gives it to you now," she said. It was big in my hand. Gold. A little greasy. Warm.

I asked her what her father's name had been, and the manic heat of her all-night burnout seemed to go cold and congeal. "Oh," she finally said, "it's one of those Chinese names I . . ." in English, faintly from another world, woozy and her throat and nostrils full of bubbly sniffles, the solemnity of the moment gone, the watch in my hand turned to cheap with the mumbling of a few awful English words. She giggled herself down to nothing but breath and moving lips. She shuffled backward, one step at a time, fox trotting dreamily backwards, one hand dragging on the edge of the table, wobbling the table, rattling the dishes, spilling cold soup. Back down one side of the table, she dropped her butt a little with each step then muscled it back up. There were no chairs in the kitchen tonight. She knew, but still she looked. So this dance and groggy mumbling about the watch being no good, in strange English, like an Indian medicine man in a movie.

I wouldn't give it back or trade it for another out of the collection. This one was mine. No other. It had belonged to my grandfather. I wore it braking on the Southern Pacific, though it was two jewels short of new railroad standard and an outlaw watch that could get me fired. I kept it on me, arrived at my day-off courthouse wedding to its time, wore it as a railroad relic/family heirloom/grin-bringing affectation when I was writing background news in Seattle, reporting from the shadows of race riots, grabbing snaps for the 11:00 P.M., timing today's happenings with a nineteenth-century escapement. (Ride with me, Grandmother.) I was wearing it on my twenty-seventh birthday, the Saturday I came home to see my son asleep in the back of a strange station wagon, and Sarah inside, waving, shouting through an open window, "Goodbye Daddy," over and over.

I stood it. Still and expressionless as some good Chink, I watched Barbara drive off, leave me, like some blonde white goddess going home from the jungle with her leather patches and briar pipe sweetheart writer and my kids. I'll learn to be a sore loser. I'll learn to hit people in the face. I'll learn to cry when I'm hurt and go for the throat instead of being polite and worrying about being obnoxious to people walking out of my house with my things, taking my kids away. I'll be more than quiet, embarrassed. I won't be likable anymore.

I hate my novel about a Chinatown mother like mine dying, now that Ma's dead. But I'll keep it. I hated after reading *Father and Glorious Descendant, Fifth Chinese Daughter, The House That Tai Ming Built*. Books scribbled up by a sad legion of snobby autobiographical Chinatown saps all on their own. Christians who never heard of each other, hardworking people who sweat out the exact same Chinatown book, the same cunning "Confucius says" joke, just like me. I kept it then and I'll still keep it. Part cookbook, memories of Mother in the kitchen slicing meat paperthin with a cleaver. Mumbo jumbo about spices and steaming. The secret of Chinatown rice. The hands come down toward the food. The food crawls with culture. The thousand-year-old living Chinese meat makes dinner a safari into the unknown, a blood ritual. Food pornography. Black magic. Between the lines, I read a madman's detailed description of the preparation of shrunken heads. I never wrote to mean anything more than word fun with the food Grandma cooked at home. Chinese food. I read a list of what I remembered eating at my grandmother's table and knew I'd always be known by what I ate, that we come from a hungry tradition. Slop eaters following the wars on all fours. Weed cuisine and mud gravy in the shadow of corpses. We plundered the dust for fungus. Buried things. Seeds plucked out of the wind to feed a race of lace-boned skinnys, in high-school English, become transcendental Oriental art to make the dyke-ish spinster teacher cry. We always come to fake art and write the Chinatown book like bugs come to fly in the light. I hate my book now that ma's dead, but I'll keep it. I know she's not the woman I wrote up like my mother, and dead, in a book that was like everybody else's Chinatown book. Part word map of Chinatown San Francisco, shop to shop down Grant Avenue. Food again. The wind sucks the shops out and you breathe warm roast ducks dripping fat, hooks into the neck, through the head, out an eye. Stacks of iced fish, blue and fluorescent pink in the neon. The air is thin soup, sharp up the nostrils.

All mention escape from Chinatown into the movies. But we all forgot to mention how stepping off the streets into a faceful of Charlie Chaplin or a Western on a ripped and stained screen that became caught in the grip of winos breathing in unison in their sleep and billowed in and out, that shuddered when cars went by . . . we all of us Chinamans watched our own MOVIE ABOUT ME! I learned how to box watching movies shot by James Wong Howe. Cartoons were our nursery rhymes. Summers inside those neon-and-stucco downtown hole-in-the-wall Market Street Frisco movie houses blowing three solid hours of full-color seven-minute cartoons was school, was rows and rows of Chinamans learning English in a hurry from Daffy Duck.

When we ate in the dark and recited the dialogue of cartoon mice and cats out loud in various tones of voice with our mouths full, we looked like people singing hymns in church. We learned to talk like everybody in America. Learned to need to be afraid to stay alive, keep moving. We learned to run, to be cheerful losers, to take a sudden pie in the face, talk American with a lot of giggles. To us a cartoon is a desperate situation. Of the movies, cartoons were the high art of our claustrophobia. They understood us living too close to each other. How, when you're living too close to too many people, you can't wait for one thing more without losing your mind. Cartoons were a fine way out of waiting in Chinatown around the rooms. Those of our Chinamans who every now and then break a reverie with, "Thank you, Mighty Mouse," mean it. Other folks thank Porky Pig, Snuffy Smith, Woody Woodpecker.

The day my mother told me I was to stay home from Chinese school one day a week starting today, to read to my father and teach him English while he was captured in total paralysis from a vertebra in the neck on down, I stayed away from cartoons. I went to a matinee in a white neighborhood looking for the MOVIE ABOUT ME and was the only Chinaman in the house. I liked the way Peter Lorre ran along non-stop routine hysterical. I came back home with Peter Lorre. I turned out the lights in Pa's room. I put a candle on the dresser and wheeled Pa around in his chair to see me in front of the dresser mirror, reading Edgar Allen Poe out loud to him in the voice of Peter Lorre by candlelight.

The old men in the Chinatown books are all fixtures for Chinese ceremonies. All the same. Loyal filial children kowtow to the old and whiff food laid out for the dead. The dead eat the same as the living but without the sauces. White food. Steamed chicken. Rice we all remember as children scrambling down to the ground, to all fours and bonking our heads on the floor, kowtowing to a dead chicken.

My mother and aunts said nothing about the men of the family except they were weak. I like to think my grandfather was a good man. Even the kiss-ass steward service, I like to think he was tough, had a few laughs and ran off with his pockets full of engraved watches. Because I never knew him, not his name, nor anything about him, except a photograph of him as a young man with something of my mother's face in his face, and a watch chain across his vest. I kept his watch in good repair and told everyone it would pass to my son someday, until the day the boy was gone. Then I kept it like something of his he'd loved and had left behind, saving it for him maybe, to give to him when he was a man. But I haven't felt that in a long time.

The watch ticked against my heart and pounded my chest as I went too fast over bumps in the night and the radio on, on an all-night run downcoast, down country, down old Highway 99, Interstate 5, I ran my grandfather's time down past road signs that caught a gleam in my headlights and came at me out of the night with the names of forgotten high school girlfriends, BELLEVUE KIRKLAND, ROBERTA GERBER, AURORA CANBY, and sang with the radio to Jonah and Sarah in Berkeley, my Chinatown in Oakland and Frisco, to raise the dead. Ride with me, Grandfather, this is your grandson the ragmouth, called Tampax, the burned scarred boy, called Barbecue, going to San Francisco to bury my mother, your daughter, and spend Chinese New Year's at home. When we were sitting down and into our dinner after Grandma's funeral, and ate in front of the table set with white food for the dead, Ma said she wanted no white food and money burning after her funeral. Her sisters were there. Her sisters took charge of her funeral and the dinner afterwards. The dinner would most likely be in a Chinese restaurant in Frisco. Nobody had these dinners at home anymore. I wouldn't mind people having dinner at my place after my funeral, but no white food.

The whiz goes out of the tires as their roll bites into the steel grating of the Carquinez Bridge. The noise of the engine groans and echoes like a bomber in flight through the steel roadway. Light from the water far below shines through the grate, and I'm driving high, above a glow. The voice of the tires hums a shrill rubber screechy mosquito hum that vibrates through the chassis and frame of the car into my meatless butt, into my tender asshole, my pelvic bones, the roots of my teeth. Over the Carquinez Bridge to CROCKETT MARTINEZ closer to home, roll the tires of Ma's Chevy, my car now, carrying me up over the water southwest toward rolls of fog. The fat man's coming home on a sneaky breeze. Dusk comes a drooly mess of sunlight, a slobber of cheap pawnshop gold, a slow building heat across the water, all through the milky air through the glass of the window into the closed atmosphere of a driven car, into one side of my bomber's face. A bomber, flying my mother's car into the unknown charted by the stars and the radio, feels the coming of some old night song climbing hand over hand, bass notes plunking as steady and shady as reminiscence to get on my nerves one stupid beat after the other crossing the high rhythm six-step of the engine. I drive through the shadows of the bridge's steel structure all over the road. Fine day. I've been on the road for sixteen hours straight down the music of Seattle, Spokane, Salt Lake, Sacramento, Los Angeles, and Wolfman Jack lurking in odd hours of darkness, at peculiar altitudes of darkness, favoring the depths of certain Oregon valleys and heat and moonlight of my miles. And I'm still alive. Country 'n' western music for the night road. It's pure white music. Like "The Star-Spangled Banner," it was the first official American music out of school into my jingling earbones sung by sighing white big tits in front of the climbing promise of FACE and Every Good Boy Does Fine chalked on the blackboard.

She stood up singing, one hand cupped in the other as if to catch drool slipping off her lower lip. Our eyes scouted through her blouse to elastic straps, lacy stuff, circular stitching, buckles, and in the distance, finally some skin. The color of her skin spread through the stuff of her blouse like melted butter through bread nicely to our tongues and was warm there. She sat flopping them on the keyboard as she breathed, singing "Home on the Range" over her shoulder, and pounded the tune out with her palms. The lonesome prairie was nothing but her voice, some hearsay country she stood up to sing *a capella* out of her. Simple music you can count. You can hear the words clear. The music's run through Clorox and Simonized, beating so insistently right and regular that you feel to sing it will deodorize you, make you clean. The hardhat hit parade. I listen to it a lot on the road. It's that get-outta-town beat and tune that makes me go.

Mrs. Morales was her name. Aurora Morales. The music teacher us boys liked to con into singing for us. Come-on opera, we wanted from her, not them Shirley Temple tunes the girls wanted to learn, but big notes, high long ones up from the navel that drilled through plaster and steel and skin and meat for bone marrow and electric wires on one long titpopping breath.

This is how I come home, riding a mass of spasms and death throes, warm and screechy inside, itchy, full of ghostpiss, as I drive right past what's left of Oakland's dark wooden Chinatown and dark streets full of dead lettuce and trampled carrot tops, parallel all the time in line with the tracks of the Western Pacific and Southern Pacific railroads.

The Eat and Run Midnight People

I FELT THE NIGHT SEA crouch up gloomy, humpbacked under the starlight, near me a dark creature in a dark cape that moved closer to me, breathing a heavy breath full of fish and weeds, sighing a bad breath that hackled the beach, that faked the sound of distant applause, the faraway screech of a treed mountain lion echoing down the hills out of the dark nightwoods, very near my feet. And I was still and shitless stone inside the lay of its breath. The wet flash of old men's Chinatown sneezes came out of the past from the sea to paw my body with stardust and mosquitoes. I was in the way here. I was always in the way.

Warm breath was everywhere over me, coddling me like a warm smelly sticky sauce all over me, serving me up as a delicacy of the night to bloodthirsty mosquitoes that winged in fooling on the sound of ricocheting snipershots and higher, the longing shrill whiz of rubber tires peeling off a long downhill streak. I was sand-and sea-coated all over except for where I lay, pounded in the sand. I was very hot and very cold and dry on my back being beaten by the fleshy stomp and throb of the sea that beat on the shore, beat on me up out of the beach like the life of a slow, slow deepbreathing, longstroking iron steam engine chugging the planet to the stars overhead. This is my ancient ship. I am the Iron Moonhunter mounted in the cab, rigged for silent running, warm in deep space, on the move for sleep and worlds beyond. Ride with me, Grandfather. Going home, Grandfather, highballing the gate down straight rail to Oakland. Ride with me on enginemen's forever longtime hungry stomach home again and again and I will sing of us to your great-grandchildren, write them home of how fathers come passing through now and then, ghostly giants roaring iron on the mainline past their backyard, maybe on holidays,

maybe on birthdays, and round Christmastime, children, you'll
hear laughter like distant dynamite rollicking in our iron lungs,
blink like sleepy dogs whose fur old men lose their fingers in, and
hear us coming from way back then, when there were rare
children in the town and the few mothers crooned the few fathers
home out of the mountains where they slept giving rocks, snow
and iron a Chinaman soul. The mountains were bed. Clouds were
breath. The giant moonhunter awoke each morning as quietly as
he could, yawning like ships at sea, sleep-petrified muscles
stretched, bending with the sounds of trees being uprooted, joints
snapped and popped like giant popcorn, children, like weighing
anchor chains, the iron fathers rounding into your yard limits
down the mainline dead slow. As quietly as he could, yes. And
carefully leaned over his mountains, sheltering the town, in order
not to hurt your ears, children, with the terrible width, height,
depth and loudness of the fiery voice, whispered of his coming
down across valleys. With the very least of the boiling breath, the
way aunts whispered what the rare children knew meant "Good
morning, town." The voice rose birds from the bushes, lifted
eagles from their nests. They spread their wings on his voice. They
rode down the flow of the giant's whisper. The shape of his
whisper could be seen in the flutter of the treetops reaching for
the town to finally shove church bells and shake snow off fron-
tyard trees. Listen, children. Ride with me, Grandfather.

A naked forty-three-year-old ex-nun was next to me, close,
naked and wet I knew. I'd seen her, I knew later, by starlight come
out blue and gleaming, streaked with black seawater, black lips,
black tongue, black eyes gleaming in swollen black assholes,
eyeing the can of Primo in her hand, blue and gleaming like her
oily aluminum skin. A palpitating beerdrinking sea organism
thrown up out of a splash of ocean sick of her through my eyes,
undetected till after the thud at the bottom of my skull, where my
mind found her, later, after all the tasty sensation of the sight was
gone, guzzling beer and touching me with all the tacky sandy
flesh. I'd left my eyes abandoned, open to the stars and darkness
like doors in my house open for a breeze, and had no consciousness in them anymore. The visual sigh. But I knew she was in my
head, on the creep in the corridors of my snores like a prowler, and
knew how she got in unchallenged and followed her quiet way in-

side, upsetting the balanced quiet of a house that had had my kids in it, and me. I was still, as she lay next to me, still again as she put a smelly damp sandy hand under my shirt, on my chest, and still again as she moved her hand back and forth, flat, round and round my breast, sanding off a nipple. She breathed in my ear, put her tongue inside, dribbled beer off her kiss roaring inside my head and I was still again.

I'd seen *North to Alaska* for laughs and waited in hibernation to see it again on her color TV. On restroom walls of Chinese restaurants and a few selected gas stations all over the American continent I'd passed my piss reading warnings against Chinamans watching too much TV on Maui. At the Greasy Chop Suey in Wailuku, the quarter-blooded Chinese cook said it was no good here for Chinese-blooded people to watch TV. Though Chinamans in Honolulu saw the exact same programming, these same Honolulu-beamed shows got charged with something sinister going through the Maui relay stations and waited, he said, they waited for a Chinaman to turn them on.

I told him I couldn't help it. TV movies were in my blood; I had to go after them from Sunrise Cinema to the end of the broadcast day. On Maui my day to day was such that all that kept me going was the afterlife I could give old times and choruses of dead extras and tap dancers by turning them on and letting the waves blurt into my room. I told him I rode the waves away from Maui. "To the city, Old Man Hong." Then I told him I would live forever too. For I have insinuated myself in the crowd scenes of movies that star stars whose movies will be seen on TV forever. I counted on seeing *North to Alaska* tonight. I wanted to see a movie to take me far from Hawaii. No beach. No palm trees. No ocean all around. The ex-nun made it important to me, urgent to my well-being on this island. In the movie about me, I'm in a war far from home, a straggler, out to kill at last, and happy enough about it to be corny, to make light of shoving my thighs through rancid water further into enemy-infested darkness. I am silence, the phantom-soldier of the water, carrying a loaded M-1 rifle with a bayonet on the end of it. I am John Ireland in *Salerno Beachhead,* brave music to myself on patrol, easygoing with all the safeties off every sense, and tuned high on the make for danger through the chatter of letters and stories being written home in my head while I watch out!

No more news and soul-searching hard words, soft words, bad words on Chinese America for me. And she asks me during a video seizure of situation comedies what it feels like. She's been locked up all her life and never saw anything like me before. From way down in comfort I tell her being a Chinaman's okay if you love having been outlaw-born and raised to eat and run in your mother country like a virus staying a step ahead of a cure and can live that way, fine. And that is us! Eat and run midnight people, outward bound. Chinaman from the Cantonese, yeah, I tell her, we were the badasses of China, the barbarians, far away from the high culture of the North where they look down on us southerners because we do not have the noble nose, because we are darker complected, because we live hunched over, up to our wrists in the dirt sending our fingers underground grubbing after eats. We were the dregs, the bandits, the killers, the get out of town eat and run folks, hungry all the time eating after looking for food. Murderers and sailors. Rebel yellers and hardcore cooks. Our culture is our cuisine. There are no cats in Chinatown. Up North they had time to wait for the mellowing of the wine. They cooked with a lot of wine, a lot of vinegar. Us, it is three-day quick whiskey and fast rice wine. We eat toejam, bugs, leaves, seeds, birds, bird nests, treebark, trunks, fungus, rot, roots, and smut and are always on the move, fingering the ground, on the forage, embalming food in leaves and seeds, on the way, for the part of the trip when all we'll have to eat on the way will be mummies, and all the time eating anything that can be torn apart and put in the mouth, looking for new food to make up enough to eat. Up north they used all kinds of grains and fancy goodies, while everything with us was the rice of long wars and bad ground. Rice. Rice. Rice. Rice flour, rice noodles, rice rice, rice paste, burnt rice boiled out of the pot for dessert and ricewater to wash it down. I'm proud to say my ancestors did not invent gunpowder but stole it. If they had invented gunpowder, they would have eaten it up sure, and never borne this hungry son of a Chinaman to run. In that tradition, the first things I learned to read were cereal boxes, bread wrappers, and coffee cans. During the war against the Axis, they made good reading.

"*North to Alaska* tonight! On JOHN WAYNE MOVIE TIME!" I heard from the house, clearly, as if the sea had dried up. Then there was a surprise of beer filling my mouth up to the backs of my teeth and laughter outside, maddening me scared back to the Fourth of July I drowned under my father's grin, and wide awake flashed on me, breathing beer, swallowing it, spitting it, shooting foaming beer out of my nostrils like slow lightning, backing it up into the chambers of my ears. My kids! I am Daddy! And she was laughing, raising sand. "Your mouth was open," she said. "You looked so funny, like a joke about catching flies. And I was lonely." The discovery of loneliness liberated her from her vaulted life of a bride of Christ. Sand was thick on the wet trails of beer and snot out of my nostrils, down my upper lip, chest, and belly. I look about for John Wayne Movie Time. "You looked too sexy!" Lily said. Her name was Lily. "And I couldn't stand it." The breath of her speaking bounced like beachballs off my face. The vibrations of her voice rained straight into the openings of my skull hard to hear above the battering of thirty-two pistons from out of the past hauling ironass home to the crazy and the kids out of the dark from Roseville, home, Grandfather, singing at me out of the steel of a bridge I crossed in high cold daylight. My grabeyes snapped the sight of her flashing between the girders as she dove. A long look that hit straight down on her back, her arms out like wings as we passed still sticks to my eyes. I never saw her splash.

"No, you don't," I said and barely heard myself through the slap and flop of her tongue beating wet against the walls round my ear like something slimy was being born in there. Her tongue seemed to have little suckered feet on it popping and squeaking footsteps inside down the interior of my ear. I did not close my eyes against her tongue, or raise my hands or say a word of stop. Her hands were damp from the sea, from holding cold sweating beer cans, from spilled beer. She was crusted with sand all over and gasping as if the sand were choking her. "You have no children, yeah?" she said, inside my ear, clouding her breath in, and I heard boulders roll aside and close in her throat, roll and knead the doughy steamy humid green weather of the lost world inside her into words that broke like storms in my head. I heard prehistoric crocodiles chomping in swamps, big lizards uprooting trees, the b-17 bomber in the movie about me lost in the fog conking out and diving inside her. "I have two children. A boy and a girl. Named after my best friend and his wife."

"Oh."

"I remember they sang 'I've Been Working on the Railroad' to me in their pajamas one night, when I came home tired from work."

"On the railroad, yeah?"

"Yeah, on the railroad."

"That was nice, yeah?"

"Yeah, it was nice."

"Yeah."

"But I didn't like it."

"Does it make you sad, yeah?"

"Yeah," I said.

"Yeah." She did not ask their names. If she asked, I knew I would tell her and I did not want to. I waited for her to ask. When she reached down for my prick and began to sand it, I knew she would not ask, that our talk was finally over.

All I could think of without going crazy, crying, beating fists, screaming all kinds of false alarms was getting back in the house for *North to Alaska* coming on the tube in twenty minutes without letting myself go, so stalling for time, I rolled over onto her sandy breasts, her sandy belly, her sandy thighs, and stuck it in. Like an old old man, I was vaguely pleased that it got up and felt the behavior of the flesh was strange. Inside her twat was like I was mixing concrete. It was wet cement and sand inside there. I moved back and then I moved in, in cold blood, in and out, fascinated with the motion, pistoning grit, digging an escape tunnel out of camp, banging down the right of way, going home, Grandfather. This is my ancient ship. The Iron Moonhunter is out of the devil's roundhouse, called out to roll a Chinaman Special down the mainline home, out of the mountains of night, children, lifting eagles out of their nests with the flow of its voice, home. The sand gave way under my knees on each stroke. I was slowly digging a hole under her butt with my knees. I grunted while I fucked. Fucked and grunted, beating up a railroad song to make sense of this Hawaii. The angle of my stroke changed slightly on each push forward and drove her crazy. She grabbed me and rubbed sand into my mosquito bites. She had sand in her cunt. I couldn't close my eyes. Keeping my eyes open kept the pain out. She moaned and groaned and poured Primo beer down her belly to wash my prick off on the outstroke. She told me it felt good, hummed "I've Been Working on the Railroad" when I struck a steady rhythm and broke the tune up with chortling and backslapping, keeping me awake, walking in place deeper into a hole, wondering into her beer-and-bennie ecstasy if she knew what she meant to me and if she was something ugly and mean doing me this way on purpose. I was falling into the hole I was digging and kneeling in it to stay inside her. I held her up with her thighs stuffed in my armpits and kept moving, anything for her not to ask the names of my children or talk to me, and leave me close to home.

My ear was against her cheek. Her breathing grew out of the sea. Her body, the moon, the beach, breath, splash, sea heaving through the sand, her body all one, grinding in my euphoric hunger pangs. Through her body stamped into the sand like a big foot, bone-jarring sea smash and snake song broke into seams and hollows of my skull, rattled and screeched there as in seashell, an abandoned cathedral, infested with rats, a deep cave, and echoed. My skull was high, cold, outer space full of ethereal singing far away, miles and oceans above my grumbling snarling stomach wringing itself out after food. A deep hysterical silence was pumping my blood up. I heard the same echoes shimmering inside her head. We were corpses skull to skull, full of worms, adjoining buildings in an earthquake. Bats in the upper hollows. Wrestlers grunted and smacked the floor with their bodies. Footsteps click out of the dark of a long corridor. Exploding war all around. All around sizzling meat. I heard the rumble before maniacal laughter. I yelled against her into the sand, lost my voice in the loudness of the noise gathering in my head. Something coming, I heard, too late to get out of the way. I'm always in the way. I felt the strength of my shouting in the tension of my chest and shoulders. Lots of muscles in my voice. I felt it work into her jawbones, break the harmonic codes of her face, loosen all the joints in her head, and vibrate her teeth to pains that thrilled straight to her cunt. Her cunt clutched me like a baseball bat. My head ached, throbbed, thumped the elephant step rhythm for the chorus of headaching echoes building in my head. Echoes of my knees pounding sand, her buttocks flopping down, of my thighs rushing through space toward sand before she repeated, "Fuck me!" again in a moist whisper. And I fucked her. I ran it in a long time, panting behind my dong, exploring the terrible length of her cavernous sigh with it, pushing toward the source of her heat. Going and going with my thing, I walked it in with my toes, my knees, pointing it into the sound of a stove cooking up a feast. Her ribs caved in. Her breasts changed shape. I was traveling to the ends of her breath. I drooled on her neck. Highballing deep into the night until her tightening grip round her can of beer crumpled it as her lips puckered and her breath went shrill dizzying me and I heard from far off, in the sound of faint wheels rolling in her breath, in ancient history, a well-fed little beautiful, flying off that Great Northern freight end over end, me! Making the stillness whistle off the shells of my ears with my speed, a little before dawn in Seattle. I was coming down. I would crack my skull, break my elbow, pass out and bleed awhile.

Before the sun has risen in the sky above the dark boxcars, above the dark shape of West Queen Anne Hill, the air glows deep, empty, cloudless, blue-white like polished sheet steel. It turns hard in the boy's eyes, children, makes tears bright with red rainbow flame and is at once deep and impenetrable.

Up. Up. And away. I used to ride. The first Chinaman to brake on the Southern Pacific line.

He stared too long with an urgency of expectation into the sky, as if he felt distant thunder in his bones or heard old World War Two P-38's inside a gust of wind tell their distance and approach softly in his ear. I was up in the air, off the train. Freer than I'd ever been.

Ride. We'd get the call that our train was ready for us to take out of town, and something would happen inside. I'd stand up wide awake, swallowing a mouthful of new drool down into coffee, on my way out, bluffing. Nothing but bluff. Bluff tall. Bluff muscular. Bluff mean brakeman going to his train. I felt sure that I'd forgotten something. You get the call, get your orders, are told the train is yours. You pick up your gear, your lantern, and step outside into a low flat world of heavy iron and steel, and again as it was the very first time, it is John Wayne stepping outside and turning a piece of the outdoors into the goddamned Old West. His West. You take possession, walk with your hands out of your pockets ready for danger. Only bums and hoboes, men in no hurry, going nowhere, can afford to pocket their cold hands. I walked knowing that I'd been sung about, that this ground, the rails and crossties, whistles, bells, switches, wheels, lights, and me messing with all that had fattened up many jukeboxes, kept people guzzling up beer late at night, made sweaty folks dance with their eyes closed. I knew most of the songs. Between us, any two or three railroad men knew all them songs. We were itchy with the reverberations of all those songs going off at once as we walked across roadbed and track to the train that was ours. I felt them humming in my bones, coming down. Damn that boy! I'll teach him to fight back. I'll throw him from the train, shake those songs out of him once and for all.

At a certain time of morning all railyards come to this moment of peculiar quiet, of muttering dark iron, locomotives going nowhere at all. All dark. Iron. Painted steel. Shadows. All the same blackness. All hold the night, while far above, the sky is bare white and throbbing, without a sun or moon.

This time of morning has no name. No rulebook name. No railroad nickname. It just comes every day, children. It is a kind of no-time, when the mudhops are no longer between tracks of boxcars writing road initials and numbers down on lists, and no trains are arriving or leaving. Everything becomes cold and old in this hour. Here in the Great Northern Interbay yards in Seattle, the three Western Pacific yards in Oakland, the Southern Pacific yards, it is all the same bright moonless sunless light right now. Some slick freak train delivered the boy here and left him in the air. If he were to see an old Santa Fe troop train now, he would not be surprised. This was the hour animals would not howl, the ghost time famous for flashlights going dud, matches scratching up no flame, visions coming on lone men caught in the open. A shifty empty-house quiet here. The breeze like a woman breathing in her sleep all around. Dogs stop in their tracks and shiver for no reason at all. An eagle soaring down the voice of the Iron Moonhunter, the vengeance train, a Chinaman Special on a special ghost run in the mountains or an old troop train coasting down the mainline would be no surprise. He'd know he was a boy. But unlike the boy he was, he'd know he would grow up and work around trains and someday on trains. His wife and kids would park by the tracks and wave at him high in the locomotive, and he'd wave back.

"Oh," she said. Her arm came up from the sand around my neck and clamped my head to hers while she finished her beer. She hummed and beat on the backs of my legs with her knees to keep me going. I felt the musculature of each of her swallows work against my body. I breathed beer into my hunger. My blood had turned to thin gas. I smelled chicken pie burning in the oven. "That feels so good," she said. "Shuddup!" I said. "Don't talk to me!" I heard the can thump into the beach down the darkness. "All the way in," she said. "Come on."

I'd see a green light on our track. "Green," I'd say. "Green," the hoghead said, and "Here we go." The loudness of our four locomotives in the hoghead's hands increased and we sat down heavily into the gathering density of sound, the rising pitch of vibrations and concussive thunders that reached right through the flesh and clutched the heart and deeper into the valves of the heart, the lips of the valves. Before actual movement I felt the strength of the engines grab and in that instant no one spoke. I leaned slightly, poised my body on the cresting powerful motionlessness that was beyond my control now, that would break into movement carrying me away no matter what. The first movement, slight, terrific, continuing, rocked my head slightly back on my spine. Through the floor, into my bones, came the bone-brightening sound of all them songs of lonesome whistles, riders of thunder, dynamite breathers scorched with speed and the twang of the wheels beginning to move. They squeaked on the dry polish of the rails. More. I'm moving. Being moved. More muscle had to be put into my relaxation. The racket of the engines had settled into my flesh, my muscle, all of me and become the sounds of me being alive. The sound of slack being taken up car by car, steel joint by steel joint, was heard crashing at my back, the crash and tug of the first car and each afterward echoed in the muscles of my back, a sudden blossoming of a dark heat up my spine and fading into the muscles of my shoulders and neck more lightly again and a hundred times again. Listen, children. I was riding. I would come home to motion, my grandfather.

An old mudhop, a thumbless former brakeman and sneaky drinker was my friend, and told me: "I was brakin for, why it musta been the I.C. Yeah, sure, it was that Illinois Central and there was this little fella, a switchman, Shannon was his name. Tough little bastard, made out of chicken gizzards and spit, he was. Whore spit. He was, too. Well, I'll be damned if he don't go and get himself coupled up. I mean coupled up. Couldn't tell him nothin for his good what he didn't take just the opposite on ya. But he had a looker for a wife. At least in those days she was a looker. Can't remember what the hell she looked like anymore. Except like a doll, small, all of her at once, her back. That's all. Old, you know. But that's why we liked him cuz he told us how his wife couldn't be trusted with any friend of his, and how many times he come home to find her in bed with one. So, you know, we all figured he should have plenty of friends. Well, there was this car. Knuckles didn't line up and wouldn't couple up. So he starts trying to move the couple over by himself and he pushes and pushes on it and then steps between the two couplings, you know, to try pulling on it from the other side. Well, he no sooner steps square between 'em then it comes around and at the same time, simultaneously you might say, the slack lets out of the cut of cars and he's coupled up. An hour later and he's still ticking away all right, cussing and making speeches while the police and doctors try to figure out how to loose him. His wife comes down and she must have spent three or four hours confessin this and that, namin names while he eats a ham sandwich and complains about the coffee bein cold. Well, finally they decide to try uncoupling the cars. Just for a lettle momentito as them couplings come apart you could see him, how he was, pinched you know. God! He died sudden. Just fell apart. Like a dam breaking: blood! Well, I quit right there! I tell you, I got drunk. I didn't care where the hell I was, no sir, I just quit and got drunk and this guy me and my pardner have been drinking with suddenly slaps his forehead and says, 'My God! I've got a funeral in three hours, and she's not ready!' Then he asks us how'd we like to help him prepare the body. Seems he was the town undertaker as well as town drunk. He seemed like a nice enough fella too, and said he'd give us fifty, well maybe not fifty but a lot of money for them days anyhow, and stake us to drinks for the rest of the night after the funeral was over. So I think I'm drunk enough to take on a one-eyed baldhead clubfoot of a whore anyway and enjoy it and I say we go, and we go. It was like a hospital butchershop icebox all at once. You walked down into it like. And there she was and he puts a hole in her vein under her armpit.

A not-bad looker, I'd say. And he hands me this thing that looks like a flysprayer, a can with a pump on it, and sticks its point (it had a needle to it) and stuck it in her navel. I sure thought that was interesting. And tells me to start pumping. Well, I was pumping embalming fluid in one end and the fluid forced the blood out the hole he'd made in her. In her armpit you know. Well, there I am a born pumper, pumping away with that pump and raising a stink too. And I start looking around the place, what the hell? Sure, you know, I was a young feller like you, all piss and vinegar and useless as tits on a ham sandwich, but don't count me out yet, no sir. I may not be able to cut the mustard, but you bet I can still lick the jar. Well, I'll be damned if I don't start wondering if I'm not become cured of el borracho, the old family dipsomania, which was bad thinking. Because stone cold sobriety is on me like white on rice, as they say, and whatshisname the undertaker, seeing my intentions to leave, must have poured a case of whiskey into me. A noble effort, prima facie noble effort, but I'm not drunk. And I know I have to be drunk to stay in this place. And, rat's ass, if it ain't snowin outside when I'm finally done. Lotta good that did me though. A check. Not a sou markee of dinero as they say and no coat too. And sober. Well, the only person I knew in this town was Shannon, meaning now, Shannon's widow, of course. Yeah. And when I tell you I went in there smelling dead drunk and looking the part. Dead and drunk. Blue blazes, cold turkey whiskey reeking and formaldahyde. I got a little careless when I sobered up there. You would too. And well, that must've been the goddamndest day in my whole life up to then at least, but that night! That night! I learned once and for all that I am rotten to the core. And she was too. Well, after we proved that, to get the smell of, well all the smells, to, as they say, come clean, we went swimming bareass naked in the middle of a blizzard. That is she did. We went out on this trestle, an old wooden one, and took our clothes off. Sure. And she dove off the damn thing. Neatest swan dive I ever saw. I looked down on her back. Goddamn that was pretty to see. It was like a doll, the shoulder blades and entire backbone. ... them butts. All of God's work in one blink of an eye right there. Oh, I'll remember that sight all right. But I put my clothes back on and went back to her place and signed the undertaker's check over to her in trade, you see, for money I found around the house. Goddamn! her arms were out so, just so, and her hair. I kick myself in the ass everytime. I never saw her splash either. Snow in my eye or something. I blinked. And then it was like she'd never been. Not a ripple. Damn! I bet it was pretty. Damn!"

A flight of pigeons flies up out of the mass of boxcars. The high steel eye-hardening light from the sky plays on the backs of their flight. Iridescent greens, lilacs, colors following their own movement, the electric colors that make slime look alive and certain jewels deep with mystery emerge out of the grey of their feathers.

I ate nothing but breakfasts all day. The dispatcher'd call me out of the dark and away from her, past the sound of the kids breathing somewhere near me not too deep in the dark. Barefoot I'd peel some steps off the cold linoleum to the front door, then sit on the scuff mat, put on my thick socks, string up my steel reinforced boots, wind my watch, then leave for breakfast in a diner near the yard among whores. At eight the trip over and hungry. Everybody's breakfasting it up, so breakfast before bed. Wake up to the call and another breakfast because that's what I eat first out of bed. Breakfast again before the trip home to the kids. I was out of town or asleep all the time they were awake. I worried about them recognizing me, on my way home, riding. Once when I came home in the dark, Barbara brought them into my room in their pajamas. They scuffled in, dazed. They blearily sang and whined, "I've Been Workin on the Railroad" to me while I unlaced my boots. "They love you," she said. "You shouldn't have made them learn that dumb song and then get them out of bed to sing it," I said. "I thought it would make you happy," she said. I said, "Thanks," tired. She went back to her room where the phone wouldn't wake her.

In this space, this quiet and time of morning, this stillness governed by the internal motion of great engines standing still, the flight of pigeons seems an event. There's no need to make sense of them and everything here. It seems he should hear them. Higher, wings curved, beating down, cupping the air, higher, gathering themselves upward into the fall of light, they turn sidewise, backs to the coming dawn, bellies to the boy. And the spread wings, the light silent strong feathers of the wings are alive with captured light. And still there is nothing heard of them. Their flight is somehow incomplete. Something else is coming. It is too late to get out of the way.

We were running straight track through noon making good time at sixty miles an hour. The tops of the tall dried summer grass were white. Shadows rippled through them. Shadows of clouds and our train. "I don't like that electric stuff on a toilet," the hoghead said. "It hums." He wouldn't use the electric toilet in the short hood of the engine. "If I gotta piss, I just stand in the doorway and piss outside," he said and did it, stood up from the controls, opened the door and stood in the doorway. He used his shoulders, elbows, and feet to wedge himself in place, and looked to the side, watching the thrust and arc and break of his stream of golden urine, past backyards, women hanging up wash, admired it standing long and whole parallel to the ground and train, a line of piss suspended in time and space by the speed. The engine rocked side to side and this affected the shape of his urine, gave it a little bend and crook. Between his legs and between his bulk and the wall of the cab, my eyes grabbed up cows, distant farmhouses, far mountains. The engines changed sound as we came out of the hills out onto a bridge, and he still pissed, sixty miles an hour. We crossed the motion of a diving girl. I grabbed fast, caught her several times in my eyes and she now becomes seen, her body between the flash of black girders, ahead of us poised for the spring, then in the air and climbing, her body arched and the sun on the tautness of her body as we were upon her, above her. I looked down on her back, saw out of the interior of thunder to her body descending toward the water. I stuck my head out the window. My neck tingled with each swish of passing girder. Each instance of shadow cut my head off as I looked for her out beyond the flash of our wheels. And saw her once. Fixed above the water. Small. I never saw her splash. I looked out the window on the hoghead's side. Only the end of the hoghead's ribbon of piss breaking up. I wonder how many bodies of engineers, heads bent down and to the right, the tips of the index fingers and thumbs of both hands lightly hoisting a penis, have been found by the side of the tracks, thawed out after winter, near barnyards or anywhere. In every engine I rode there was the possibility that I would become the intelligence of its thrusting tons. I felt like pushing the man out, let him fall out of a train with his pecker out, and leave me alone up here, at the head end of sixty miles an hour.

"Oh," she said on each closed stroke. "Oh."

A cut of cars stopped when, he doesn't know, and long gone with its engine released one car he hears drifting down the track now. The hollow ping of the wheels breaking up small stones that have been thrown on the track by the speed of other wheels, the click click of slick rolling steel across the joints between lengths of rail, though they haven't been heard so close by in a long time, are incomplete in their effect. The sounds of the railyard don't compose music. Listen, children. Grab eyes. Men pissin in sinks — ridin down breakfasts . . . that was us.

It seems, to hear the flutter of pigeon wings, the squeaking hinges of pigeons working flight would make music of these noises. Something must be wrong with him. And still I wasn't done, not all in. I'd shoved her out of breath out of voice into a dead faint and was still shoving, into her dizzy. I must have been funny off the train, a whirling ball, funnybook heap of fast feet and raggedy hands, nothing but hands and feet whoosh off that train with the goat painted on the sides. I made the air whistle with my speed. And I was still going in, easy, watching a mile long of me wind in and disappear into ooh baby, instead of yelling at that stupid flying boy, though I knew I'd come down again. I had the hurt waiting ready for my arrival home. I heard it in the smashing of the sea running out of the pores of her flesh, the big crashes ventriloquized out of her head, something out of the past passing the creeps through her yelling skull into mine. A kind of kiss smacking across deep centuries. A kind of memory of a smile, making me smile. I would fall. I would come down. I had come down before, heard it in my head, felt my hands go numb and cold in the ends of my arms before I was out. I knew I would come down. Nothing could stop me. I was perfecting that moment here. I held onto her. We were slipping into the hole. Sweating. Sand climbed my body like meteors slamming into a molten virgin planet. I felt them all and fucked in a runaway wild engine indifference, digging a hole under us, running from the crash of an idiot Chinatown brakeman about to come down hard off a running freight, some time ago, before my kids were gone, before other screams and collisions that sung in me now, making me rich with fear like aged cheese. I was older this time down. Happier, more miserable, angrier. On an island without real trains, or great highways. And afraid this time. I would take fear into my throat, my breath, I'd take it into me and let it have me like outlawed wine, let it occupy me organ by organ, grow fat on me, mother me, make me a monster. Then I'd let it out from time to time. In front of friends, women, strangers whose looks I didn't like. The sea, snuffling the beast of night, I was breathing up sounds I had heard sitting in an idling locomotive ready to go, but softer, it broke again, hissed and broke again into wreckage. I heard my wreckage falling home to the roadbed and the hollow ringing rolls of big steel wheeling past me, polishing across me, beyond me, humming a mile away all around carrying my hearing across the iron valley, thin sound down to the merest thunder shuddering in the flesh. Listen, children, I've picked up distant thunder like a radio ever since, been blood kin to dark storms and bad weather. I heard the sea become wreckage. She screamed. I heard myself diminishing in her scream, voyaging deep into the vastness of her heavy fluttering breath after its source. Toes, feet, hands, fingertips avalanched on me and my knees buckled. She poured beer down my spine and screamed. I was still stroking. Ride with me, Grandfather. Her twat was feeding on me. It gnawed on me with fat lips, bone gums, bombardments of marshmallows, rosy slugs, swelling dough. The beer down my spine killed everything of me but my prick. The prick that grew bigger than New York and nudged the moon in outer space was loose. I lost all sense of breathing, of being alive. I couldn't locate my hands, my eyes, my lungs, any part of my body in here. I'd been shanghaied by my monster dong that was rocketing me away with one long hysterical streamline sensation toward parts unknown. I was the great rider, Jonah in the whale, a load of shot in my dad's primed hardon pumping grease out of Ma's little cunt that night in a backyard chickencoop, in Chinatown, Oakland, California.

The Chinatown Kid

A TINY CHAMELEON climbed up the throat to his Adam's apple, became a reed for his whistling breath, excited his teeth, excited the
moisture in his mouth, then danced in the glue lining his throat a
moment before being coughed up to the back of his tongue and
swallowed. The skin was diaphanous; he knew his skin, was per-
sonally acquainted with his skin, but real. Nature's insulation.
The skin was diaphanous, a seamless nylon stocking hardly
muting the pink veins swelling and collapsing from the pressure
of muscles whose shadows appeared through the skin like
glimpses of chameleons swimming through cloudy water. In the
dark no one would mistake capillaries in whole networks blossoming red and pink, grey and coffee-colored hallucinations of movement through his skin for a mood. No one would put a hand on
his shoulder and ask him about his feelings, while their eyes in-
sidiously tried to read him as if he were a thermometer. No jokes
about the color of his skin turning Mexican as if the ghost of his
dead Mexican wife swelled through his flesh to press and gasp for
vengeful rebirth against skin when he was angry. He was never
angry. He was never angry. No one lived in his skin. But, perhaps
his skin did stain or perhaps the eyes of the people wanted a mood
in him stained; their eyes colored from having so little to see in
him; the sight of cheeks trembling from a satisfying sigh became
an indication of rabies. His skin colorless in the dark. Nude breathing face like a woman taking the air with all her clothes off. All
touch. All heat. And nobody. Not any kind of voice in this room
playing games with a dead Mexican who had died in childbirth in
vain, thinking a child, their child, would be irresistible fruit, the
binding force between the proud descendants of Montezuma
and Kung Fu Tze. Some Colorado jade and Chinese gold bought
for twenty-five dollars on Grant Street in 1948 and pinned on the
costume of a corpse. A stick of burning joss and her other golden

crucifix. No idea of heaven for a Mexican married to a Chinaman, no magic in the incense or out of the photograph of a bride and groom, but something to buy, something to smell and watch, something to do to unload a death off his shoulders as he had rocked and sung one Chinese lullaby to a daughter. What would she think of the name he had given her, when she grew older, he wondered. All touch. All heat. The eyes, thank God, rioting futilely, withering in the darkness not designed for touch and useless. All touch, all heat, all sound, he closed the distance toward his daughter's sleeping, instinctively knowing where her head lay.

Colorless, moodless, he was unmistakably the shape of a concerned mother chasing after the sound of a child who had shrieked. Still a baby, only larger. No more diapers to change, but still the occurrence of the ripe odor of urine now and then. Still organizing sounds she made into what he told her was language. In what nameless colors, what forms and shapes, in what language did tensed flesh dream? How does the sound of your voice comfort a growling dog?

A blue hint of light and the louder sound of hissing and clicking and the sensation of warmth was her head, was her oily Mexican hair, her mongrel eyes neither Oriental nor Mexican, her flat baby's nose, hardly perceptible cheeks with a prophecy of highness, all dark, four-year-old young, aging quality whiskey of sleeping unpredictable girl. He loved her. She was loved by ghosts. He was not her mother's angel. He was not ghostlike or even dead. A few inches from her face, his eyes fearing claws, his nose slightly more daring touching her cheek without her feeling, he longed for her to be his flesh, to live within him more his, longed more than he would for an arm torn from his body by animals. "Hyacinth." The darkness and silence quieted him, urged his voice back into the realm of juicy chameleons. He was no ghost. "Hyacinth, you were groaning. You screamed, dear." Chinese, the only language he could command in a whisper. Did she dream in Chinese? He licked his fingers and smoothed her hair. His little auxiliary engine. His own iron lung.

"You crying, Hyacinth?" His nose collided with her cheek gently. Darkness married into darkness, fur to fur. A trace of moisture on his nose. "Are you all right now?" softly to not wake her. His voice the sound of mad butterflies beating themselves to pulp within his lungs, the sound of flesh hammered into a voice through the ancient plumbing of his throat. Softly imitating softness, a night animal stalking, trying to insinuate himself into her sleep. He held her, squeezed her body against his with remnants of strength and felt her slipping away, fading into another element the longer, the tighter he held her. Pete shunning himself like the rest of his family. A thief of a man believing thieving a slight pleasure from his own innocent daughter like a man siphoning gas from a car feeling watched. The darkness, the night was his smile, an echo of when he had been a dinosaur, the Chinatown Kid in this same suit that had been in fashion then, starchily sitting down in a pose with his cigarette, his wide lapels, hat worn indoors and hands with femininely long fingers. Naked fingers like miniature showgirl's legs. Hands as menacing as loose crabs touching his throat as he spoke. And gentle. Gentle, controlling himself, his switchblade spring-steel dinosaur body because he felt graceful leashing what he thought was malevolent power, felt an accumulation of sensation in being so much of a man doing nothing, being an apparition of ease, gentleness, sincerity. "If you marry her," his sister had said, "we won't be able to bear seeing you all the time." His hands played with walnuts with increasing noisiness, an irritant against the silence of his sister's sleeping daughters. "Are you angry with me, brother?" She smiled sheepishly, her eyes behind the thick lenses changing size, clear, ever staring like the eyes of a doll seemingly held open with weights. Yet the eyes focused, worked with a curious energy of their own, making her face always in subtle motion, always moving from one pretty arrangement of cheeks, shadows, lips, and winking nostrils to another. Their eyes were a matched set, he knew, except hers were weak and had been destroyed by her zeal to support and encourage a young Chinese optometrist rather than any natural erosion. He shut his eyes, her eyes, hid them under flaps of muscle and skin because she expected him to weep. "Say something, brother," his sister had said. "Please." She's pleading, he thought, and allowed the plea to fade into nothing and breathed himself impregnable calm behind his eyelids.

"Well?" he said in loud English. "Dat're dat." He stopped speaking immediately.

"You," his sister said, "come by on the family days now and then. I don't want to drive you out of the family. We shouldn't do that . . ."

"We?"

"I'm thinking of the children," she said, "Rose, Minnie . . . the girls, ah-Pete."

"Yes," in Chinese, a grunt, "the girls."

"Will you stay here?"

"No," Pete said. "I'll go right now. Let me finish my tea."

His sister chuckled and touched him. He faded from the spot where she touched, looked curiously at her fingertips on his hand and left it on the table. "I meant — you can stay as long as you want, ah-Pete, of course — after. I meant after you get married, will you stay in Oakland?" Her hand unconsciously performed artificial respiration, fingering a dead crab, and occupied his interest a moment. He was utterly dissatisfied. Alert. Bored. His left hand with a cigarette between the index and middle finger moved mechanically toward his face and pressed its thumb against his forehead, pushed the brim of his hat back and rested fingertips into his hair. The hand, like a pitiful half-lifeless woman come to comfort, come to touch him and feel generally useful about a tired man, massaged his brow, aroused an illusion of being cooed at, and him — sickened, listless — being performed upon like a piece of dough.

Still blinding himself, deafening himself against the lingering sister pleasantly groping with her pleasant breath into his guts, groping and coaxing him to say something to her, he married the Mexican woman. He wanted to see Maria happy, to ease the grip of boredom and death on him. With faulty decayed muscles and the weight of tastelessly taken food grinning the taste of his own liver into his flesh, he assembled a smile, set in motion a mimicry of the Chinatown Kid's walk and was not obviously — even to himself — certain of failure, half believing Maria's faith in their joint future. Mexicans would be happy, and he, at least could observe. The minister, a friend of hers, a Mexican Protestant wasn't obviously unhappy, Pete saw. They spent two days before their marriage in the minister's house. His wife — the image of a glamorous woman melted and bent by a funhouse mirror — visited her husband, tantalized him with a false reunion, in the end came only to see her childhood friend marry a lanky Chinaman. The minor and petty noises of the minister trying to talk inconspicuously with pet names and obvious references to their mutual secrets were overwhelmed by the woman's spectacular presence. She was forever on stage, singing opera, her huge voice gobbling up the minister's thin-bodied endearments like the shadow of an elephant lost in a solar eclipse. She made sandwiches for lunch. Her pearls dangled onto each mayonnaised slice of bread. She acted like she was at home. The minister acted like she was at home. She and the minister nodded at each other and smiled as they bumped each other walking around the table picking up a cup here, a soiled plate there, becoming more absent-minded as they wore on through washing dishes together and laughed at the minister wearing an apron. At night the minister's wife sang opera. The minister smiled and swallowed a great deal, awkwardly listened for a pleasant word from his wife, hoping she listened, and praised her singing, no matter she didn't listen, and she had no pleasant word. He told Pete and Maria that his wife had a great career ahead of her, that she had a theatrical agent and her own studio where she spent most of her time singing and sharpening her art. He smiled after not having exactly lied and sat heavily, absolutely finished and transparent. Everyone knew what they weren't talking about.

Finally the wedding in a converted grocery store. Wai-mun, Rose's young husband, very bewildered and here without any enthusiasm or good reason, followed Pete walking aimlessly through the church and trying to be a loyal friend and loyal to Rose's mother, his sponsor into this country, simultaneously. Dangerously. Maria very tiny in white, blushing, apologizing, presenting her eyes to him through a lace veil worn by her mother at her wedding, suddenly ashamed of herself, thought herself worthless and not good enough for Pete because her parents refused to attend the wedding, because the church was a converted grocery store and not the Church, because the minister was actually a poor weak Mexican boy who must appear shabby and foreign and small to Pete and Pete's friend. "It'sa a'righ', Maria," Pete said smiling, outlawing all sad sounds from getting deep into his ears for now, "We're gettin marry and bein happy." He put all his life into that squeeze of her hand he gave her. He promised her grandeur and unheard of gaiety at their wedding supper at the DRAGON RES-

TAURANT CHOP SUEY and winked at her. A joke. Complete miss. Amazing that she should love him, he thought, as gauze, lace, silk, all white and noisy clung to him, grew a face, and kissed him on the neck. The minister blushed, explained that he had promised to umpire a baseball game later that afternoon and that the boys were here and were happy that his friends were getting married. Of course no one minded the boys sitting quietly in the back row and watching the ceremony. The minister thanked everyone, spread his arms, and introduced eight boys.

Everyone looked happy dressed in their best. They sat close together with their knees pressed together and ate the opera singer's homemade cake off paper plates, smiled, cleared their throats, and suddenly were engaged in a marathon session of complimenting the woman's cake and urging her to sing. The ceremony was over. The boys had taken their cake outside. They could be heard bouncing a baseball against the walls. "Tell her the cake is good," Wai-mun said now and then. "My pal like this cake very much, man," Pete said. Then the reception was over. Then the dinner at the restaurant was over. Then Pete was a widowed father, much older, feeling his stomach to never have healed from his sister's tea, damp sandwiches, and a dinner the both of them suddenly tired of eating to look at each other's laughably stomach-affected faces. "Twenty? No. Less. A little over ten years of marriage. Good marriage, I tell you too." A memory uncurled a beginning. He shook his head violently and whacked it out. "*Chee-rice, man,* I don't even remember what happened," Pete had said. "And well. She dies."

"Your sister says you and baby can come home and live," Wai-mun said. "She's sorry, older brother." Still *dai gaw* and *sai low* "older brother" and "little brother" to each other, the Cantonese courtesies. How entirely Chinese Wai-mun was right now. Like Buck Rogers stepping out of his crashed spaceship on a strange planet. Wai-mun's Confucian universals of revenge hadn't discovered the Confucian uses of American-born Rose's Christian universals of "Revenge is Mine! sayeth the Lord!" and "Turn the other cheek." But he would, like so many of the fast-footed shiny-eyed Chinamen on the make, and Wai-mun would go for the women and the money, in that order, and get them, and keep them in a way that the Chinatown Kid had gotten them and lost them. Wai-mun wouldn't turn the other cheek when it counted. And he would when it counted. All warfare is based on deception, they say. Now the innocent who would soon put Christ and Shakespeare to shoulder Confucian work was in less than awe of the God of Christendom, and not feeling guilty about it. Pete, the American-born Chinatown prince, the Chinatown Kid, son of a great Chinatown madame, used to have a Havana in his mouth, a nickel-plated revolver in a shoulder holster, and women of many colors on each arm as he gambled high stakes in the plushest hushed-up games in town. Now Wai-mun's here with the family's rude humiliating condolences without grief for Maria's passing, and Wai-mun and Rose have a son, and Wai-mun a business he runs badly because of the time he spends chasing women.

"Sorry for me? I'm sorry too, little brother," Pete said. Look at this room. She lived here." He glanced around, fingered things with his eyes, chuckled at the sight of gay little kitchen curtains over the room's one large window, salt and pepper shakers with sterling silver caps in need of polishing, her Holy Bible — a look at Wai-mun as the Bible came into view — the diary, a pile of new baby clothes Rose had sent over with Wai-mun, everything not quite as she had left them; it seemed he had moved everything aside, flattened the table cloth, straightened the pictures, changed the sheets to make the room new without driving her out. "I thought of having her here. Then I thought she'd weigh five hundred pounds or more in her coffin, and the hallway's so narrow, and the stairs. And look at the street outside."

Pete looked at Wai-mun's face as if he expected the man to answer, then said. "These clothes! God, I need a bath. They colored her grey hairs. Did you notice that? That's what I get from living with her, a little Mexican accent in my Chinese. You say, come home for the death anniversaries, ah-Pete. My sister says, you're still in the family and my wife Rose, my niece, says, you're a magician with bean curd, Uncle Pete. And you, you little dumb Chink, tell me what they say and add that you're sorry. Well . . ." He didn't want to touch the baby in Wai-mun's presence, yet he didn't want the man to leave. "Look at this room. She lived here," he said again and wanted to say it again, because the sound of those words in his voice reminded him of her.

"Ah-Pete-Ah!" Wai-mun said and touched Pete's wrist. Wai-mun wept. Very Chinese, Pete thought, the way you weep, ah-Wai. His arms at his sides, eyes wide open, not a step forward or backward, and the tears over his eyes and spilling over his lids, like a leaky building. Pete embraced Wai-mun, and Wai-mun gently wrestled himself loose. "They think you're crazy, an old man selling newspapers at night, living alone and . . . raising a baby by yourself," Wai-mun said. "You are an old man, ah-Pete. I think you're a great man!" An idiom he's picked up, Pete thought, and mumbled a few words about at one time having wanted to hear those very words on someone's lips. Someone from his sister's family. Hopefully one of his sister's daughters. One of their husbands had to do. Then the silence. The absence of little tensions. Emotionless, expressionless muscles limp like metal fatigue, like giant machines and intricate parts left to cool and rust in oblivion after a war. The flesh bleaching, fossilizing around relic nerves, sprouted mold and gentle mushrooms. A white blindness. A man without an attitude, purely loving his daughter, like a lung romancing oxygen.

"Don't cry, baby. It was a bad dream."

"I ate pickle before I sleep. 'Sa right, don't be a scare, daddy. I won't dream no. I'll sleep now."

For something cold against my forehead. To relax. Oh, God, I've grown old. So old that there seems very little left of me that's any good for anything. There's no more God, no goodness, no evil, nothing but time for the old men like me, no hope, no hopelessness, no fear; just dilution, evaporation.

God be with this little girl. See, I say, nothing's happened. No halo glows around her head, no tinkle of gold in my heart, no hum of ghosts in my ear. I'll survive fully conscious, be conscious of being a constant temperature. And to this I say, Amen. I put a thick blanket over my daughter to do something on this hot night. I cover her. I watch her look comfortable and drift off into sleep, into her own country and I cover her, feel like swearing and would swear if there would be anything original about it . . . not a thought in Pete's head or an emotion but his flavor, his color.

Out of the concentration of being seated, Pete with his arms extended and Hyacinth, her arms bent at the elbows, all their hands working her buttons, their faces long numbed to reflecting the constant touching of each other as they became aware of the afternoon, marking them in time as they noticed the blood and flesh respond to the intelligence of another afternoon, like so many chameleons changing color. Like so many snakes molting. Like worms seeking moisture. Miracle! On the edges of consciousness, visibly the palpable shallows of evening before the moths rose into the mirror image in breeze and color of a morning. But, not disappointingly, Pete knew it was an afternoon. Without looking up or adjusting, they were conscious of each other within the other's indelicate stare as the shadows were suddenly present and continued. The afternoon, the dusk, the breeze rattling the grimy glass of the window was a language between them. This afternoon. Consciousness soaked into a depth of tedium, focused to the perfection of buttoning rows of buttons on a blouse covered by a row of buttons on a sweater and perfectly buttoning the coat — each buttoned seam a maniac's work of art — he gently ached himself dead to the sounds around him. Ticklishly insensitive, suffocating his agitation with the brilliance of tedium, he was for a lapsed moment not dressing his daughter before leaving for a celebration to the family dead or toward anywhere — he was merely dressing her.

"What's that you're sing?"

"A *Star-Spangled Bammer*. It has guns ennit."

"Who say dat?"

"I forgot."

"You are Merican."

"Sure, I knows it."

"Umk," Pete grunted. The sound of her voice had been quick, reviving her presence above his occupation with her clothes. Her voice had made the moment with her and the specific length of the already played-out sound immediately precious to him in memory like a tiny little fleshy thing gone dead in his hand. He gloated. Dressing the girl had been an act of revenge; he was a master baker ornamenting a poisoned wedding cake, something white and preciously beautiful that would mindlessly be eaten alive. He didn't know how to tell her. Then gloating passed into a waning momentum. He was an engine at minimal pressure on an incline. Here. Alone. From now to then, there would be nothing more to remember than what he knew now. He was finished buttoning his daughter, and, now seated, was realizing that the moment had dissipated into an expansion of innocuous processes, as after strenuous, half-believed desperate prayer. In agitation the working of the still body processed through his staring into an unknown cheese. He was wholly still, a mountain around tunnels of effervescent bloods, a gap between phases. He was a man standing hungry in a doorless corridor. All he could do was want to say something.

He was old beyond superstition, he thought. Now with his daughter he was old, realizing emotion through artificial respiration, waiting for the heat to reach him through rusted pipes. Seeing his daughter dressed in clothes bought by the family in Oakland was an ornamented, simply incommunicable sensation. Being near the girl now was an unpleasant habit. He knew he must be actually old and was old through his body and in the action of blood mesmerizing decay to fractionally living flesh. In a silence calculated not to offend, he was silent, accepting into the senses the pressure of his age like wine. At the same moment silence was a terrifying emotional pallor. He wasn't able, of himself, to contrive enough motive force to so much as arouse a whisper, to whisper, "Goodbye, Hyacinth." How do you make a child care about leaving you forever? How do you make a cute dumpling satisfy you that she's human by shrieking when you leave? Better to not hear her shriek.

"Well, hi! hi! hi! Come in, now don't mind me, *ah-Kow*," —Pete was *ah-Kow*, the mother's brother—"I'm just a bundled of nerveses," suddenly a tone higher in Chinese. "Take off your coat. How do you expect to stay with your coat on?" Rose was radiant. But metal grinning strenuously involving every muscle of her face and neck, even making little fists against her legs as tremulously before Pete's eyes the fibers strained in relief and threatened to burst through her skin at the throat and lips. Rose's rouged cheeks and her hair were warped from the steam and floating grease of a day's cooking. He was late. Usually, on the death anniversaries, he did the cooking for the family while the girls played with Hyacinth — taught her to kowtow before the dead and serve the dead rice while he cooked and had handed to him a five or ten dollar bill from Wai-mun, who always said it came from the old woman, Pete's sister. Now Rose was half-dead and stunned to see the still night outside the house. Unconscious of the tiny jangle of her complicated earrings, she spoke face to face with Pete loudly in constant still-motion like carbonation in a bottle, with the effect of a woman hysterically screaming murder in the streets. "Oh, ah-Kow, don't just stand there." Pete recognized her indifferently. He treated her like an old photograph he might have found fallen on the floor and would soon return to its album.

The uncanny silence. The air had no sound. The air was hot. Hot and void, the apparatus for breathing was smothered, out of reach in the prickly silence of his flesh. The flesh hummed about him as if he were alone in a sleeping city, as if he were walking surrounded by the hum of a sleeping city, hearing in his, the only ears functioning, the fitful coughs, the crickets, the cracks of expanding stones. The flesh hummed like the sleeping sick in whom he dreamed indifferently, the dream soaking him into its marrow, materializing him, the city of flesh into the house which was cooler, a refrigerator-house, lit like an alley with the face of his sister, the white scar of a removed cancer and her chilled eyes all grey, the faces of her daughters, Rose and Minnie, resembling each other in odd parts of their different faces, resembling the woman, his sister, the old women with their jade bracelets tight as tourniquets swelling the veins on their thin arms, the children all images of suppressed hilarity, all like the colors of circus posters plastered on fences and walls he passed. They looked at him like posters. Looked at him as if choking back a nightmare. They spoke. "Hello, Pete." "Look who's here." They spoke to him without disturbing the indifference of a dreamer's body. He watched them perform, dreaming his presence, speaking to him as if he weren't there, speaking to no one he knew. He might dance and laugh in their faces without disturbing them, and then laugh, tweak their noses, sniff in their armpits — being invisible all the while — if he thought his heart would stand the strain, if he could be sure of enjoying himself being an invisible spectacle before his family turned into mortuary furniture. Nothing left of them here but pasteboard faces, clothing, and rattling jewelry. But, still as they were, faces gone to vegetables and colored cloth made heavy with rocks, they were real. And he was real. Really indifferent cushioned in stringy flesh agitating like soda pop in a bottle, as he watched the real and remote world being dreamt for him, including him as if after all this was his nightmare.

"She doesn't like pork," he said. He held a hand below his daughter's chin while she grimaced and drooled lumps of chewed pork, drew strings of it out of her mouth with her fingers and put them into Pete's hand, counting "One, two, three..." aloud. "She likes bacon, though. It's the only kind of pork she'll eat." The women lowered their eyes at the sound of his voice and immediately, as if shocked into motion, cooed at Hyacinth through puckered lips, ignored Pete with their whole physiognomy and reached across the table with their thighs braced against the edge of the table and their small haltered Chinese breasts hanging near the crests of piled food and mounds of broken chicken bones picked clean. They arched over the table with long red smiles to wipe Hyacinth's face after Pete had wiped it or leaned to remove a bone from her plate after Pete had put it there for Hyacinth to chew. "Bones are good for her teeth," he said matter-of-factly.

"What is she, a dog?" a voice asked and no one laughed. Glancing around the table, searching for the speaker, the faces were all alike, strenuously convivial and silent as if he had heard nothing.

Another antiseptically taken dinner. Another glimpse of his sister, sad and enduring woman at the head of the table surrounded by her children and grandchildren and her walls cluttered with pictures of herself and her children taken at various ages at various times of day. She was already dying, accumulating weariness like a pus that would send her crashing to the floor of her room in a puddle of her last urine. Dead above him, her thud to the floor gone unnoticed in his near-deaf ears as he smoked Bull Durham cigarettes he had rolled with her in the kitchen, on this very stool, years later when it was too late, too many pains and agonies later to say a kind word to her without irony, to say the most mundane cliché without baring for a moment some running sore. Not speaking to her in the kitchen where they sat together peeling onions and shelling peas, not listening to Rose scolding her son Dirigible for hitting Hyacinth in the other room where mah-jong was in progress, Pete played with his sister, set his flesh humming to attract a familiar sign out of her body.

The Chinese in America seemed to live that long, live beyond endurance, beyond the limits of interest and curiosity and die slowly like cities blacking out a light bulb at a time, and even then not dead; a few more years of being not quite dead, a living corpse painfully sensing what he wanted to say, what she wanted to say but not caring to speak or to have to hear. When children or one of the girls opened the old photograph albums, they might glance and recognize themselves, Pete and his sister Lena standing on either side of their ancient parents. They remembered what they felt in their faces, the grinning mock-grin owlish look they projected when they were young. The longer they looked, the less they recognized. Once dead, the old woman was utterly dead to Pete; the stopped heart, the rigor mortis, the funeral were merely embellishments. The funeral parade past the house, the laying to rest of his sister's deserted body was a long walk, a long wait, Pete the survivor below death's threshold of appreciation, coming to the death anniversaries to cook and eat his own cooking with his family.

He wasn't looking at his sister surrounded with her relics, as if she would die. "The whole world is waiting to not have ever cared for me when I die" was not a thought in his head or an emotion. He looked at his sister. "So you're buying my Hyacinth from me," he said abruptly, momentarily ending what he no longer wanted to listen to.

"I think the children should clear the table now," his sister said. "You have a way of speaking, a way of ... of ..." The old woman's eyes blinked prettily. She sighed. The silence was passionless. Finally they told him again, all of them added to the pile of words. They were giving him two thousand dollars. They were ashamed of him, but it wasn't his fault. They loved him and knew he would be unhappy for awhile without his daughter, but he must know himself, if he was honest, that he was much too old to raise the girl, that living the way they did in one room wasn't healthy, that he shouldn't be bothered really because Hyacinth was, after all, still in the family, so no need for a long argument. They stopped speaking, realizing that Pete had not argued, that he didn't seem bothered.

"They say you look like a bum," someone said with a vehemence that froze and became isolated in his silence. He observed his family disintegrating, dying, loving him, needing a recognizable sound from him to set them right again.

But he was too wretched.

Ever hear about the time, about the time, I say, did you ever hear about the time the Chinatown Kid gave an exhibition of the secret Chinese fighting form Kung-fu and Japanese Judo and Karate at the Chinese New Year's celebration, when I challenged single-handedly and blindfolded a dozen professional wrestlers and never had a finger, not a foot, laid on me? And under the influence, that is to say under the influence of a darkness darker than the darkness of the black blindfold, a darkness where only the sensations in my teeth — never knew teeth had feelings, had nerves and perhaps, just think, perhaps have livers and little hearts and teeth of their own, for the teeth felt being chewed at from within, and not tooth decay or bad breath, no, never had a cavity in my life — but only the internal dancing of the teeth told me where my head was, and which way was up and in that darkness — listen, not a sound! — which influenced me, I crawled, crawled like a worm through my arms, through my legs into my body searching for the joints and holes of sensation like crawling through the bowels of a slide trombone and I gave an exhibition of Kung-fu, Judo, and Karate and screamed like bloody banzai-charging yellow imps and took on twenty full-grown men and never had a finger, not a finger, laid on me. In the stands sat the Mexican girl with a hyacinth tattooed between her thumb and forefinger who, one day had, I say she did one day finally on a certain day when I was a Hindu in my sari and carrying tinfoil to give myself a nice suntan, she turned around, turned her head and saw me just as the sun sparkled and reflected off my body, just as I gently caressed her shadow with my foot, and she said, "Oh!" And it was love, my dear, LOVE in the tanning rays of a California Sun. She rushed, and like the ghost of the great Quetzalcoatl, I dropped dead, leaving her in the petals of her tattoo to console her. And I was dead, losing my tan fast as she kissed her tattooed hand and mourned the dead Aztec monster who she knew was dead.

Then I was alone on the pavement. Then night, my medium, came, breathed into me, soaked into my pores, through my viscera into the muscle tissue to the blood, to the heart, to the teeth and I breathed with the night and lived in its life.

Then the sun came casting upon the scene
The sun that is but a single dying star
Alone a rusting round ghastly machine
As in an empty lot, a bright abandoned car

I rose painfully from the pavement, a little confused. The streets were empty that morning, no one around to confirm whether or not my being alive was an illusion. I spoke to hear my voice. I urinated in the gutter and saw that my urine was real and solid enough to make a noise on the ground and slither around the small stones embedded in the asphalt. I almost tasted it, but touching it, wetting my finger in it and smelling it was enough. I swore in amazement and was thrilled with the sound of my living voice. I spoke hefting the weight of my voice in the air. Yes sir, I was no longer dead. But I was, for there, at my feet, was a puddle of me, an old flesh ripened to shit wrapped in tinfoil. I stepped out and had my picture taken by the Mexican girl and it was love. But I was naked. The first person I encountered in that life would have had to be a Mexican, a girl. That is to say, the one who had mourned me, yes. She arrested me for being naked, for leaving refuse on the street. I told her that that was me on the street, that was my decayed corpse lying there. "Look there," I said. "You can still make out where my face was. Of course the bones are all gone. The bones are in me. I saved them." And you should have heard her laugh. The night saved them, the bones. Cleaned them and built me around them. Together out of the dung that was left of me we began to dry out and weave clothes for my body. And she with her camera was in the crowd cheering me giving a Kung-fu, Judo, Karate exhibition. Not a finger laid on me. Not a foot. Then I spit the terrible secret Kung-fu Chinese spit that sent tons of people reeling in a stun before they had time to draw their handkerchiefs. The tattooed Mexican girl reaching for her handkerchief bared her hand and the tattoo. Me peeking out of my pores with Chinese eyes loved her. I rushed the hand, attacked the girl and using Kung-fu Karate, Judo Chinese-Japanese secrets I demonstrated what no other Kung-fu Karate master black belt ever thought of revealing to the public. It was all of Mexico there, I tell you. Breaking bricks, cracking steel anvils with my bare hands seemed nothing, was forgotten by the crowd, it was so innocuous compared to what they saw then.

And blindfolded!

And those terrible Kung-fu Karate Judo Chinese-Japanese imp grunt banzai, gung-ho screams and Mexican noises of such volume and loudness that it seemed impossible even to me, that the Chinatown Kid, that such sounds should be emitted, I say, that such sounds should come out of a human body. It was night behind the blindfold. The China Sea, the Japan current, the trade winds, the horse latitudes, and the workings of the earth raging in my, in our, bodies, as I, clad in fiber woven from a dead mock-Quetzalcoatl, used my hands and body to ravish as no one has ever seen or felt or heard before. That night in Chinatown on New Year's a whole generation of monks, celibates, men swearing off forever, to take up the cloth or turn queer, was created, a generation of madwomen was created. The twenty-five fully grown professional wrestlers felt their hair turn white and were struck dumb, were cursed by the huge head of heat created by the world's last public Kung-fu Judo Karate exhibition. Now and then the tattooed hand rose and twined out of the lightning Karate movements. I saved her hand. Then once again, I say, once again I was arrested for being naked. The whole world was arrested for being naked.

> *Then the sun came building light on the scene*
> *That forlorn bachelor star never nocturnal*
> *Always in daylight, poor Sol not even a queen*
> *Not a dirty old man but innocent eternal*

It came somber as a priest to make our sweat gleam. "Man, what a hell of a night," I said to Maria after I had cut our way out of jail with my bare Karate horny hands. They were poor sore hands that morning. Sore hands and bodies and minds drained, exhausted like gas out of a tank, we went our respective ways home to sleep and hopefully, dreamlessly die again to wake again and weave clothes from the bodies of the dead.

"Ah-Pete, say something, won't you?" his sister pleaded. In the light, grotesque, through the skin, blue and pink veins swelled and collapsed from the pressure of muscles whose shadows appeared like glimpses of chameleons swimming through cloudy water.

Home to a tiny museum, where through laziness and profound indifference boxes of oatmeal, cheerful kitchen curtains, a pile of small socks would never be touched again — home would be a better place than here for a body to rest. The young women with his sister insisted that he have the decency to weep when they hurt him. Afterwards they would soothe him and be soothed by feeling their internal organs being moved to pity at the sound of a creature sobbing. How would they ask him to think of the money he would save on food and the expenses of her nursery school without making fools of themselves? And what would they say if he asked them to consider an old man in his room, penknife in hand, eating fresh peaches? The Chinatown Kid's most potent moment. Under the white felt hat, inside the pinstripe shirt and wide lapels, the Kid lived savoring a silence that was entirely his, so much of a man doing nothing. Livers and little hearts and, listen to this, teeth of their own, never knew the teeth had sensations before. Finally, to break the monotony of repetitive melodrama that must have been wearing the women thin, to not hurt their feelings and get out of here, he cracked his face like a coat of paint, strained at the valves and retired machinery of his face and started to weep for them, like a gardener watering a small lawn. He sadly, hatefully shammed sadness and accepted their hands on his shoulders, their sorrowful encouraging words as a kind of applause for an athletic feat. "Don't cry, Daddy. I won't play anymore," Hyacinth said. Poor little girl was fooled like the rest of the family. "Don't cry, Hyacinth," he said. All touch. All sound. He sincerely twitched for them and wept drily behind his tears as he tried to make his daughter laugh and not be frightened of his weeping.

The Only Real Day

THE MEN played mah-jong or passed the waterpipe, their voices low under the sound of the fish pumps thudding into the room from the tropical fish store. Voices became louder over other voices in the thickening heat. Yuen was with his friends now, where he was always happy and loud every Tuesday night. All the faces shone of skin oily from the heat and laughter, the same as last week, the same men and room and waterpipe. Yuen knew them. Here it was comfortable after another week of that crippled would-be Hollywood Oriental-for-a-friend in Oakland. He hated the sight of cripples on his night and day off, and one had spoken to him as stepped off the A-train into the tinny breath of the Key System Bay Bridge Terminal. Off the train in San Francisco into the voice of a cripple. "Count your blessings!" The old white people left to die at the Eclipse Hotel, and the old waitresses who worked there often said "Count your blessings" over sneezes and little ouches and bad news. Christian resignation. Yuen was older than many of the white guests of the Eclipse. He washed dishes there without ever once counting his blessings.

"That's impossible," Huie said to Yuen.

Yuen grinned at his friend and said, "Whaddaya mean? It's true! You don't know because you were born here."

"Whaddaya mean 'born here'? Who was born here?"

"Every morning, I woke up with my father and my son, and we walked out of our house to the field, and stood in a circle around a young peach tree and lowered our trousers and pissed on the tree, made bubbles in the dirt, got the bark wet, splattered on the roots and watched our piss sink in. That's how we fertilized the big one the day I said I was going to Hong Kong tomorrow with my wife and son, and told them I was leaving my father and mother, and I did. I left. Then I left Hong Kong and left my fami-

ly there, and came to America to make money," Yuen said. "Then
after so much money, bring them over."

"Nobody gets over these days, so don't bang your head about
not getting people over. What I want to know is did you make
money?"

"Make money?"

"Yes, did you make money?"

"I'm still here, my wife is dead . . . but my son is still in Hong
Kong, and I send him what I can."

"You're too good a father! He's a big boy now. Has to be a full-
grown man. You don't want to spoil him."

Yuen looked up at the lightbulb and blinked. "It's good to get
away from those *lo fan* women always around the restaurant.
Waitresses, hotel guests crying for Rose. Ha ha." He didn't want
to talk about his son or China. Talk of white women he'd seen
changing in the corridor outside his room over the kitchen, and
sex acts of the past, would cloud out what he didn't want to talk
about. Already the men in the room full of fish tanks were speaking loudly, shouting when they laughed, throwing the sound of
their voices loud against the spongy atmosphere of fish pumps
and warm-water aquariums. Yuen enjoyed the room when it was
loud and blunt. The fishtanks and gulping and chortling pumps
sopped up the sound of the clickety clickety of the games and kept
the voices, no matter how loud, inside. The louder the closer,
thicker, fleshier, as the night wore on. This was the life after a
week of privacy with the only real Chinese speaker being
paralyzed speechless in a wheelchair. No wonder the boy doesn't
speak Chinese, he thought, not making sense. The boy should
come here sometime. He might like the fish.

"Perhaps you could," Huie said, laughing, "Perhaps you could
make love to them, Ah-Yuen gaw." The men laughed, showing
gold and aged yellow teeth. "Love!" Yuen snorted against the
friendly laugh.

"That's what they call it if you do it for free," Huie said.

"Not me," Yuen said taking the bucket and water pipe from
Huie. "Free or money. No love. No fuck. Not me." He lifted the
punk from the tobacco, then shot off the ash with a blast of air into
the pipe that sent a squirt of water up the stem. "I don't even like
talking to them. Why should I speak their language? They don't

think I'm anything anyway. They change their clothes and smoke in their slips right outside my door in the hallway, and don't care I live there. So what?" His head lifted to face his friends, and his nostrils opened, one larger than the other as he spoke faster. "And anyway, they don't care if I come out of my room and see them standing half-naked in the hall. They must know they're ugly. They all have wrinkles and you can see all the dirt on their skins and they shave their armpits badly, and their powder turns brown in the folds of their skin. They're not like Chinese women at all." Yuen made it a joke for his friends.

"I have always wanted to see a real naked American woman for free. There's something about not paying money to see what you see," Huie said. "Ahhh and what I want to see is bigger breasts. Do these free peeks have bigger breasts than Chinese women? Do they have nipples as pink as calendar girls' sweet suckies?" Huie grunted and put his hands inside his jacket and hefted invisible breasts, "Do they have . . .?"

"I don't know. I don't look. All the ones at my place are old, and who wants to look inside the clothes of the old for their parts? And you can't tell about calendar pictures . . ." Yuen pulled at the deep smoke of the waterpipe. The water inside gurgled loudly, and singed tobacco ash jumped when Yuen blew back into the tube. He lifted his head and licked the edges of his teeth. He always licked the edges of his teeth before speaking. He did not think it a sign of old age. Before he broke the first word over his licked teeth, Huie raised his hand. "Jimmy Chan goes out with *lo fan* women . . . blonde ones with blue eyelids too. And he smokes cigars," Huie said.

"He smokes cigars. So what? What's that?"

"They light his cigars for him."

"That's because he has money. If Chinese have money here, everybody likes them," Yuen said. "Blue nipples, pink eyelids, everybody likes them."

"Not the Jews."

"Not the Jews." Yuen said. "I saw a cripple. Screamed 'Count your blessings!' Could have been a Jew, huh? I should have looked . . . Who cares? So what?"

"The Jews don't like anybody," Huie said. "They call us, you and me, the Tang people 'Jews of the Orient.' Ever hear that?"

"Because the Jews don't like anybody?"

"Because nobody likes the Jews!" Huie said. He pulled the tip of his nose down with his fingers. "Do I look like a Jew of the Orient, for fuckin out loud? What a life!" The men at the mah-jong table laughed and shook the table with the pounding of their hands. Over their laughter, Yuen spoke loudly, licking the edges of his teeth and smiling, "What do you want to be Jew for? You're Chinese! That's bad enough!" And the room full of close men was loud with the sound of tables slapped with night-pale hands and belly laughter shrinking into wheezes and silent empty mouths breathless and drooling. "We have a Jew at the Eclipse Hotel. They look white like the other *lo fan gwai* to me," Yuen said, and touched the glowing punk to the tobacco and inhaled through his mouth, gurgling the water. He let the smoke drop from his nostrils and laughed smoke out between his teeth, and leaned back into the small spaces of smoke between the men and enjoyed the whole room.

Yuen was a man of neat habits, but always seemed disheveled with his dry mouth, open with the lower lip shining, dry and dangling below yellow teeth. Even today, dressed in his day-off suit that he kept hung in his closet with butcher paper over it and a hat he kept in a box, he had seen people watching him and laughing behind their hands at his pulling at the shoulders of the jacket and lifting the brim of his hat from his eyes. He had gathered himself into his own arms and leaned back into his seat to think about the room in San Francisco; then he slept and was ignorant of the people, the conductor, and all the people he had seen before, watching him and snickering, and who might have been, he thought, jealous of him for being tall for a Chinese, or his long fingers, exactly what he did not know or worry about in his half-stupor between wakefulness and sleep with his body against the side of the train, the sounds of the steel wheels, and the train pitching side to side, all amazingly loud and echoing in his ears, through his body before sleep.

Tuesday evening Yuen took the A-train from Oakland to San Francisco. He walked to the train stop right after work at the restaurant and stood, always watching to the end of the street for the train's coming, dim out of the darkness from San Francisco. The train came, its cars swaying side to side and looked like a short snake with a lit stripe of lights squirming past him, or like the long dragon that stretched and jumped over the feet of the boys carrying it. He hated the dragon here, but saw it when it ran, for the boy's sake. The train looked like that, the glittering dragon that moved quickly like the sound of drum rolls and dangled its staring eyes out of its head with a flurry of beard; the screaming bird's voice of the train excited in him his idea of a child's impulse to run, to grab, to destroy.

Then he stood and listened to the sound of the train's steel wheels, the sound of an invisible cheering crowd being sucked after the lights of the train toward the end of the line, leaving the quiet street more quiet and Yuen almost superstitiously anxious. Almost. The distance from superstitious feeling a loss or an achievement, he wasn't sure.

He was always grateful for the Tuesdays Dirigible walked him to the train stop. They left early on these nights and walked past drugstores, bought comic books, looked into the windows of closed shops and dimly lit used bookstores, and looked at shoes or suits on dummies. "How much is that?" Yuen would ask.

"I don't know what you're talking," Dirigible, the boy of the unpronounceable name, would say. "I don't know what you're talking" seemed the only complete phrase he commanded in Cantonese.

"What a stupid boy you are; can't even talk Chinese," Yuen would say, and "Too moochie shi-yet," adding his only American phrase. "Come on, I have a train to catch." They would laugh at each other and walk slowly, the old man lifting his shoulders and leaning his head far back on his neck, walking straighter, when he remembered. The boy. "Fay Gay" in Cantonese, Flying Ship, made him remember.

A glance back to Dirigible as he boarded the train, a smile, a wave, the boy through the window a silent thing in the noise of the engines. Yuen would shrug and settle himself against the back, against the seat, and still watch Dirigible, who would be walking now, back toward the restaurant. Tonight he realized again how young the Flying Ship was to be walking home alone at night through the city back to the kitchen entrance of the hotel. He saw Dirigible not walking the usual way home, but running next to the moving train, then turning the corner to walk up a street with more lights and people. Yuen turned, thinking he might shout out the door for the boy to go home the way they had come, but the train was moving, the moment gone. Almost. Yuen had forgotten something. The train was moving. And he had no right. Dirigible had heard his mother say that Yuen had no right so many times that Dirigible was saying it too. In Chinese. Badly spoken and bungled, but Chinese. That he was not Yuen's son. That this was not China. Knowing the boy was allowed to say such things by his only speaking parent made Yuen's need to scold and shout more urgent, his silence in front of the spoiled punk more humiliating. Yuen was still and worked himself out of his confusion. The beginning of his day off was bad; nothing about it right or usual; all of it bad, no good, wrong. Yuen chewed it out of his mind until the memory was fond and funny, then relaxed.

"Jimmy Chan has a small Mexican dog too, that he keeps in his pocket," Huie said. "It's lined with rubber."

"The little dog?" Yuen asked. And the men laughed.

"The dog . . ." Huie said and chuckled out of his chinless face, "No, his pocket, so if the dog urinates . . ." He shrugged, "You know."

"Then how can he make love to his blonde *fangwai* woman with blue breasts if his pocket is full of dogpiss?"

"He takes off his coat!" The men laughed with their faces up into the falling smoke. The men seemed very close to Yuen, as if with the heat and smoke they swelled to crowding against the walls, and Yuen swelled and was hot with them, feeling tropically close and friendly, friendlier, until he was dizzy with friendship and forgot names. No, don't forget names. "A Chinese can do anything with *fan gwai* if he has money," Yuen said.

"Like too moochie shi-yet, he can," Huie shouted, almost falling off his seat. "He can't make himself white!" Huie jabbed his finger at Yuen and glared. The men at the table stopped. The noise of the mah-jong and voices stopped to the sound of rumps shifting over chairs and creaks of table legs. Heavy arms were leaned onto the tabletops. Yuen was not sure whether he was arguing with his friend or not. He did not want to argue on his day off, yet he was constrained to say something. He knew that whatever he said would sound more important than he meant it. He licked his teeth and said, "Who want to be white when they can have money?" He grinned. The man nodded and sat quiet a moment, listening to the sound of boys shouting at cars to come and park in their lots. "Older brother, you always know the right thing to say in a little pinch, don't you."

"You mother's twat! Play!" And the men laughed and in a burst of noise returned to their game.

The back room was separated from the tropical fish store by a long window shade drawn over the doorway. Calendars with pictures of Chinese women holding peaches the size of basketballs, calendars with pictures of nude white women with large breasts of all shapes, and a picture someone thought was funny, showing a man with the breasts of a woman, were tacked to the walls above the stacked glass tanks of warm-water fish. The men sat on boxes, in chairs, at counters with a wall of drawers full of stuff for tropical fish, and leaned inside the doorway and bits of wall not occupied by a gurgling tank of colorful little swimming things. They sat and passed the waterpipe and tea and played mah-jong or talked. Every night the waterpipe, the tea, the mah-jong, the talk.

"Wuhay! Hey, Yuen, older brother," a familiar nameless voice shouted through the smoke and thumping pumps. "Why're you so quiet tonight?"

"I thought I was being loud and obnoxious," Yuen said. "Perhaps it's my boss's son looking sick again."

"The boy?" Huie said.

"Yuen stood and removed his jacket, brushed it and hung it on a nail. "He has this trouble with his stomach . . . makes him bend up and he cries and won't move. It comes and goes," Yuen said.

"Bring him over to me, and I'll give him some herbs, make him well in a hurry."

"His mother, my boss, is one of these new-fashioned people giving up the old ways. She speaks nothing but American if she can help it, and has *lo fan* women working for her at her restaurant. She laughs at me when I tell her about herbs making her son well, but she knows . . ."

"Herbs make me well when I'm sick."

"They can call you 'mass hysteria' crazy in the head. People like her mean well, but don't know what's real and what's phony."

"Herbs made my brother well, but he died anyway," Huie said. He took off his glasses and licked the lenses.

"Because he wanted to," Yuen said.

"He shot himself."

"Yes, I remember," Yuen said. He scratched his Adam's apple noisily a moment. "He used to come into the restaurant in the mornings. I'd fix him scrambled eggs. He always use to talk with bits of egg on his lips and shake his fork and tell me that I could learn English good enough to be cook at some good restaurant. I could too, but the cook where I wash dishes is Chinese already, and buys good meat, so I have a good life."

Huie sighed and said, "Good meat is important I suppose." Then put his mouth to the mouth of the waterpipe.

"What?" Yuen asked absently at Huie's sigh. He allowed his eyes to unfocus on the room now, tried to remember Huie's brother's face with bits of egg on the lips and was angry. Suddenly an angry old man wanting to be alone screamed. He wiped his own lips with his knuckles and looked back to Huie the herbalist. Yuen did not want to talk about Huie's brother. He wanted to listen to music, or jokes, or breaking bones, something happy or terrible.

"His fine American talk," Huie said. "He used to go to the Oakland High School at night to learn."

My boss wants me to go there too," Yuen said. "You should only talk English if you have money to talk to them with . . . I mean, only fools talk buddy buddy with the *lo fan* when they don't have money. If you talk to them without money, all you'll hear is what they say behind your back, and you don't want to listen to that."

"I don't."

"No."

He received a letter one day, did he tell you that? He got a letter from the American Immigration, and he took the letter to Jimmy Chan, who reads government stuff well . . . and Jimmy said that the Immigration wanted to know how he came into the country and wanted to know if he was sending money to Communists or not." Huie smiled wanly and stared between his legs. Yuen watched Huie sitting on the box; he had passed the pipe and now sat with his short legs spread slightly apart. He was down now, his eyes just visible to Yuen. Huie's slumped body looked relaxed, only the muscles of his hands and wrists were tight and working. To Yuen, Huie right now looked as calm as if he were sitting on a padded crapper. Yuen smiled and tried to save the pleasure of his day-off visit that was being lost in morbid talk. "Did he have his dog with him?" he asked.

"His dog? My brother never had a dog."

"I mean Jimmy Chan with his rubber pocket."

"How can you talk about Jimmy Chan's stupid dog when I'm talking about my brother's death."

"Perhaps I'm worried about the boy," Yuen said. "I shouldn't have let him wait for the train tonight."

"Was he sick?"

"That too maybe. Who can tell?" Yuen said without a hint, not a word more of the cripple shouting "Count your blessings!" at the end of the A-train's line in Frisco. It wouldn't be funny, and Yuen wanted a laugh.

"Bring the boy to me next week, and I'll fix him up," Huie said quickly, and put on his glasses again. Yuen, out of his day-off, loud, cheerful mood, angry and ashamed of his anger, listened to Huie. "My brother was very old, you remember? He was here during the fire and earthquake, and he told this to Jimmy Chan." Huie stopped speaking and patted Yuen's knee. "Yes, he did have his little dog in his pocket . . ." The men looked across to each other, and Yuen nodded. They were friends, had always been friends. They were friends now. "And my brother told Jimmy that all his papers had been burned in the fire and told about how he came across the bay in a sailboat that was so full that his elbows, just over the side of the boat, were in the water, and about the women crying and then shouting, and that no one thought about papers, and some not even of their gold."

"Yes. I know."

"And Jimmy Chan laughed at my brother and told him that there was nothing he could do, and that my brother would have to wait and see if he would be sent back to China or not. So . . ." Huie put his hands on his knees and rocked himself forward, lifting and setting his thin rump onto the wooden box, sighed and swallowed, "my brother shot himself." Huie looked up to Yuen; they licked their lips at the same moment, watching each other's tongues. "He died very messy," Huie said, and Yuen heard it through again for his friend, as he had a hundred times before. But tonight it made him sick.

The talk about death and the insides of a head spread wet all over the floor, the head of someone he knew, the talk was not relaxing; it was incongruous to the room of undershirted men playing mah-jong and pai-gow. And the men, quieter since the shout, were out of place in their undershirts. Yuen wanted to relax, but everything was frantic that should not be; perhaps he was too sensitive, Yuen thought, and wanted to be numb. "You don't have to talk about it if it bothers," Yuen said.

"He looked messy, for me that was enough . . . and enough of Jimmy Chan for me too. He could've written and said my brother was a good citizen or something . . ." Huie stopped and flicked at his ear with his fingertips. "You don't want to talk anymore about it?"

"No," Yuen said.

"How did we come to talk about my brother's death anyhow?"

"Jimmy Chan and his Mexican dog."

"I don't want to talk about that anymore, either."

"How soon is Chinese New Year's?"

"I don't think I want to talk about anything anymore," Huie said, "New Year's is a long ways off. Next year."

"Yes, I know that."

I don't want to talk about it," Huie said. Each man sat now, staring toward and past each other without moving their eyes, as if moving their eyes would break their friendship. He knew that whatever had happened had been his fault; perhaps tonight would have been more congenial if he had not taken Dirigible to the used bookstore where he found a pile of sunshine and nudist magazines, or if the cripple had fallen on his face, or not been there. Yuen could still feel the presence of the cripple, how he wanted still to push him over, crashing to the cement. The joy it would have given him was embarrassing, new, unaccountable, like being in love.

"Would you like a cigar, ah-dai low?" Huie asked, with a friendly Cantonese "Older Brother."

"No, I like the waterpipe." Yuen watched Huie spit the end of the cigar out onto the floor.

"You remind me of my brother, Yuen."

"How so?"

"Shaking your head, biting your lips, always shaking your head . . . you do too much thinking about nothing. You have to shake the thinking out to stop, eh?"

"And I rattle my eyes, too." Yuen laughed, knowing he had no way with a joke, but the friendliness botched in expression was genuine, and winning. "So what can I do without getting arrested?"

"I don't know," Huie said and looked around, "Mah-jong?"

"No."

"Are you unhappy?"

"What kind of question is that? I have my friends, right? But sometimes I feel . . . Aww, everybody does . . ."

"Just like my brother . . . too much thinking, and thinking becomes worry. You should smoke cigars and get drunk and go help one of your *lo fan* waitresses shave her armpits properly and put your head inside and tickle her with your tongue until she's silly. I'd like to put my face into the armpit of some big *fangwai* American woman . . . with a big armpit!"

"But I'm not like your brother." Yuen said. "I don't shoot myself in the mouth and blow the back of my head out with a gun."

"You only have to try once."

Yuen waited a moment, then stood. "I should be leaving now," he said. Tonight had been very slow, but over quickly. He did not like being compared to an old man who had shot himself.

Huie stood and shook Yuen's hand, held Yuen's elbow and squeezed Yuen's hand hard. "I didn't mean to shout at you, dailow."

Yuen smiled his wet smile. Huie held onto Yuen's hand and stood as if he was about to sit again. He had an embarrassingly sad smile. Yuen did not mean to twist his friend's face into this muscular contortion; he had marred Huie's happy evening of gambling, hoarse laughter, and alcoholic wheezings. "I shouted too," Yuen said finally.

"You always know the right things to say, older brother." Huie squeezed Yuen's hand and said, "Goodnight, dai low." And Yuen was walking, was out of the back room and into the tropical fish store. He opened the door to the alley and removed his glasses, blew on them in the sudden cold air to fog them, then wiped them clean.

For a long time he walked the always-damp alleys, between glittering streets of Chinatown. Women with black coats walked with young children. This Chinatown was taller than Oakland's, had more fire escapes and lights, more music coming from the street vents. He usually enjoyed walking at this hour every Wednesday of every week. But this was Tuesday evening, and already he had left his friends, yet it looked like Wednesday with the same paper vendors coming up the hills, carrying bundles of freshly printed Chinese papers. He walked down the hill to Portsmouth Square on Kearney Street to sit in the park and read the paper. He sat on a wooden bench and looked up the trunk of a palm tree, looking toward the sounds of pigeons. He could hear the fat birds cooing over the sound of the streets, and the grass snap when their droppings dropped fresh. Some splattered on the bronze plaque marking the location of the birth of the first white child in San Francisco, a few feet away. He looked up and down the park once, then moved to the other side of the tree out of the wind and sat to read the paper by the streetlight before walking. Tonight he was glad to be tired; to Yuen tiredness was the only explanation for his nervousness. Almost anger. Almost. He would go home early; there was nothing else to do here, and he would sleep through his day off, or at least, late into the morning.

HE ENTERED the kitchen and snorted a breath through his nose. He was home to the smell of cooking and the greasy sweat of waitresses. His boss wiped her forehead with the back of her arm and asked him why he had come back so early; she did not expect him back until dinnertime tomorrow and was he sick? He answered, "Yes," lying to avoid conversation. All warfare is based on deception, he thought, quoting the strategist Sun Tzu, the grandson. He asked the young woman where her son the Flying Ship was, and she said he was upstairs in his room sleeping, where he belonged. Yuen nodded, "Of course, it's late isn't it," he said, avoiding the stare of her greasy eyes, and went upstairs to his room across the hall from the waitresses' wardrobe. He looked once around the kitchen before turning the first landing. He saw the large refrigerators and the steam table, and realized he was truly tired, and sighed the atmosphere of his day off out of his body. "You're trying to walk too straight, anyway, Ah-bok," his boss, Rose, said, calling him uncle from the bottom of stairs. He did not understand her joke or criticism or what she meant and went on up the stairs.

At the top of the stairs he turned and walked down the hall, past the room of his boss and her paralyzed husband, and past Dirigible's room, toward his own room across the hall from the wardrobe and next to the bathroom. Facing the door was the standup wardrobe, a fancy store-bought box with two doors, a mirror on the inside, and a rack for clothes, where the waitresses kept their white-and-black uniforms and changed. A redheaded waitress was sitting inside the wardrobe smoking a cigarette. She sat between hanging clothes with her back against the back of the wardrobe, her legs crossed and stretched out of the box. One naked heel turned on the floor, back and forth, making her legs wobble and jump to the rhythm of her nervous breathing.

Yuen walked slowly down the hall, his head down, like a car full of gunmen down a dark street, his fingers feeling the edges of his long hair that tickled the tops of his ears. He looked down to the floor but could no longer see the bare legs jutting from out of the box, the long muscles under the thighs hanging limp and shaking slowly to the turning heel. He knew she was ugly. He snorted and walked close to the far wall; he would walk past her and not at her. She did not move her legs. He stopped and leaned against the wall and lifted one foot after the other and gingerly swung them over the waitress's legs. As his second foot went over her ankles, he glanced into the box and saw her pull a strap over her shoulder and giggle. Dry rock and unnatural white teeth in there. He hopped to keep his balance. She kicked. "Hiya, Yuen," she said to him stumbling down. He felt his shoe scrape the waitress's leg, skin it a little, heard her yelp, and fell on her. "Oh, my God!" she growled and went crazy, tangling her legs and arms with his, jumping into the box to stamp out the cigarette she had let fall from her mouth laughing. The smell was sweet, dusty, and flowery inside the box, like a stale funeral. Huie wanted to stuff his head into a *fangwai* woman's armpit, did he? Yuen looked, as he stumbled to his feet out of the sweet choking smell, and could not make out any distinct armpits in the flurry of flesh and shiny nylon slip and uniforms, and flying shoes, shouting and pounding after her cigarette. He couldn't find his hat. He looked under the waitress.

The waitress stood from out of the wardrobe up to her skinny and flabby self and pulled her slip straight around her belly. She looked down to Yuen, his head nodding and dangling on his neck. He looked like a large bird feeding on something dead, and the waitress laughed. "Come on there, Yuen," the waitress said. "I was just playing." She bent to help the man up. She took his shoulders with her hands and began pulling gently. The door to the bathroom was open and the light through the doorway shone white on the front of her powdered face. Yuen saw her face looking very white with flecks of powder falling from light hairs over her grin, a very white face on a grey wrinkled neck and a chest warped with skin veined like blue cheese. He did not like her smiling and chuckling her breathing into his face or her being so comfortably undressed in front of him.

"Are you all right now, Yuen?" she asked. He did not understand. He felt her holding him and saw her smiling and saw her old breasts quiver and dangle against her slip and the skin stretch across her ribs, not at all like the women in the calendars and magazines, Yuen thought. He took his shoulders closer to his body and she still held him, squeezing the muscle of his arm with strong hands, and pulled him toward her and muttered something in her rotten-throated voice. He leaned away from her and patted his head to show her he was looking for his hat. He chanced a grin.

She looked at his head and moved her fingers through his hair. "I don't see a bump, honey. Where does it hurt?"

Her body was too close to his face for him to see. The smell of her strong soap, stale perfume, layers of powder hung into his breathing. He was angry. "My hat! My hat!" he shouted in Chinese. He took an invisible hat and put it on his head and tapped the brim with his hands.

The waitress, also on her knees now, moved after him and felt his head. "Where does it hurt?" she said. "I don't feel anything but your head."

He stood quickly and leaned against the wall and glared stupidly at her.

"I was just trying to see if you're hurt, Yuen," the waitress said. "Did I touch your sore or something?" She held her arms out and stood. A strap fell from her shoulder; she ignored it and stretched her neck and reached toward him with her fingers. "I was just joking when I kicked you, honey. I thought it was funny, the way you were stepping over me, see?" All Yuen heard were whines and giggles in her voice. He shook his head. He held his coat closed with his hands and shoved at her with his head. "*Chiyeah!* Go way! *Hooey la!*"

A door opened and Dirigible stepped into the hall in his underwear. "What'sa wrong?" he asked. The waitress turned then, fixed her slip, and brushed her dry hair out of her face. "Make him understand, will you?" she said pointing at Yuen. She jabbed her arm at Yuen again. "Him. He's . . ." She crossed her eyes and pointed at her head.

"She's drunk!" Yuen said. "Tell her to go away."

"I was joking! Tell him I didn't mean to hurt his old head."

"Don't let her touch you, she's crazy tonight. Ask her why she here so late. What's she been doing here all night?"

"Do something! I can't."

"What? What?" Dirigible said. "What? I don't know what you're talking," sounding as if he were being accused of something.

The waitress was in front of the boy now and trying to explain. Yuen stepped quickly down the hall and pushed the boy into his room and closed the door. "Go to sleep . . . you'll get a stomach ache," he said.

"What'd you push me for?" the boy asked in English. He kicked the door and tried to open it, but Yuen held the knob. The boy shouted. His anger burst into tears.

"Coffee," Yuen said to the waitress and pointed at her, meaning that she should go have coffee. The waitress nodded quickly, took a robe from the wardrobe, and went downstairs.

Yuen went to his room without looking for his hat. The boy opened his door and followed the old man. He stood in the doorway and watched Yuen hang his overcoat in his closet. Yuen did not notice the boy and locked the door in his face.

The old man put a hand under his shirt and rubbed the sweat under his armpit. He loosened his belt and flapped the waist of his underwear before lying on top of his bed. He felt under the pillow for his revolver; it was big in his hand. Then he swallowed to slow his breath and sat up to take off his shoes and socks.

He saw the dark stain of blood on the heel of his right shoe, and dropped it onto the floor. 'I guess, I can't tell,' he thought. 'She'll say I kicked her.' He rapped the wall to speak to Dirigible. "*Wuhay! Ah-Fay Shurn ahh*, don't tell nutting, okay?"

"I don't know what you're talking. You..." Yuen heard nothing through the wall. He wished that Dirigible spoke Chinese better than he did. What the hell was he learning at that Chinese school if not Chinese?

"You hit me in the face," Dirigible said.

"I did not."

"You did, and it hurt," the boy said. Dirigible. The flying ship that doesn't fly anymore. The boy had the name of an extinct species. He was playing himself more hurt and younger than he was. "Don't be a baby," Yuen said.

"You hit me in the face."

"Uhhh," Yuen groaned, and rolled away from the wall. He would buy the little Dirigible a funnybook in the morning. He would buy Dirigible a dozen funnybooks and a candy bar in the morning. He leaned back into bed and began unbuttoning his shirt.

He stopped and blinked. Someone knocked at his door again. He'd almost heard it the first time. He almost felt for his revolver. He heard, "Ah Yuen bok, ahhh! I got some coffee, uncle. Are you all right? Anna says you hurt your head?" Rose, his boss, Dirigible's mother.

"Go away, I'm sleeping."

"But Anna says you asked for coffee. Have you been drinking?"

"I don't want any coffee."

"Since you're here, I told the colored boy not to come in tomorrow morning... What's your hat doing in the bathroom?"

"Leave it," Yuen said. "Just leave it. I'll get it in the morning." He coughed and rolled over on the bed and coughed once into the pillow.

"By the way, you got a letter today. Your American name on it. Nelson Yuen Fong... Your name looks nice," the voice outside said.

"What?"

"Nothing. I'll keep it until tomorrow for you."

He coughed phlegm up from his chest, held it in his mouth, then swallowed it. His face was warm in his own breath against the pillow. He relaxed the grip of his lids on his eyes for sleep. The hat was probably all dirty if it was in the bathroom, he thought and did not get up to urinate, get his hat, or shut off the light.

The hallway outside was quiet now. He felt his eyes smarting and felt stale and sour. He was not sure whether or not he was a-sleep. It was late; the night was wider, higher without lights on the horizon or lengths of sound stretching down the streets. The air was not silent but excited, jittery without noise. Yuen heard sounds on the edge of hearing, and listened for them, the small sounds of almost voices and cars somewhere. He occasionally heard nothing. Perhaps he was sleeping when he heard nothing. If he opened his eyes now, he would know . . . but he could not open his eyes now. He decided he was asleep, and was sleeping, finally.

What had the waitress been doing up here all this time? Entertaining the man who would never play a Japanese general or Chinese sissy sidekick who dies in the movies ever again, if he ever did, by inflicting her flesh on his mute, immobile, trapped, paralyzed self? Or perhaps a show, a long striptease for the boy to watch from his room through his keyhole. Or had she been inside his room? He had no right. How had they met? Come up the stairs one day from a smoke of the waterpipe in the cool dry room where the potatoes and onions were kept and peeled, looking forward to an hour on his bed with one or two picture magazines full of strippers showing their breasts. The sight of the boy, nine or ten years old, holding his revolver stopped the man from stepping into his own room. The unexpected boy caught Yuen dirty-minded, his mental pecker hanging out. He had a loaded gun in his hand, between Yuen and his girlie magazines. His son. The knees. The boy's knees. That was funny. That was laughable now.

Tomorrow he would buy Dirigible a dozen funnybooks and a big candy bar, even if he was not angry or scared anymore.

And now truly asleep, he was sitting at a table with this boy, but the boy was his son, then Huie's dead brother with bits of scrambled eggs drying on his lips. The flesh all over the skull looked as if it had been boiled in soup to fall off the bone. Yuen wiped the boy's lip but more egg came up where he had wiped the egg off. Then the lips were gone. The lipless boy laughed, took Yuen's hand, and pulled him up. They walked from the table and were in a field with not a bird in the sky above them, smooth as skin, blue as veins. The boy pointed, and there, on the edge of the world was the peach tree. They dropped their trousers, aimed their peckers to the horizon, and pissed the long distance to the tree and watched the streams of their yellow liquid gleam and flash under the bright sky before it arched into the shadow of the mountains. They pissed a very long time without beginning to run out. Yuen was surprised he was still pissing. He squinted to see if he was reaching the tree. The boy was laughing and pissing on Yuen's feet. Yuen was standing in a mud of piss. "What are you doing?"

"Coffee," the boy answered in the waitress's voice and laughed. Birds. They were in the sky out of nowhere and dove on him, silent except for their wings breaking the dive. I'm going to die. Too moochie shi-yet. I'm going to die. And continued fertilizing the peach tree on the horizon. He had not shouted. "It's true!" He woke up to the sound of his voice, he was sure, and heard only the curtains shuffling in front of his open window. He felt under the sheets around his ankles to see if there was any wet. There was not. He hadn't wet the bed. He got up and spat into the wash basin in the corner. He didn't curse the spring handles on the taps. He turned out the light, sat on the edge of his bed, and listened for a hint of waitresses lurking in the silence outside his door, then returned to sleep.

He bathed with his underwear on this morning and plugged the keyhole with toilet paper. He combed his hair and returned to his room. He had found his hat on the lid of the toilet. He did not like the hat any longer; it was too big and the band was dirty. The dream had left him by the time he went downstairs for breakfast, but he knew he had dreamed.

He sat down at a table at the end of the long steam table. He could hear a waitress laughing shrilly outside in the dining room, not the same waitress as last night, he knew, for the breakfast waitresses were different from the ones at dinner. He took a toothpick from a tin can nailed to the end of the steam table and put it in his mouth and sucked the taste of wood and read his Chinese paper. He did not goodmorning his boss. She was younger and should be the first to give greetings, out of respect. But she was his boss. So what. He was reading about Chiang Kai-shek making a speech to his army again. He liked Chiang Kai-shek. He decided he liked Chiang Kai-shek. Chiang Kai-shek was familiar and pleasant in his life, and he enjoyed it. "He made another speech to his army, " Yuen said.

Dirigible said, "He made one last week to the army."

He's forgotten last night, Yuen thought, and answered, "That was to the farmers. This time it's to the army. Next week to everybody." This was part of every morning also.

Rose wiped her hands on her apron and sat down next to Yuen. She took an envelope from her pocket and unfolded it. Before removing the letter, she turned to Dirigible and said, "Go upstairs, change your pants. And comb your hair for a change."

"I'll be late for school. I gotta eat breakfast."

"Go upstairs, huh? I don't have time to argue!" Rose said.

"Can I use your comb, ah-bok?"

"You have your own comb. Don't bother people. I wanta talk to ah-bok."

Yuen gave Dirigible his comb, which he kept in a case. Rose watched the boy go past the first landing and out of sight and then took the letter out of the envelope. "I read this letter of yours," she said. She looked straight at Yuen as she spoke, and Yuen resented her look and the way she held his letter. "Who said you could?" he asked, "It might have been from my son. What do you want to read my mail for, when you don't care what else I do?"

"Now, you know that's not so!" Rose said. "Anyway, it's addressed to your American name, and it's from the U.S. Immigration."

"Well . . . What did Anna tell you about last night? You know what she was really trying to do, don't you? I'll tell you I don't believe a word that woman says. She eats scraps too. Right off the dirty dishes.

"Oh, Yuen bok, you're so old, your brain's busting loose. She was just trying to see if you had a cut or a hurt on your head was all."

"Aww, I don't like her no matter what," Yuen said. He went to the steam table and ladled cream of wheat into a bowl and sat down to eat it. "What are you looking at? You never seen me eat before?"

"Don't you use milk?" Rose asked.

"No, you should know that."

"But your letter, Yuen bok. You're in trouble."

"What for?"

"It's from the immigrators, I told you. They want to know if you came into this country legally."

Yuen looked up from his cereal to the powder and rouge of her face. The oil from her Chinese skin had soaked through and messed it all up. She smiled with her lips shut and cheeks pulled in as if sucking something in her mouth. He did not like Rose because she treated him with disdain and made bad jokes, and thought she was beautiful, a real femme fatale behind the steam table with an apron and earrings. And now she did not seem natural to Yuen, being so kind and trying so to soften the harshness in her voice. "That's a bad joke," Yuen said.

"I'm not joking. Do I look like I'm joking, ah-bok? Here, you can read it for yourself if you don't believe me." She shoved the letter to him. He pushed his cereal bowl aside and flattened the letter on the table. He put his glasses on, then without touching the letter, bent over it and stared. He saw a printed seal with an eagle. The paper was very white, and had a watermark that made another eagle. He removed his glasses and licked his teeth. "You know I don't read English."

"I know," Rose said. "So why don't you eat your breakfast and I'll tell you what the letter says. Then you can get the dishes done."

Yuen nodded and did as she said. She wiped her hands on her apron and told him that the letter said the immigrators wanted to know if he had any criminal record with the police in the City of Oakland and that he was to go to the Oakland Police and have his fingerprints taken and get a letter from them about his criminal record yes or no. "I will talk to Mrs. Walker who was a legal secretary and she can help me write a watchacall, a character reference for you."

"Why tell people?"

"They ask for letters making good references about you, don't they? You want to stay in this country, don't you?" She folded the letter and ran her thumb along the creases, leaving grey marks where her fingers had touched. Yuen took the letter and unfolded it again and put on his glasses again and stared down at the piece of paper. He took a pencil and copied something he saw in the letter on a napkin. "What's this?" he asked, pointing at the napkin.

"That's a т," Rose said.

"What's it mean?"

"It doesn't mean anything. It's just a т."

"Did I make it right?"

"You are not going to learn to read and write English before this afternoon, ah-bok."

Yuen lost interest in his т and wiped his face with his napkin. "т Zone wahh. Camel cigarette!" he mumbled. He remembered cigarette ads with the pictures of actors' heads with a т over their mouths and down their throats. Rose didn't know everything. She was not his friend. He sighed and straightened in his seat. He was sure Rose heard all the little gurgles and slopping sounds inside him. It ached to sit straight. He had to sit straight to feel any strength in his muscles now. The ache gave a certain bite to the fright. He thought about aching and wanting to ache, like nobody else. Every white muscle in his body felt raw and tender, from the base of his spine, and the muscles from his neck down to his shoulder, and the hard muscles behind his armpit. He was conscious of every corner and bend in his body, and all this was inside him, private, the only form of reliable relaxation he had. He wanted to sit back and enjoy himself, ignore the letter and travel the countries of his aches. He looked to Rose. She looked away. He saw she knew he was frightened. He did not want her pity, her face to smile some simpering kindly smile for his sake, for he had always pitied her, with her reasonable good looks, her youth, and a husband she keeps in a room like a bug in a jar, who won't be going to Hollywood after all. He didn't want to need her English, her letter full of nice things about him, her help.

Rose patted Yuen's shoulder and stood up and went to the foot of the stairs and called for Dirigible to come down. "You'll be late for school!" Then to the old man, "I'm going to have to tell him, you know."

"Dritchable?" Yuen said, botching the name.

"Everyone will know sooner or later. They come and ask people questions. The immigrators do that," Rose said. They could hear Dirigible stamping on the floor above them.

Yuen put the letter in his shirt pocket and removed his glasses and put them and the case in the tin can with the toothpicks. His place. He went around the steam table to the dishwashing area, lit the fires under the three sinks full of water, and started the electric dishwashing machine slung like an outboard motor in the well of the washing sink.

He put a teaspoonful of disinfectant into the washwater, then a cup of soap powder. He watched the yellow soap turn the water green and raise a cloud of green to the top of the water. He turned and saw Dirigible sitting at the table again. "*Wuhay!* Good morning, kid," he shouted over the noise of the dishwashing machine. Dirigible looked up and waved back, then looked back at the breakfast his mother had set in front of him. "Come here, Dritch'ble, I got money for funnybooks!" Yuen switched off the machine and repeated what he'd said in a lower voice.

"Dirigible's late for school. He has to eat and run," Rose said. She turned to Dirigible and said, "Be sure you come right home from school. Don't go to Chinese school today, hear?"

"It's not my day to read to Pa."

"Just come home from school, like I told you, hear me? She leaned through a space between a shelf and the steam table to see the boy, and steam bloomed up her face and looked like a beard.

"Oh, boy!" Dirigible said, and Yuen saw that the boy was happy.

"What did you tell him?" he asked Rose.

"That he didn't have to go to Chinese school today."

"Why? Don't you want him to be able to talk Chinese?"

"I want him to take you to the city hall this afternoon and do what the letter says," Rose said. She lifted her head back on her neck to face Yuen, and Yuen looking at her without his glasses on saw her face sitting atop the rising steam.

"I don't want a little boy to help me," he said. "You think I'm a fool? I'll call Jimmy Chan and ask him to help me. Dritch'ble too young to do anything for me."

Rose flickered a smile then twisted herself out from between the shelf and the steam table. "You've been watching too much television, ah-bok. Chinatown's not like that anymore. You can't hide there like you used to. Everything's orderly and businesslike now."

"How do you know Chinatown? You watch television, not me. I know Chinatown. Not everybody talks about the Chinese like the *lo fan* and you. You should know what you're talking about before talking sometimes. Chie!"

"Ham and!" a waitress shouted through the door.

"Ham and!" Rose repeated. "I'm just as much Chinese as you, ah-bok, but this is America!"

"The truth is still the truth, in China, America, on Mars... Two and two don't make four in America, just because you're Chinese."

"What?" the waitress said, jutting her head through the kitchen door, in the rhythm of its swing.

"Eggs how?" Margie asked.

"Oh, basted."

"Basted," Margie said, and reached for the eggs. "Listen, ah-bok. I don't want to get in trouble because of you. I worked hard to get this restaurant, and I gave you a job. Who else do you think would give you a job, and a room? You're too old to work anywhere else, and you'd have to join the union and learn English. You don't want to learn English. That's your business, but if you get in trouble here, I'm in trouble too. Now just do what the letter says. And just don't argue with me about it. No one is trying to hurt you." She brought three cooking strips of bacon from the back of grill toward the center where she kept the iron hot.

"Me make trouble for you? You said I am in trouble already."

"I am trying to help you the best way I can. Now let me alone to cook, and you get back to the dishes. Can't you see I'm nervous? Listen, take the day off. I'll call the colored boy. I shouldn't have told him not to come in. I don't know what I was thinking... Now, please, ah-bok, leave me finish breakfast, will you?"

"I'm sorry, I'll get the dishes ... " Yuen said.

"I said take the day off." Rose said. "Please." She quickly slid the spatula under another egg order on the griddle and flopped them onto a plate. She forgot the bacon.

"The bacon," Yuen said.

She ignored him and said, "Dirigible, you don't have time to finish your breakfast. Take that little pie in the icebox for your teacher and go to school now."

Dirigible looked to Yuen. "I'll walk you to school," Yuen said. Rose snapped, "Be back in time for the dinner dishes ... Oh, what ... Forget I said that, but both of you be back after school."

Looking down the street, they could see the morning sun shattered in the greasy shimmer of Lake Merritt. The grass on the shore was covered with black coots and staggering seagulls. Yuen had his glasses on and could see the trees on the other side of the lake and sailors walking with girls, and he could smell the stagnant water as he walked the other way with Dirigible.

The boy watched the ground and stayed inside Yuen's shadow as they walked. Yuen glanced at the boy and saw him playing his game with his shadow and knew the boy had forgotten last night, the waitress. They were beyond the smell of the lake now and inside the smell of water drying off the sides of washed brick buildings, and Yuen's morning was complete and almost gone. "What're you carrying there?" Yuen asked.

"A pie for teacher," Dirigible said.

Yuen smiled his wet smile. They stopped at the street that had the train tracks in the center. "Mommy said your hat was in the toilet."

"Do you want to go to San Francisco with me?"

"I can't. I have to go home right after school. You too."

"I mean right now. Would you like to go to San Francisco on the train, right now?"

"I have to go to school."

"I'll take you to my friend's and he'll give you some herbs that will make your stomach stop hurting again." Yuen put a hand on the boy's shoulder and stood in front of him. What happens to boys born here? Are they all little bureaucrats by ten years old? They no longer dreamed of the Marvelous Traveler from the outlaws of Leongsahn Marsh come to deliver an invitation to adventure? "I'll buy you five funnybooks and a candy bar."

"But it doesn't hurt."

"For when your stomach does hurt. These herbs and it won't hurt again." Then inspiration in his instinct had the words out of his mouth before they'd come to mind. "How about I buy you special Chinese funnybooks? Chinese fighters with swords and bows and arrows, spears, big wars, heads cut off. And the head cut off spits blood in the face of its killer. You'll like them."

There were more people on the train now than at night. The train was dirtier in the day. They caught the A-train at the end of the line near Dirigible's school. As the train started to pull, it rang its electric bell, screeching like a thousand trapped birds. They hummed and rattled across Oakland, onto the lower level of the

Bay Bridge toward San Francisco. Dirigible ate the little pie and
Yuen put his arm over the boy's shoulders when people boarded,
and let go on the bridge. He was glad to have the boy with him.
Good company. He was young and didn't have to know what
Yuen was doing to have a little adventure. Yuen enjoyed being
with the boy. That was something he could still enjoy.

The train moved quickly, swaying its cars side to side over the
tracks. Yuen looked only once out of the window to the street full
of people. He had been in Oakland for twenty years now, and he
still felt uncomfortable, without allies in the streets. On the train
he could sit and did not have to walk among people with hands
out of their pockets all around him. The train moved him quickly
out of the moldy shadows between tall buildings, and was moving
down a street lined with low wooden houses now. He could see
Negro women with scarves around their large heads. Elephant-
hipped women with fat legs walking old and slow down the street.
The feelings he had for them were vague and nothing personal,
but haunted him. The train passed them, and now there were no
more houses. They whirred into the train yards, and the A
screamed its crazed electric birds toward the bridge.

They passed broken streetcars and empty trains in the yards,
and saw bits of grass growing up between the crossties. Beyond
the yards they saw the flat bay and the thick brown carpet of dung
floating next to the shore. And they could smell the bay, the cooking sewage, the oily steel. Last night he slept past this part of the
trip. "Shi-yet," he said sniffing. The boy smiled. Yuen realized now
what he was doing. He was trying to be brave, and knew he would
fail. He felt the letter in his coat pocket without touching the letter and thought of how he would take the letter from his pocket
to show Jimmy Chan.

The sounds of the wheels on the rails changed in pitch and they
were on the bridge now, with shadows of steelwork skipping over
their faces. They were above the bay and could see the backs of
seagulls gliding and soaring parallel to them, their beaks split in
answer to the electric bell. Yuen could see the birds stop and hang
on the air with their wings stiff, then fall and keep falling until the
bridge blocked his vision, and in his mind he counted the splashes
on the bay the seagulls made. He looked down to Dirigible again
and saw pie on the boy's lips. Dirigible took his hand out of the

paper bag and grinned. "That's bad for your stomach," Yuen said.
Too nervous to smile. No, not nervous, he thought, angry. Calm,
numbly angry. It wasn't unpleasant or aggravating or lonely, but
moving very fast, train or no train, he without a move felt himself
hurtling home. The electric birds screamed and they were moving
in a slow curve toward the terminal at the San Francisco end of
the line.

Chinatown was very warm and the streets smelled of vegetables
and snails set out in front of the shops. Among the shopping
Chinese women, Yuen saw small groups of *lo fan* white tourists
with bright neckties and cameras pointing into windows and playing with bamboo flutes or toy dragons inside the curio shops.
Yuen stopped in front of a bookstore with several different poster
portraits of a redfaced potbellied, longbearded soldier in green
robes. "Know him?" Yuen asked. The boy glanced, "Sure, I've seen
him around."

"Who is he?"

"He's you," the boy said, looking caught again. Yuen took him
inside and bought an expensive set of paperbound Chinese funnybooks that looked like little books and came in a box. Yuen
opened up one of the books to the pictures and chuckled,
delighted. "See, here?" He snatched at the tale of the 108 outlaw
heroes of legendary Leongsahn Marsh in curt, chugging Cantonese babytalk the boy might understand. "Heh heh, look like a
Buddhist monk fella, huh? Very bad temper this guy ... Now this
guy, look. He catch cold, get drunk on knock out 'Mickey Finn'
kind of booze, not knock out, and gotta cross the mountain. *Don't
cross that mountain alone!* they say. *Fuck you!* he says. *Oooh, big
tiger eat you up there. Better not go!* they say him. *Don't try to fool
me!* he says and he goes and they can't stop him go. Up the mountain at night. The tiger jump him! Whoo! He gotta sniffle and
sneeze. Runny eyes and cough. And he drunk too much wine suppose to knock people out. And he thinks maybe he should not
have come up to the mountaintop after all, but gotta fight anyway,
and *kawk kawk kawk kawk!* punch and kick and push the tiger's
face in the dirt and punch and kick 'em and kill that tiger. They
call that one Tiger Jung. He's my favorite of the 108 heroes," Yuen
said and sighed, smiling. "One by one, you know, all the heroes are
accused of crimes by the government. They say he commit a

crime he didn't and they make him run, see? And one by one, all the good guys made outlaw by the bad government come to Leongsahn Marsh and join the good guy, Soong Gong. Yeah, sure. *Sam Gawk Yun Yee, Sir Woo Jun,* I memorize 'em all. All the boys like to see who know more. Then you see them in the opera, and . . ." Yuen signed again and wouldn't finish that thought. "Soong Gong. They call him the Timely Rain, Gup Sir Yur. Every boy like you in the world for awhile is like these guys. Before you lie, before you betray, before you steal. You know if you stay honest, don't sell out, don't betray, don't give up even if it means you run all alone, someday, someone will tap you on the shoulder and, *You!* the Marvelous Traveler will say. *Our leader, the Timely Rain, has long admired your gallantry. Soong Gong says he is a man of no talent, but asks you to join us and our rebel band and do great things.* But you grow up. You sell out, you betray, you kill . . . just a little bit. But too much to expect the Marvelous Traveler to come with any message from the Timely Rain."

The dining room of Jimmy Chan's restaurant was dark with the shadows of chairs stacked and tangled on the tabletops. A white-jacketed busboy led Yuen and the boy between the tables sprouting trees of chairs to the office. Yuen left Dirigible outside to read his funnybooks, then went inside after removing his hat. Rose's lessons in American servility got to him at the oddest times.

Jimmy Chan's bow tie was very small against his fat bellying throat. The tie wriggled like the wings of a tropical moth when he spoke. Jimmy Chan's dog walked all over his desk and Jimmy laughed at it when Yuen came in. Instead of greeting Yuen, he said, "It's a chee-wah-wah. How about that? Please, have a seat."

"How are you?" Yuen asked. "I've been trying to catch you to ask you out for coffee and see how you are. But a busy man about town, like Jimmy Chan . . ." Yuen said, opening with a courtesy, he hoped. The knack for saying the right thing. Huie said Yuen had it. Or had Huie just been saying the right thing himself?

I'm busy all right. Busy going bankrupt to hell and damn."

Yuen nodded, then too quickly put his hand into his coat pocket, as if he'd been bitten there. Then, "I got a letter from the United States of America," Yuen said.

"I can't help with letters from the government. I can't tamper with the government. I'm going to be naturalized next year, but I know people who think I'm a communist. Why? Because I have a big restaurant. What kind of communist owns a restaurant with a floor show and a fan dancer? I'm going bust, I tell you the truth. People say Jimmy Chan is a smuggler. I'm not a goddamn-all-to-hell smuggler any more than you are. But what the hellfuck are my problems compared to yours? Where's a crooked cop when you need one, huh? You need money for a lawyer? What you need is a lawyer to tamper with the government, you know that?"

"Maybe you could read the letter?" Yuen held the letter out. Jimmy Chan put a cigar into his mouth and took the letter. The dog walked over to sniff Jimmy's hands and sniffed at the letter. "Don't let the dog dirty the letter," Yuen said.

"You should let him piss on it. Ha ha. It's a chee-wah-wah. You think I'd let my chee-wah-wah walk on my desk if it was going to dirty things up? You think these papers I have on my desk mean nothing? . . . I'm sorry if I seemed short-tempered just then, uncle, you asked with such force. You see, men with letters like this have come in before, and never, ever, have they ordered me or asked me anything straight out. I was surprised. You should be in business. You should be a general!" Jimmy turned and held the letter up to the light and stared at the watermark. "Fine paper they use," he said, and patted the dog.

"I thought you could give me some advice,"

"You don't want advice," Jimmy Chan said. "You want me to help you. Perform a miracle. But you said advice. I'll take you on your word and give you advice. If you have no criminal record, you have nothing to worry about. There is no advice to give you. Just do what the letter says. Want me to translate it? It says go to the police. Get your fingerprints made and sent to Washington. Get your record of arrests and have the police send a copy to the government. It says it's only routine. Right here, just like this. I am routine."

"They might send me back to China."

"Not if you're all legal."

"Well, still . . ."

"Uncle, my sympathy is free. My advice too. I sympathize with you. You can't hide from them. They even have Chinese working for them, so you can't hide. I sympathize with you, but the only Chinese that get ahead are those who are professional Christian

Chinese, or, you know, cater to that palate, right? You didn't know that when you came here, and now you're just another Chinaman that's all Chinese and in trouble. I can't help you."

"You could write a letter for me telling them I'm all right," Yuen said. He leaned back as Jimmy Chan pushed papers to both sides with his hands and elbows.

"Uncle, I don't know you're all right. And I don't want to know. I can help when I can help because I don't ask for secrets, I don't ask questions, and I don't trust anybody. I'd like to help you. I'm grateful to your generation, but your day is over. You could have avoided all your trouble if you had realized that the *lo fan* like the Chinese as novelties. Toys. Look at me. I eat, dress, act, and talk like a fool. I smell like rotten flower shop. And the *lo fan* can't get into my restaurant fast enough. They all call me Jimmy. I'm becoming an American citizen, not because I want to be like them, but because it's good business. It makes me wealthy enough to go bankrupt in style, to make the *lo fan* think I belong to them. Look! They like the Chinese better than Negroes because we're not many and we're not black. They don't like us as much as Germans or Norwegians because we're not white. They like us better than Jews because we can't be white like the Jews and disappear among the *lo fan*. But! They don't like a Chinaman being Chinese about life because they remind them of the Indians who, thirty-five thousand years ago, were Chinese themselves, see? So...!" Jimmy Chan clapped his hands together and spread them with the effect of climaxing a magic trick and looked about his office. He adjusted his bow tie and grinned. "This is being a professional Christian Chinese!"

"Indians?" was all Yuen could say that made sense.

"But helping you would be bad for me. So I write a letter for you. I get investigated, and then I get a letter. I don't want to be investigated. I want to become a citizen next year. Nobody likes me. Your people don't like me anymore because I'm really nobody, and you'll say I stepped on you to become a citizen and a professional Chinese. I have no friends, you see? I'm in more trouble than you."

"I'm going then. Thanks," Yuen said, and stood.

"Listen, uncle," Jimmy said from his seat, "don't do anything goddamn silly. If I can help with anything else, I'll be happy to do it. Want a loan? A job?"

"No," Yuen said and started to leave.

"Uncle, I trust you. You know what I mean. I know you have a job and keep your word and all that." Jimmy stood and took a long time to walk around his desk to Yuen's side. He put an arm around his shoulders. "You are a wise man . . . If you die, die of old age. I feel bad when I can't help, and I feel real bad when men die." He grinned and opened the door for the old man. "But you are a wise man."

"Didn't even offer a drink," Yuen said outside with the boy.

Pigeons dropped from the sky to walk between the feet of people and peck at feed dropped from the cages of squabs and chickens in front of the poultry shops. "Stupid birds," Yuen said. "Someone will catch one and eat it." He laughed and the boy laughed.

"I'm hungry," Dirigible said.

As they left the restaurant, Yuen walked quickly. He held Dirigible's hand and pulled him down the streets and pointed at fire escapes and told him what Tongs were there and what he had seen when he had been at parties there, and he walked over iron gratings in the sidewalk and pointed down inside and told Dirigible that at night music could be heard down there. They passed men sitting next to magazine stands and shook hands. Then Yuen went to the bank and withdrew all his money in a money order and borrowed a sheet of paper and an envelope, and in Chinese wrote his song: "This is all the money I have. You will not get anymore. I'm dead. Your father," and signed it. He put the letter and the money order in the envelope, addressed it, then went to the post office branch and mailed it. San Francisco was nothing to him now. He had said goodbye to his friends and seen the places he used to visit. They were all dirty in this daylight. The value of his death, to himself, was that nothing in his life was important; he had finished with his son that he hadn't seen in twenty years or more, and his friends, and San Francisco. Now he was going home. The tops of the buildings sparkled with their white tile and flags, Yuen saw. Jimmy Chan was wrong, he thought. But he helped me start the finish. The Grandson, Sun Tzu, the strategist says, "In death ground, fight." I am. I'm a very lucky man to know when all I am to do in life is done and my day is over. Jimmy Chan is too professional to know that. He doesn't see the difference between me and Huie's dead brother. Too bad. No cringing. No excuses. He walked quickly down the hill, believing himself to the bus stop. Dirigible had to run to keep up with him.

"What did you take him to San Francisco for? And why go to San Francisco, anyway? Do you know I had to wash all the dishes and cook, too? That colored boy wasn't home, you know," Rose said. "Criminey sakes, you think I'm a machine or something?"

"I'm sorry," Yuen said. Rose wouldn't understand anything he said right now. Better she not know what good shape he was in. No explanations.

"Well, you have to hurry, if you're going to get back in time to help me with the dinner dishes. I'm sorry, I didn't mean that, ah-bok, I'm just worried. All right?" She put a hand on his shoulder.

"All right."

Rose took the letter from Yuen's pocket and sat down at the kitchen table and read it over. Yuen sat down next to her and put a toothpick in his mouth. Rose stared down at the letter and began scratching a slow noisy circle around her breast. She talked to Dirigible without looking at the boy. "Uncle's in trouble, dear, I mean ah-bok has to go to the police and get his pictures taken. And you have to take him there and help him answer the questions the police will ask in this letter."

"I've been walking all day, Mommy. I don't wanta walk no more," Dirigible said. "Why don't you go?"

"You got a car," Dirigible said, stepping backward.

"Listen," Rose said. "You take this letter." She lifted the letter and pinned it with a safety pin inside Dirigible's coat. "And you go to where the fingerprint place is and you tell them to read the let-ter, that the United States Immigrators want them to read it, and that everybody, everybody, likes Yuen-bok, okay? And you take him." She gave the boy some crackers to eat on the way and helped Yuen to his feet.

"Do you know how to get there?" Yuen asked at every corner. They walked streets full of rush-hour traffic, walked past parking meters and a bodybuilding gymnasium. Yuen put an arm about Dirigible and held him. "Where are we in all this?" Yuen asked and pushed Dirigible toward the edge of the sidewalk with each word.

"We have to go fast now, ah-bok, or the police will close," the boy said.

The streets were not crowded, but everywhere on the sidewalks along the sides of the buildings Yuen saw people walking, all of their eyes staring somewhere beyond him, the pads of fat next to their stiff mouths trembling with their steps. They all moved past him easily, without actually avoiding him. Yuen held the boy's hand and walked, numbing himself to the people.

The long corridor of the city hall was full of the sound of feet and shaking keys against leather-belted hips, and waxed reflections of the outside light through the door at the corridor's end, shrunk and twisted on the floor, as they walked further down, past men with hats on and briefcases, policemen picking their noses, newspaper vendors with aprons. "Where do we go?" Yuen asked.

"I don't know," Dirigible said. "I can't read all the doors."

In a low voice, almost as smooth as an old woman's, Yuen said, "Do you see any Chinese around? Ask one, he'll help us." His hand rested on the back of the boy's neck, and was very still there as they walked.

"Excuse me . . ." a large man said, walking into them. They all tried to walk through each other a moment, then fell with the large man holding Dirigible's head and shouting a grunted "excuse me." Their legs all tangled, and they fell together in a soft crash. The man stood and brushed himself off. "I'm terribly sorry. Just barged out of my office, not thinking. Or thinking when I should have been watching my step. Are you all right? Your father looks a little sick."

"I have a letter," Dirigible said, and opened his jacket to show the letter pinned to the inside of his lapel.

"What's this?" the man asked, bending again. "A safety pin. All you people are safety pinning each other, my god!" he muttered. He took the letter and took a long grunt to stand up. Dirigible turned and helped Yuen, who was still on the floor, waiting, and staring with drool over his lip up at the strange *lo fan*. Yuen lifted himself to a crouch, rested, then stood and held himself steady, leaning on the boy.

"Immigration people want him fingerprinted," the man said. "You poor kid." He brushed his hair under his hat as he spoke. "I'll take you there. It's upstairs. Don't worry, if things go badly, you can call me, Councilman Papagannis." He adjusted his hat with his fat fingertips and walked quickly upstairs, swinging his arms with each step. They walked into a narrow hall with benches. At a desk, sitting on a high stool, in front of a typewriter, his sleeves rolled sloppily over his elbows, was a police sergeant, typing. "You can wash that ink stuff off your fingers in there, through that office, you see?" he was saying as they walked up to his desk. "What do you want? You'll have to wait in line. All these men here are in a hurry to get fingerprinted too."

"But I got a letter and supposed to tell you how people like Yuen-bok. Him." Dirigible pulled Yuen to the desk.

"What?" the police sergeant asked.

"Immigration people want him fingerprinted, photographed, and a copy of his record," Councilman Papagannis said. "Here's the letter. I'm Councilman Papagannis. I'd like to see them out of here in a hurry, you know, for the boy's sake." The councilman shook the sergeant's hand, then removed his tight-fitting hat.

"It says here, they want a copy of his record, too," the sergeant said.

"Well, do it!" the councilman said, stuffing himself between Yuen and the boy. The police sergeant took out a form and put it in the typewriter; then he picked up the telephone and asked for the city's record on Nelson Yuen Fong. He put the telephone down and looked up to the councilman. "Never heard of him," he said.

"Surely you have a form for that contingency, sergeant."

"Surely."

"Who said, 'The mills of the gods grind slow, but they grind exceedingly fine'? or something like that. The mills of the system are a-grinding, young man," the councilman said, marveling at the sergeant's checking boxes on a form. The police sergeant removed Yuen's hat with a short motion of his arm, "Hair color, grey," he said and began typing. He dropped the hat onto Yuen's head.

Yuen took the hat from his head and looked inside the brim. "What for?" he asked.

"Nothing," Dirigible said and took the hat and held it. Yuen watched now, his eyes wide with the lids almost folding over backwards. This was a fine joke for Yuen now. They were all so somber for his sake, and he had finished already. He could say any-thing and they would not understand, but Dirigible might under-stand a little, and Dirigible was too young to see the humor of the situation. Dirigible shouldn't be here, Yuen thought. I'll buy him a funnybook on the way home. He'll like that and won't feel so bad.

Dirigible yanked Yuen up to the edge of the police sergeant's desk and held his sleeve tightly. "How much do you weigh?" the police sergeant asked.

"He don't talk American," Dirigible said.

"What is he?"

"He's alien," Dirigible said.

"I mean, is he Filipino, Japanese, Hawaiian?"

"He's Chinese."

"Fine people, the Chinese," the councilman said.

"Fine," the police sergeant said and typed. "Now ask him how much he weighs."

Dirigible pulled at Yuen's coat until the man half-knelt. Dirigible's first word was in English and jittery. Yuen frowned, then smiled to relax the boy. The boy stamped his foot and snapped his glare burning from the police sergeant to Yuen. Yuen should have known the boy would hate him for not being able to speak English Longtime Californ'.

"You how heavy?" Dirigible said, blushing, sounding stupid to everybody, and cracked the accent on the *choong* word for "heavy" in a flat accent, but meaning "onion" when high-toned. Both the boy and Yuen heard "heavy" waver into "onion" and blushed. "What do you mean?" Yuen asked instead of laughing. "Take it easy, kid."

"You are how many pounds?"

"What's your old man say, boy?"

"We don't talk good together yet," Dirigible said, crunching his tongue into English, while still lugging his tongue in gutless Chinese, "You are HOW MANY POUNDS?" The boy stood straight and shouted, "How heavy the pounds?" as if shouting made it more Chinese.

"Oh, how many pounds do I weigh?" Yuen grinned and nodded to the police sergeant and the councilman. The police sergeant nodded and pointed at Yuen's stomach then patted his own belly. "Hundred and thirty pounds heavy," Yuen said.

"One hundred and thirty pounds," Dirigible said. The police sergeant typed.

After the questions, the police sergeant stepped down from his high stool and held Yuen's arms. "Tell him we're going to take his picture now, boy." Dirigible told Yuen what he'd heard old Chinese say to children all the time, and Yuen asked Dirigible to ask the police sergeant if he could comb his hair before being photographed. The men laughed when Dirigible asked.

Dirigible stepped away from Yuen and snuck a pinch of the blue stripe of the police sergeant's trousers, to see if what looked like shiny wire was metallic to the fingertips and wasn't sure. Yuen turned his head and combed his hair with his pocketcomb.

The police sergeant kicked a lever that turned Yuen's seat around. He snapped a picture. Yuen yelled once as the chair spun ninety degrees with the snap and stunned humm of a huge spring in the floor. "Atta boy, Nelson!" the police sergeant cheered. "Now for the fingerprints." He took the frames from the camera and tapped Dirigible next to the ear. "Tell your father to get down now."

"Ah-bok ahhh, get down now."

They walked home with the first blue of the dark night coming. Yuen patted the boy's shoulder and kept asking him to stop and buy some funnybooks, but the boy pulled Yuen's sleeve and walked on quickly, saying he was hungry and wanted to get back to the hotel kitchen. "Come on, ah-bok. I'm hungry," Dirigible said whenever the old man stopped to sit on a garbage can and nod his head at every streetcorner with a city trashcan. He sat as if he would sit forever, without moving his body or fixing the odd hairs the wind had loosened, his head nodding slowly like a sleeping pigeon's. "Are you mad at me?"

"No," the boy said in a hurry.

"Your mother's waiting for us, isn't she?" Yuen said. He stood and walked a little and said, "You're a funny son . . ." He muttered to himself louder as they neared the Eclipse Hotel. All his old age shook and fattened up the veins in his hands as he tried to touch Dirigible's nose or his ears or poke the soft of the boy's cheeks. "You're almost as tall as me . . . Did you see the policeman's face when he saw me?" In his slouching walk Yuen and the boy were very close to the same height. Yuen took a breath and tried to straighten up a thousand years, then sighed. He was too tired. Not important. "And that chair . . . "

He walked slower as they came to the back door of the restaurant. He looked up to the light over the door with pigeon droppings painting the hood. That light had gone out only once while he lived here, and he had changed the bulb himself. He had polished the hood and wiped the bulb. It was his favorite light in the whole restaurant, perhaps because it was the light that helped him open the door when he returned tipsy from San Francisco, or perhaps because it was the only light outside, back of the building. Thinking about a light bulb is stupid, he thought. He could enjoy stupidity now, after all this time of trying to be smart, trying to be tall, stupidity was inevitably on the way to rounding out the circle and resting it in silence.

Yuen could hear Margie shouting the names of foods back to the waitresses as if cussing them out and didn't seem to hear a thing. He could hear the little screech of ice-cold meat slapped flat onto a hot steel griddle before the grease cackles, running water, the insulated door of the walk-in refrigerator stomping shut, and didn't hear a thing. He held Dirigible's wrists together with one hand. Then to his horror, both his hands and all his strength, which felt considerable, twisted Dirigible's wrists. He could see from the ease with which the boy moved his arms that his considerable strength was nothing. "Help me upstairs," he said. "I don't feel well."

He leaned heavily on the boy, pushed himself upright against the wall as they climbed. Dirigible was very strong, Yuen felt, very strong. And very angry. The boy pushed at Yuen, upping the old man onto the next step up, up the stairs to his room.

In his room, Yuen did nothing but sigh and sigh and fall backward onto his bed. He stared a moment at the ceiling. The boy did not leave the room. Yuen closed his eyes and pulled at his nose and wiped it with his fingers and stared at the boy. He saw the boy clearly now, and the smile on his face closed shut, then the mouth opened to breathe. It no longer felt like his face he was feeling, no part of him. The old man's fingers, nothing felt like anything of his now. It all felt like old books in old stores. "I have an idea," he said slowly, and took the gun from under his pillow. "We used to try to swallow our tongues to choke ourselves when we were scared, but we always spit them out, or couldn't get them down. I want you to watch so you can tell them I wanted to."

"I don't know what you're talking." Dirigible eyed the gun.

"I'm going to die by myself," Yuen attempted in Chinese for dummies.

The boy stared, eyes big as black olives, "Who? You ... what are you doing?"

"Your mother can find another dishwasher. She's a good businesswoman."

"Who'll buy me books?"

Yuen pointed the gun at one ear, then switched hands, and pointed the gun at the other ear. He looked at the gun and held it with both hands and pointed it at his mouth, aiming it into his mouth, toward the bulge at the back of his head. He could be angry at the boy, even knowing the boy knew nothing else to say, he could be angry, but wasn't. Dirigible hit himself with a fist and shouted, "Ah-bok!" Dirigible leaned and fell backward, stepped once toward the old man before stopping against the towel rack. The boy was weeping and groaning, holding an imaginary pain in his shoulder.

Yuen looked over the gun and watched the boy's rhythmless stumblings in the close room. He eased the hammer to safe and sighed a longer sigh than he had breath. He went to the boy and pulled him to the bed and sat him and wiped his face with his hand. "It's all right, Dritch'ble." Yuen worked for enough breath to speak. "Get up. Go downstairs, now." He bent to untie his shoelaces, dropping the gun to the floor when his fingers could not work them. "Wait. Will you help me bathe? I feel very weak." He'd failed. But he had known he would. He'd expected it.

"Yes."

"I have soap. All kinds. You can have some . . ."

"I have soap too."

He patted the boy's shoulders with his hands and clutched into them with his fingers as he pulled himself to standing. You're an odd son," Yuen said, before turning to undress. "Help me with this."

Dirigible held a towel about Yuen's pale waist as he took him out of his room to the bathroom and helped him into the tub. Dirigible plugged the tub and turned on the water, with Yuen curled up on the bottom, waiting. He didn't complain about the temperature. He leaned forward and asked the boy to scrub his back. His body was loose over his bones, and the same color as his colorless wrists with fat spongy veins piping through the skin. He took the boy's hand and looked into his face with eyes covered with raw eggwhite. "You didn't write me," he said clearly and, his body quivering, rippling water away from his waist, Yuen died. He closed his eyes with his mouth opening to breathe or sigh, and at the end, his chest was low, his ribs showed, and he was dead. There was no more for him. He had finished it.

Dirigible lifted his hands from the water and put his cheek on the edge of the tub. Yuen's death had seemed nothing special, nothing personal. He had given up the boy also. The boy tried to work a tear loose. He felt he should. Tears not all for Yuen, but for himself, because Yuen had been *his*.

Rose came up the stairs and walked down the hall noisily, saying, "Well, how did it go, you two?" before she leaned her head into the bathroom.

Yes, Young Daddy

Hi Dirigible,

Guess hoo! Ya man, It's me, you know hoo-ooo! That fat lazy thing that lives somwere across the bay. Well, I thought I'd drop a few lines or two 'cause I's got nothing to do with myself. Seriously though, I thought it would be fun to write to you; and I know 24 hours a day isn't enough for you, you know college and drawing and all your girlfriends, but if you do get a tiney second; I would love to hear from you.

Do you know what I'm doing this summer? Well to put it flatly 'NOTHING'! The most I would do is go to the movies (with the kids of course since mommy's never home). The rest of the time I'd go to the church, clean house, stay home and look at TV. Oh, yes, if you do come to the city once in awhile for pleasure, I'm always free. That is if you don't mind my company. Your the only boy I think mommy will let come up, since she don't like strangers to see how a mess we live in, and she says I can't go out until I'm 18!

You know what, I got my school ring today and it's "Beautiful" (That's what I think anyway?) I know what your thinking. How come I have my ring now? You see, I don't want to pay $22.52 for the ring now? and just wear it for my last term in school. I believe it's a waste of money; so this way I can wear it through my junior and senior years.

Brother! Am I ever glad tomorrow will be the last day for my finals. Oh! It's driving me nuttie. To top off this week my English teacher hands back our term paper outlines just yesterday and said to hand in the finished term paper and he want it at least five pages long. He said we had to do a book report too, on TEST even! The termpaper and the book report is due tomorrow. What makes me so mad is that he has NO HEART, he doesn't care if you have tests in other classes or not!; and he's so last minuted. Oh, he makes me want to jump into the bay for all the other things I'd have to do plus those.

Well that's enough about my troubles, how've everything with you? Find of course. I bet you have a nice time there living so independent in your own apartment and everything. Well goodbye for now I've got to clean up the house.

Hope you'll always be very successful in what ever you do.

Lena

Dirigible waited two days to answer. He opened Lena's letter and shook it, trying to shake the smell of unimaginable dead flowers out of the paper. Finally he wrote.

Dear Lena,

Your loneliness must be very profound, indeed, to send me, your cousin, a perfumed letter. It's still smelling up my whole apartment, and soon, I'll have to hang it out the window. Really, I appreciate your letter and your *cousinly* affection. I don't have as many girlfriends as you say, and I do have a "tiny second" to write you.

Your spelling and grammar are miserable (this is cousinly concern now). "Find" is a verb meaning to discover. "Fine" is an adjective meaning, in colloquial English, "well." "I find you feel fine." Also you have your "your's" mixed up. "Your" is not "you're," okay? Now, I'm going to talk like father would talk, only in a cousinly way. You might show this to your mother if you like. I think it's time for you to start dating. I know you think about it. I know boys ask you out. You've told me, remember? And I know how your mother carried on when she found you and me and ma dancing to those old records at my house a couple of years ago, and it's not right. Why don't you work out a plan of going out every other week-end with some nice Chinese boy that your mother likes and promise to come home by midnight? If you don't go out this summer some time, a girl of your vitality might start sneaking out and meet up with the wrong kind of guy, you know the kind of guy that has "one thing on his mind" and steals cars, reads poetry and drinks, gambles, hates his mother and George Washington, calls San Francisco "Frisco" and rolls drunks . . . the kind of guy my mother thinks I am. But honestly I know that's the way a girl could go...don't ask me how I know, I know, okay?...And maybe, when I have time, a friend and his sister (about your age) and me and you can go to the zoo or Playland or something in the daytime, okay? No promises, just maybe. Practice your grammar, don't disparage school, be a good girl, give little Boo Boo a haircut...you're not fat.

> Your eldest and outcast cousin,
> *Dirigible* (*Dirge* for you)

He began by crossing out "Dirge for you." Time to break the habit of answering to that nickname. Let the old Chinamans and his relatives get his name right. The letter was right, he thought, a vocabulary that would make her use a dictionary, plenty of commas and semicolons; it was the right tone, he was sure, concerned without giving anything away. "Some nice Chinese boy" he read aloud from his letter. Well, he thought, Lena and some nice Chinese boy would go good together. She's not ambitious, and she's young...maybe smarter'n I think, and if she listens to her cousin's advice, tempers it with what she sees? He stopped planning his cousin's life, mailed the letter and forgot it.

Her next letter was not perfumed.

Dear, young Daddy;

All my girlfriends at the church call you that now, how 'bout that? I showed the letter to them and they finded it real fine. Why don't you come back and help build the church and get some of Buddha's *gum hay*? Whatever that is in English nobody has heard, right? The church is really needing help with it. Mommy is out in Los Angeles getting people to donate stuff for it (she's so pretty in her Chinese dress!) and you know what that means ME AND THE KIDS. Say! Howcome you made me look up all those funny words in the dictionary? You think I'm a brain or something?

Mommy lets some of the girls from the church come over to the apartment (what a mess it's) and we lock ourself in the bathroom and make ourself up with lipstick and stuff we buy. But that's girlses business and shuld not tell boys. But your a man, I'd forgot. Boy! do we look funny in the mirro sometimes. You should see us. Why don't you come over and watch TV with us? They all want to see you. They think your so handsome? They all remember you at the church and think you was "cute" and oh, so tall! And your smart too.

Oh! Don't get mad now. I forgot to show your letter to mommy. She was talking so much about Detroit and some girdles she got them to donate to build the church and stuff; but I's going to do it soon's she gets back from L.A. Ok? I am too fat! Boo Boo wants you to cut his hair. It's so LONG!

So long "Young Daddy."
Lena

Just one x

    Enclosed in the letter was a photograph of Lena in a miniature bridesmaid gown. Dirigible remembered the photograph; it had been his grandmother's favorite. He put it in his steel ammunition box where he kept his letters and social security stub and wrote.

Lena,

    You have to stop this "young daddy" jazz. People will think you have an Oedipus complex and are crazy. And I wish you'd stop showing your friends my letters. I'll write to them (I won't really) if they're so interested in my prose style . . . though I am flattered . . . a little. I'm sorry to be so curt with you (I know you'll understand) but I'm having a time with a poem I'm working on. I'm trying to figure out whether or not dawn really looks like the sound of a thousand muted pops of champagne corks or not, and if it does, what is a good word that rhymes with "corks"? . . . this is just a short note, dear cousin. Don't worry about your looking fat or thinking you're fat; you're not. No matter your mother came back from Detroit with girdles instead of girders. Actually I think girdles are what the church needs more than structural steel. Me. I'm skinny, and I don't worry about girdles or girders. Put ribbons on Boo Boo and tell him he's a girl. Show the first letter to your mother. Your spelling is not much better . . . but better.

As ever,
Dirigible

I concede 1/2 an x

Dear Dirigible;

I know how really busy you're now, writing poems and draw-ings. By the way! I finded a bunch of words that "rhyme" with corks. There're porks storks forks and works and torque and bork (I heared that one on the radio.) Anyways why don't you come over sometime when your not busy with your girlfriends or nothing? I'm always free I told you, and mommy is gone for awhile. I losed three WHOLE POUNDS, man! And I can't do nothing with the kids here.

What are you doing these days? Busy, I know.

Your friend,

Lena

P.S. You can see my new ring if your coming xxx

Dirigible felt the same sour embarrassment, pity, and disgust that he felt after seeing a cripple wearing trousers too long for his legs, selling colored carnations in front of a theater. Lena had such a happy way of writing her loneliness, he thought, like the cripple, bent and ugly, half-dancing in front of the crowd and shouting, "Flowers! Quarter! Half a dollar!" Sentimentalist! Dirigible thought to himself. But he always had a quarter, the flowers he never kept. He knew he would visit his plump cousin. He opened his ammunition box and put her note inside. The smell of per-fume was all through the papers inside and bloomed into his face as he lifted the lid. He wished suddenly that Lena was not his cousin, that he never knew her. And he was ashamed when he thought that she might remember them at his grandmother's house, bouncing on the cold sheets of the bed with a flashlight that made the skin look like soap. Ashamed wasn't it. He was still afraid she would, after all these years, tell on him. Perhaps if her name wasn't Lena, he thought, as if her name were to blame, then kicked the box under his desk where it belonged.

She lived in an apartment house owned and lived in by her dead father's family. Everybody in every one of the apartments here belonged to the same family and the same Buddhist church. The apartment house was far enough above Chinatown to have a hedge and a few flowers planted around it. A boy was doing a Chinese battle dance, using a broom for a sword in the front hall. He stopped and opened the door before Dirigible could press the buzzer. "Are you Boo Boo?" Dirigible asked.

"No. He lib up da stair," the boy said. He stabbed toward the stairs.

"You're not bad with that kung fu fighting," Dirigible said. "Where do you study?" toward the stairs.

"I go see lod a Chinese moobies!" the boy shouted after him.

The vague familiarity, not all that forgotten, not all that grabbing, short of nostalgia and déjà vu he found in the apartment house, the shadows in the corners, the worn rug with the pattern more walked out of it, made Dirigible realize the long time he had been away. At one time he had known everybody in the house, had lived here on weekends and gone down to help build the Buddhist church with them. But he did not regret leaving, for like the boy downstairs who was like all the boys in this house, everything was the same. The same and familiar beyond recognition, stagnant. That was why he had left and forgotten his cousin, all this part of the family, except for his glittering aunt, his mother's glamorous sister, Lena's mother. No, he thought, reaching the second flight of stairs, it's not comfortable at all to be back, even to be nice.

Lena opened the door, "Hello, Dirge, how're you?" She could write his name but still couldn't get it out of her Chinatown mouth. None of his relatives could. What a great name his mother had given him. No one else in the family could pronounce it. "Well, come on inside stranger." Her face was made up as if she had been practicing a long time, and she wore a pair of her mother's earrings. And she did not trip on her high heels when she stepped backward, making room for Dirigible's first step inside. Dirigible blushed, then turned his head to stifle a laugh. He had never seen his cousin with breasts before. Nice breasts.

"Chiyaaaaah! Hite!" they heard shouted from deep downstairs.

Lena smiled at Dirigible and still held the door. "I guess he killed a dragon or something," he said, nodding toward the stairs.

The walls of the apartment were covered with child-high crayon drawings, of trains, gardens, and battles that had been half washed off. A doorknob was missing from one of the doors, but the apartment was neat in a logical, if not attractive, sort of way, like a war surplus store. "Same old place," Dirigible said.

"It's a mess. I'm sorry."

"Oh, no. It's fine. You should see my place if you want to see a real mess." Dirigible laughed.

"When?"

"When what?"

"When can I see your messy apartment?"

"Oh, some time." He spoke quickly, looking over Lena's head. He shoved his fists into his pockets and nodded as he laughed. It was difficult trying to find the right tone, the right slouch with which to assuage his cousin's loneliness. Diplomacy. Psychology. Dirigible wished he had not come, or at least that he had dressed to match his cousin. "I didn't know you were going to dress up," he said and it didn't sound right. He sounded like a kid with his voice changing, and cleared his throat.

"Well, that's all right." She stood in front of him and he looked at her chest. "I like to dress up for . . . oh, company," she said. She closed the door with one hand, not moving from her stand in Dirigible's stare. He looked down and watched the muscles of her calves bulge as her body leaned slightly after her arm, throwing the door shut. "Where are the kids?" Dirigible asked.

"Downstairs with auntie. They're gonna be there all night."

"Oh," Dirigible said. "The first auntie, Foon Foon's mother?"

"No, she died."

"Oh, I'm sorry," Dirigible said, looking quickly about him for something to make a joke about.

"Don't be sad! Are you? She died a long time ago." Lena grabbed the swell of Dirigible's forearm, near the elbow. Her hand stopped and held tightly. Dirigible patted the back of her hand and smiled. "No, I'm fine. I should've sent flowers."

"That reminds me," Lena said quickly. "Look!" She gripped her arm and squeezed, clenching her teeth in a savage smile. "You can see all the veins and blue blood. I never knowed there was so many before! Ever! Remember when we used to did that?"

"Yeah," Dirigible stepped a step back from Lena, who was squeezing her own arm white.

"Let's see yours." She grabbed Dirigible's arm and squeezed with both hands, her body coming close to Dirigible's chest. She put her head next to Dirigible's face. She smelled like her letter, only the smell was louder in his head. "All I can feel is muscle, all your muscle," Lena said, impressed.

"Can we sit down? My legs kind of hurt."

"Where?"

"In the . . ." He looked into what had been the living room and saw a chest of drawers and a bed with a violin case on it. "Wherever the living room is."

"Where does your leg hurt? I can rub linaments on them?"

"Oh . . ." He looked up and down his cousin's short body. She was wearing one of her mother's silk *cheongsams* slit halfway up the thighs. And she began looking very new with her young body to Dirigible. He looked again. Her wrists and ankles were too thick for her small hands and feet, and again, he had never seen her with lipstick before. "No . . ." he said finally, "I think I'll just sit down somewhere. Though it's a charming idea." He made a laugh.

"Then I'll do it! Okay? I used to do it with daddy before. I know how to rub linaments."

"No, really, Lena. I'd just like to sit down. I'm tired of standing in the hallway. I feel stupid standing in the hallway." He laughed again. Too loud.

"You don't want me to?"

"Nope . . ."

"You think I'm fat and ugly and stupid and don't know how to do anything!"

"No, I don't. I never said that. Now, come on and tell young daddy how you've been and quit acting like a little girl, huh?"

"I am a li'l girl. You're older'n me. I want to do just that . . . Nobody lets me do nothing no more. Just stay home! All the time!"

Dirigible made a face with his eyes wide and stared at her. Her logic sounded simple and sound to him, and safe enough, perhaps because he wanted it so. And he did. "Okay," he said, shrugging. And she clapped her hands and was down the hall toward the bathroom and telling him to go to the bedroom and slip into one of her daddy's bathrobes. "Okay."

He lay down on Lena's mother's bed, on his stomach, and piled his hands under his cheek and closed his eyes to the light. A small belch burst up his throat before a long groan into relaxation at the sudden first slap of Lena's hands. Whap! Both hands. Now her hands were kneading the muscles of his calves, her hands gripped and slid slowly upwards, now at the soft spot behind the knees. Her hands were small and he enjoyed her fingers twisting the muscles over his bones. He felt the tightness drain out of his legs, and his legs felt softer, more relaxed than the rest of him.

As she beat him into a half-sleep she talked about her mother and her friends from the church, and her mother's new dresses, and taking care of Boo Boo and Cindy and her youngest brother whose name she took a long time to remember. Dirigible barely listened to her, felt only her hands rubbing the insides of his legs now. He imagined her bent over him, pushing with her shoulders and body as she rubbed and kneaded; he wondered if her breasts were trembling. "What's that?" she asked, and touched the soft spot behind his knee with her fingertips. She kissed it quickly then tapped it again. "There it'll be weller now."

"What'd you do that for?"

"You had a sore thing there."

"How can I have a sore there?" He raised himself to his elbows and twisted to see behind his back. He lifted his leg back by his ankle and looked behind his knee. "Yeah, I do, don't I?" he said and put the skirts of the bathrobe over his legs. He shook his head and sat up. He was awake now. He looked at his cousin sitting on the edge of the bed, the silk of her *cheongsam* shining where she swelled, but silk and sequins and lipstick could not change her eyes. After all these years they were the same eyes of the same little cousin she had always been to him, just like his photograph. They were young eyes, seeming younger surrounded by powder and rouge, and they were shallow-colored and so open. He did not know whether he liked them or not. He said, "I think you'd better stop or I'll forget you're my cousin and..." He shrugged and found a new ending for his sentence, "be sorry...."

"Really?" She grinned and edged closer toward him, her rump sitting lightly against his bare calf. Does she know what she's doing, doing that? he wondered. He did not move. He felt his pulse climb up the sides of his neck into his ears. What a dumb time to blush, he thought. Couldn't I just keep this thing to a hero worship or something? Too late.

He leaned toward her then stopped. A slight lowering of her shoulders and a quick blink of her eyes showed him what she wanted. He looked away quickly and shoved a finger up in the air and shouted, "Aha!" as if to throw his disgusting desire out of himself with a jerk. He slapped his thighs and laughed to noise the flower petals out of the air.

"What's wrong?"

"You . . ."

"You're laughing at me." She put her small hands along her hips, then quickly pulled off her mother's earrings.

"No," Dirigible laughed. "Do you know what you're doing?" He felt a chill up the outside of his legs and put the skirt of the bathrobe tighter around them.

"I didn't know I's doing nothing. Was I doin' something wrong?"

"Listen, oh, Lena." He sighed and looked at her. "You were trying to . . . I didn't think that you . . ." He stopped and jabbed at her with his fist. "I'm your cousin. God!"

"Well, gee whiz. What you want me to do? I can't help it if I like you!"

He sounded stupid to himself saying, "You're too young!" Stupid and hypocritical. "I mean, young. You don't know if you like me. I mean, I like you too. I have to, we're relatives."

"I don't mean that kind of 'like.' I mean 'like' like liking."

"What do you have to be so honest for? Why can't you be evasive like nurses or sorority girls or high school teachers?"

"Because I don't know how!" she shouted. "I don't even know what you're talking about." He knew this was true, and it was funny in a sour slimy sort of way. She began to cry.

"Don't cry," he said. "I'm not mad. See?" He touched her shoulder.

"Well, I am!" she said between gulps.

"Come on," he said. He took both of her shoulders and she leaned against him, her hair against her cheek and lips and the side of his nose. "Sooner or later you'll . . . well, you'll know better."

"You think I'm a baby. I don't want to know better. I do know better now. Better'n you!"

"Well, you don't know better than to try to be like your mother yet."

"What're you talking?" She looked at herself and cried. "You're dumb."

Dirigible looked down the length of his body to her. He leaned and touched her shoulder. "Lena?"

"Don't touch me. Get out. You think I'm a joke!"

"No . . . I . . ." Dirigible sat back and closed his eyes. It would be awkward for him to leave now, yet he could not stay.

The front door slammed and Lena's mother stepped into the room. "So dis is what goes on behind my back, huh?" Lena's mother said. She hiked her *cheongsam* up her thighs and walked quickly over to the bed and looked down at Dirigible, dressed in her dead husband's bathrobe. "And you! You should know better! Don't you know how old she is? She's your little cousin! What kind of dirty mind you got anyway?" Old makeup fell in small chips from her hairline as she spoke. Flesh shook on her arms like bread dough.

"You have the dirty mind here, Aunt Dee. I didn't do nothing."

He suddenly realized that what he was wearing didn't make sense of his righteous huff and puff. "She only put linament on my legs, because they were sore!"

"Boy, you wait till I tell your mother! What do you mean only put linament on your legs? That's what I do! Did! I'm going to take her to Dr. Jim downstairs tomorrow, man. And if . . ."

Dirigible glanced at Lena. She was sitting trying to hide herself behind her arms and crying. "And where'd you leab the kids? Can't I trust you with nothing?" Lena stood and said that she'd get them and left. Her game of Pretend was over, Dirigible thought, and she was, really was, prettier than her mother was now. Years ago they'd been under the sheets together with a flashlight and seen and touched each other in cookie-sized illuminations and never been caught, and never forgotten it, if that would be any consolation to her; it bothered him, as he left. It wasn't déjà vu, but he'd been here before. It was better when he'd been eight years old.

The trouble with his mother, he knew he could survive; he was always super-logical and composed when he was with her, but he was worried about Lena. But not anymore, he decided. No more worrying about anybody but number one for me! he thought, all to himself, not looking back to the house as he left, walking down the hill toward the lights of Chinatown and the nearest bus home.

Dirigible;

I founded your address from Lena. You're lucky this time. They said that you'd be like you're now when you left the church, remember? It's not too late to come back, you know. It would be nice if you'd work here and give your hours to your grandma. You know what me and Lena did? We earned up a hundred hours and gave them to Grandma, and now she has a million more years in heaven. So you see? The church ain't so bad after all.

I talked to your mother. I told her to be kind this time. Lucky for you. Lena and I go for Chicago next week. Think about what I told you.

Your loving aunt,
Deanna

Dear Dirigible, Hi;

It's me again, man! Ya! I'm find, really. You was right, yes, young daddy, mommy's letting me go out to town with some boys now. And I'm so happy; and I's not mad at you, ok? Boy! Next week mommy's going to Chicago for the church to talk to some magazinebook about a story for the church, and she says she's going to take me for one whole WEEK! The kids're going to stay at your mommy's hous.

I'll write you if you promise to write me, okay? Deal!

This is just a tiny letter, but I got to go down to the church now. May you be successful in whatever you endeavor.

Yours truly,
Lena

Dear Lena,

To be brief, our roles have reversed, almost. I'm the wrong man for your "young daddy." So long.

Dirigible

Dirigible re-read his note; it was brief, a pleasant tone. She would believe it, he thought. *So even the hero is gone.* He opened up his ammunition box. Her perfumed letters had gassed everything. That smell would be there forever. He took out all of Lena's letters and a piece of paper with typewriting on it. He read:

> *Dawn came up looking like the sound of a*
> *thousand pops of champagne corks*
> *And the sun with it, full of daylight and*
> *tines of forks.*

It was bad, he decided, terrible. He threw the whole bundle into the wastebag. He slapped his hands against his thighs after knotting the bag and then stepped on it.

"Give the Enemy Sweet Sissies and Women to Infatuate Him, and Jades and Silks to Blind Him with Greed"

THE AIR was very black for all the lights of the celebration. The rain was heavy. The rain was thorough. The shattered water came glistening fishscales, down, gigantic noisy tin and silver dandruff crashing out of nowhere in a constant, hypnotic, illogical noise people ceased to hear, ceased to realize was working on their nerves like termites in the woodwork, he knew. Dirigible knew the rain was working on him. He knew the rain was working on everyone. The people were stupid. They were numbed stupid. One by one, he saw people glazed and glistening from the rain, like madmen spit in the face asking why in delirium. The tapping of the rain, the shrill flutelike cleanliness of the rain, the wet, worked in all the nerves, in every organ, in every globule of fat, every ounce of hearing. It confused him he realized, as no one else realized they were confused by the rain working on them, making them grope and blink to perceive the grand spectacle of the New Year's celebration through faulty senses, through encumbrances, picking bits of the lion dancers, the string of fifty thousand fat firecrackers through the static over shortwave radios. "I don't like crowds," he shouted into Mrs. Hasman's ear. She heard no words, he realized. She had merely heard him joining the monstrous musical instrument of the crowd. She turned to him and put her small hands up into the sleeves of his coat and rested them on his bare arms like cold things out of the wet and cold. "Do you like that?" she asked. "I love it."

"I don't like crowds!" he shouted.

"Why? They're so happy! What do you have against them?"

"Nothing! I don't have anything against them. They're just stupid. They don't look happy. How do you know they're happy?"

"They wouldn't be out here in the rain if they weren't happy, silly!" Why was it all the women who couldn't resist him called him "silly" with the same petting voice? Or was it the pet name of the day?

He did and didn't tell her his father had been paralyzed from the neck down since he was nine and he read the news to the man for a half-hour every evening, for years, until he recovered and fulfilled his ambition of playing evil Jap generals and Chinese who die and seeing Tempest Storm strip live. "You know the Chinese, I've heard, have a way of being alone, you know, uncrowded, I mean, oblivious, you know? in crowds, and," gulping rain every work, "it's a great thing. Like my old man, he could sit on a crowded bus just as easily and comfortably as if he was in a hot tub, completely no self-consciousness, unselfconscious. Of course, it used to embarrass the hell out of me and bothered everybody else, seeing him sighing and sinking into himself . . . being so easy and unconcerned is an obscene thing in public, you know." The only Chinaman to crave the part of Charlie Chan's Number One Son. Now he seems about to get it. He's off in Hollywood, a chosen ageless Oriental and might as well be dead and gone to Heaven, for all he is to his Chinatown home. Dear old Dad. "But I wonder how he does it? It must be great to be that way, you know. I'd like to take you through this crowd as easily as if all these people were just flowers and grass in a field. I'd sure like to do that, wouldn't you?"

"Welcome! Welcome! One and all! Happy New Year. *Goong hai fot choy!* Happy New Year. Wind a Ford carrer! Wind a Ford! Help build a church!" came the voice of Dr. Larry. Like an itch entering the consciousness occupied by an ache, the puffing, winded cheerfulness of Dr. Larry's voice mingled and irritated with an anger into the rain, the gemlike blackness of the night, the crowd, the confusion of glitter and ooze compounded into a monster of unfathomable dimensions of incommunicable grumbling intellect that was tonight, and made him feel a helpless fool. Nobody incarnate. Shouts were drawn out of his mouth, shouts and sounds and expressions on his face were drawn out of him. His nerves in self-defense stood out stingingly against the trample of colorfully meaningless sensations. He felt himself being invaded, ransacked, and looted by nothing tangible, nothing of perceptible value, by merely being conscious. "Wind a Ford, ladies and gennulmens! Help build a church. One of the noblest acts man does . . . to help build a church! Happy New Year!" The sound of Dr. Larry's voice became less cheerful, less desperate after practiced hearing. "Sounds like W. C. Fields," Dirigible said.

"Aren't you having fun? Aren't you happy?" she asked.

"Sure. I wouldn't be out in the rain if I weren't happy, would I?" he said. "Silly."

"We don't have to stay here, if you don't want to," she said. "We can go someplace on the other side of town and wait for the theater crowd to come in and drink Irish coffee, if you'd rather. I don't want you to stay just because of me."

"I won't," he said.

"You know what? Please don't play games with me, Dirigible. Be sweet."

"I won't stay here just because of you. Good old Mrs. Hasman."

"Don't call me Mrs. Hasman," she said. "And," she squeezed his arms and put her cheek against his chest and chuckled there, "don't talk about me that way. You make me sound like one of your old school teachers."

"You are one of my old grade school teachers," Dirigible said.

"Ask me if I'm having fun, now," she said. For no reason at all he was wiping her wet hair with his hands and feeling dissatisfied when it didn't squeak.

"See the Bodhi tree! See the Bodhi treeee! The treeeee of enlightenment . . . ent. Come inside, folks. Freee! Freee!"

"Are you having fun, good old Mrs. Hasman?"

"Freee! Freee!"

"He sounds like Rex Ingram coming out the bottle. Are you having fun?"

"Yes," she said. "Now, I am," and hugged him. The wet clothes between them met and crushed bloated fabric against bloated fabric like sodden sponges. She hugged him. He vaguely felt her hands caressing the back of his overcoat as if it were his bare skin. He felt her curling inside her clothes, felt her going warm as if she were tucked into bed and taking him with her like a precious toy. For a moment he was a fat proprietor overlooking his repertoire of familiar feelings. The people rushing past him down the slight hill toward the undulating swarm of old ladies in black coats, of tourists and children with white faces chilled to jello—he saw them too, not looking at him—rushing crippled by the mud to mass on the fringes of the parade route and glint green and blue and red out of their wet clothes like bluebottle flies and crickets quietly buzzing a delicate insect violence over sweets made him, in his stillness, feel invisible, strangely a set of senses working without identity, a little god without a religion. The faces weren't seeing him with meaningful eyes as they looked at him. He discovered he had no feeling about their looking at him and they, in turn, didn't care, which was pleasant. "Hmmm," he said, and was acutely half asleep, dumbly patting her shoulder and rocking her, the senses in the arms about her and the vibrations of his humming, reminiscent of his mother's nervous hum, as she mysteriously progressed toward paralysis after her husband, an inch at a time, a numb at a time till she was wheelchair-bound, now, her hum measurable arrived home like letters from distant friends, and he had to admit to himself, self-enviously, that having the body of a pretty girl in a wet coat stop shivering and start snuggling against him, in the rain, on Chinese New Year's to be all this quiet in all this noise and wet was very pleasant. The same feeling he felt when he knelt on the sidewalk to take a chuffing suspicious dog in his arms or helped an old lady cross a street. There should be more to it. "You're quite a guy, Dirigible," she said, taking a cue from something in the crowd, perhaps Dr. Larry's evangelistic Buddhism over the loudspeakers atop the construction office. "Hmmm," Dirigible said, and shook his head once. "Yessir," to salute the fake childhood his midget self had lived. "Yessir, you know, good old Mrs. Hasman, I'm quite a guy. Man, when I think about myself, whew." He chuckled and patted her on the shoulder.

"I love you too," Mrs. Hasman said.

"Trite but true, babe, good old Mrs. Hasman, very trite, but true. Very true," he said and patted her head. Too much patting. The wet hair smacked with an interesting fleshy sound that held his attention. He took her declaration of love like a man, riding the humor in her voice, as if he hadn't heard all she meant to say. Very familiar. Uncomfortably familiar. In a glance, a shiver, a cluck of the tongue perhaps, but soon, he knew, the novelty with himself her company generated would fade and disappear like the odors of last night's digested dinner out of the emptied kitchen. Too bad. "Yessir, good old Mrs. Hasman, baby. I'm one fine Chinaman."

"You're my Chinaman's chance."

"That's very funny, what you just said, you know that?"

"Were you thinking about Cuba?"

"Cuba? No, why should I think of Cuba? Am I the minority of the month?"

"What then? Secret?"

"No."

"What were you thinking then?"

"Me. I was thinking about me."

"Is that all?"

"That's all."

"Seriously?"

"You. I thought about you. And me. You and Me. Us. I always think seriously, good old Mrs. Hasman." Very familiar and dusty this growing mood of lateness, the feeling of unrest at having overspent, overplayed, overstretched.

"Hurry! Hurry! *Goong Hai Fot Choy-eeeeee!*" faded into a low growl, then electronic silence. "*Goong Hai Fot Choy-eeeee.* Everyeee Body-eee. Wind a Foh-rerrred Car-errr. Wind a Foh-errred Carrreerrr. Help. Build uhhhh Churrrrstchhh."

"Goo'leven-ing elley bolly, lady anner gennuhmans, anna walcome to dis Chinatong, Sa'F'acisco, U-S-A, fo' ris happy Chinee New Ye'r, celebrate anna par-ray! Donk fo'geh dah affer-wars be ah Chinee opper anna finer kung fu judo ex-hibbee anna be introduced fo' you dah wonnerfooey booyootifor anna charmin Misser ah-Chinatong. U-S-A. Anna *Goong Hai Fot Choy!*" echoed suddenly from the speakers up and down Kearney Street. For a moment the loudspeakers from the Buddhist church on Washington and the reviewers stand on Kearney impacted their sounds among the crowd.

"I happen to know for a fact that there isn't a Chinaman in the world named Anna Goong Hai Fot Choy. That man's a liar," Dirigible said.

"Aww, come on, Dirigible, you know that's not what he said."

"Yes, he said that. He said in impeccable English, 'Ghoul' right? 'Ghoul leavening hully gully, lady entertainments, etc. etc.,' and '... Miss Chinatown, Anna Goong Hai Fot Choy.' That's what he said, and he's a liar," Dirigible said. "And he's a liar. I went to school with Anna Goong Hai Fot Choy, and she's ugly!" Mrs. Hasman laughed because she was the only person with him, which was familiar to Dirigible, all just as he remembered. Perhaps he had a rotten memory. Perhaps he was manufacturing the past now at the expense of all the women in his life. Even the familiarity was true. The distortion wasn't a lie for he was the purest most honest person he could trust, whether or not he knew what he was talking about, no matter what people thought of him, or how many people he shut out of the realm of meaningful consciousness and left buzzing on the fringes to be treated like flies bouncing off a screened window. *Prohibit superstitious practice and rid the army of doubt. There'll be no trouble till the moment of death,* the strategist known as the Grandson said. Did his mother know what Chinese New Year's meant to him? he asked himself once just to feel the satisfaction of knowing specifically that she didn't know. He grimly enjoyed standing in the rain to be at a scientific distance from the doctor in his shirtsleeves, sitting in a cramped room full of helium tanks and balloons and Kewpie dolls, going hoarse into a microphone, while his mother in her wheelchair, her face flaking off and turning to mud, tended the hotdog stand. "Hi, Ma!" He was out in the open with a white woman, appreciating the hilarious irony of the doctor calling people into his church to enjoy a circus where Ma all but said to each customer, "I hope you like the church, I'm going to lie in state here soon." Not that the fat holy rolling Buddhist M.D. was Ma's boyfriend. He was her doctor and her reverend minister, the medicine man who couldn't cure her and raced to finish his church in time to hold her funeral.

Dirigible held Mrs. Hasman as if she were beautiful. He held her as if she were Sharon, he knew, the princess of this church,

and couldn't make it seem any more realistic than if he were holding a sack of rice. They all weigh about the same, a hundred-
pound sack of rice, Sharon, Mrs. Hasman, his long headache.

"You know something? We're childhood sweethearts," he had
said to her. The night inside the clothing store among the head-
less dressed dummies and racks of jackets had seemed as large as
tonight's bright darkness full of rain. Any night, when he was in
the mood, seemed like that night. If he was in the mood, a coffee
and donut at Fong Fong's pastry shop at noon seemed like that
night. He was that old. But he remembered the words he had
made up to remember accurately. "How about that?" he had said.
"Childhood sweethearts. What a kick."

Larry and his chain-smoking mother along with Sharon's
parents and grandmother were on the other side of the door, in
the sewing factory part of the shop watching television. On
Fridays the room was the meeting place of the Buddhist church.
He heard them now, as he had not heard them then, when he had
been with Sharon being selectively silent, turning up the volume
of the television to not listen to it louder as they strained their
hearing to penetrate sounds and walls. "They say I can go out with
you for awhile tonight. Once," she said.

"Ma says you really have a cute way of talking, you know?" he
said to what he thought had been Sharon's own peculiar handling
of English, compounded with nervousness. He hadn't known how
perfectly she had spoken. He couldn't blame her for that. He tried,
and made himself fail to believe she had known what she was talking about, that she had known exactly what she said and meant it.
She was cute. He had studied her face until she was hardly recognizable to him when he saw it whole. She would grow up into an
unbeautiful chimpanzee-faced cute Chinese woman. He had told
her so. He told her he knew exactly what they would look like in
their old age and blushingly said he had recently been torn between revulsion and lovely heartbreak at the sight of very old
wrinkled, toothless people in a movie saying they loved each other
and kissing on the lips with tears in their eyes after their only son
had died in the Swiss Alps. "They were Swiss and cute foreigners,
you know what I mean, and so had me anyway, like they do," he
rushed on to say and continued, "and I want to know how old we
should grow to, huh?"

"Oh, I don't know," she said dejectedly. "Dirigible, I want to go *out* with you once! Right now!"

"I'll go tell 'em where we're going."

"No, That's all right. They know I'm going out that's all. Let's go!" she said. "Please!"

The buzzer on the door buzzed somewhere in the sewing factory as they opened it. They heard a wordless voice and a chair creak and the television set being snapped off, and they were off, he dragging her by the hand and giggling as they ran by the movie house, Filipino poolroom and barber shop, the tiny grocery to his car by the fire hydrant, and into the car, and in the slamming home of the doors they were gone from the world, invisible, into his car.

"Here I am, a grown man. You know how old I am?"

"You're still a young man, aren't you?" Mrs. Hasman said.

"I'm the oldest young man you'll ever see, I'll tell you."

"You were about to say . . ."

"Here I am an old young grown-up man, with a grown-up woman, you, beautiful woman, I might add. Also. And. And . . . there's the word. And! I'm thinking about this little Chinese girl I liked when I was a kid, a childhood romance."

"So?"

"I'm thinking her up. I'll show you a picture of her later, and she's really a little girl, but I don't remember being a little boy, and here's the kick. Here's the thing! It's really perverse too, really sickening. Look at me. See the lines in my neck? There's how you tell how old Chinamen are. They have ruts in their necks. See? And see my eyes? Old eyes right? See the scars on my face from years of pimples? Well, I'm thinking about a little girl. Lecherously! Wow, that's bad. And my arms around you, and through my gloves, and through your coat and your dress and your underwear I'm kind of hefting your breast through layers of stuff and it's like copping a feel off her right now, you see? But! The thing is she was flat-chested. And I never! Never thought . . . yes, I guess I did think of copping a feel off her too, come to think of it, but I never did. But now, I do. Yes, go right ahead, grin and squeeze me and put your wet head on my shoulder because I'm laughing. But you know. You know it's not so much funny as plain silly. Hmmm. Good, good old Mrs. Hasman, my own little puppydog, do you mind me copping a feel off a dead girl from you?"

"The way you talk! As a long as it's just me who knows what she's missing," Mrs. Hasman said. "You really don't know how Chinese you really are. That's why I like you so."

Dirigible and Sharon had finished their shrimp cocktails and thrown away the paper cups. They were bored with sitting on a wooden bench and sucking their fingertips, which no longer tasted like spiced catsup, and sighed and made sounds through their noses at every variation in the movement of the fog over the bay, over the boats. He knew their clothes were touching. He knew precisely how far inside the sleeve like a bug in a cocoon his elbow was from the wall touching the wall of her coatsleeve and half-imagined their elbows, like prisoners in adjoining cells, whispering to each other too low for his big ears tuned to big sounds to hear. "What're you thinking?" Sharon asked.

You, would have been a good answer. And easy out of his mouth. And not far from the truth. *You. Your family. My aunt Dee who married into your family of wacko evangelistic Buddhists who hold all-night meetings every other Friday night in your sewing factory. Big industrial sewing machines pushed together against the wall. Rows of steel folding chairs on the floor. And under the portrait of the redfaced Kwan Kung, his blackfaced squire and his adopted son with the whiteface, sat a woman in a dowdy sweater who looked like she worked there behind a sewing machine. "Auntie," on the platform before us, she was the* Gum Geng, whooo! *the Golden Mirror, the cosmic auntie, sucking oxygen through a plastic mask hooked up to a huge tank tended by Dr. Larry, under the portrait of the Buddha, had visions in Chinese. Ma had visions I'd learn Chinese here clearing my mind every other Friday to tremble before the* Gum Geng, *our Auntie. Never called her "Golden Mirror." Never translated* Gum Geng. *Auntie, we called her. Auntie. Auntie with her big tank of oxygen with the fittings and valves, clockfaced gauges, and tubes flopping around, as Auntie sucked gas, clouded the transparent mask with her breath, closed her eyes and, with Dr. Larry's eyes hard on me, out of his face fatter than three Buddhas, had a vision about the vision her nerd nephew who had eyes for you, Sharon, had about me. No more visions of money out of the pockets of the poor to convert the Club Manila into a modern church building. The practical visions of money and architecture satisfying the soul got personal enough. So what! I caught your eye* in the mirror on mine, when I said, "I wouldn't give a dime to see Jesus walk a tightrope, so why should I give my lunch money to Buddha, instead of eating a hot lunch?" You laughed. I saw it in your eyes. Eleven wasn't so long ago when I drove you to Fisherman's Wharf in Ma's Chevy. We were still kids. I never came close to believing your cousin Nerdy Nerd, Dr. Larry's heir apparent to the golden handle controlling the gas of Buddha's visions, went into any kind of trance, when he saw my open grave. I saw his eyeballs move like knees under a blanket. A shovel next to the grave. Who cares! Next to the coffin, he saw a hairy thing walking away. It wasn't even a good movie. No imagination. I didn't figure it out in the month Auntie gave me. Never gave it a thought. The Movie about Me is not a lame Bergman movie, but a western. Why didn't you remember us together, in the shell of the Club Manila, in our overalls and helmet liners for hardhats, workgloves, under the stairs, while the old folks and kids scraped bricks clean, you said it was clear to you, you were either going to be Mrs. Me or Mrs. Nerdy Nerd because you had to stay in the church. Did I mention it? Did you? It hadn't been that long ago. We still liked each other. We were still kids. You were still catching my eye in the mirror and playing with me the night, a month later, Auntie's revelations about the vision about me had the church in suspense and terror. Only the matriarch, the big mother, widow of the wildeyed founder, looking like the bigeyed mummy of a newborn bird, with white hair, and a black cheongsam too big for her, sat facing the congregation, at her glass table, doing what she always did. Chain-smoke Camels, and fold the foil linings of the cigarette packs into toy boats. All night long, cigarettes and folding boats. Auntie sucked her oxygen. The little big mother poured smoke out of her nostrils and mouth and unfolded empty cigarette packs. The fat doctor working on his Th.D. from a Stockton religious college, bit his lower lip, and glowered at me, and translates for Auntie. I am eleven and foul, evil, and dangerous. The bear is me. The grave is mine. I have stepped out of the open coffin reincarnated as a bear. Perhaps a California bear. Everyone knew cousin Nerdy Nerd dreamed of going to Cal Berkeley, like his uncles, become a doctor, become a minister of this church. Not only would I be reincarnated as a bear, I would live forever as a bear, and be hunted down by men forever. Whoops! Did I say it? Did she hear it above the whimpering and sniffling slopping out of people on my behalf? The million-year-

old newborn bird mummy creaked and rasped to her fleet of tinfoil
boats. She never spoke at meetings. Never had visions. Audiences in
her huge room in her huge house, yes. But never visions. "The bear
is smoking a cigarette. If I don't make it back to good before my
eighteenth birthday — legal smoking age in California — I will die."
The fat doctor translated. So she'd spoken in the voice of my soul,
not hers. Owooooo! The big bad wolf is a mama. That's how much
they thought you loved me.

"You like boats?" Dirigible asked.

"I like boats all right."

"I like watching them jiggle around like that in the water, you
know? I like them better than trains or airplanes, for one thing.
You know, I like watching them kinda knock each other. How
about you?"

"It's very nice."

"Yeah, I really like it. I like it a whole lot, you know? You know,
I like it so much I could do it all the time. It's really nice."

"I think so too," Sharon said. She put her hand on his sleeve,
slowly collapsed the sleeve on his arm.

"Man, I wish I had me a boat."

"Yeah, in a way. Boats? They're all right. I guess. I don't know,"
Dirigible said, "What's wrong?"

"Do I make you feel like there's something wrong? Aren't you
having fun?" Was she the first to ask him that? "Aren't you having
fun? Aren't you happy?" They all asked him. First call him silly
then ask him if he's happy. The question still made him feel so important. She'd asked the right question at the right time. The right
good girl. And he'd faked it away, instead of answering. Then, as
now. "Yeah!" he said, fast. "Yeah, man I'm having fun. It's just that
you're so quiet, you know, Sharon."

"It's all right being quiet, isn't it? I like you to talk to me. I like
to listen," Sharon said. "You talk to me nicely. Everybody notice
it."

"Hey it's been *Guys and Dolls* with us since we made faces to
each other, remember? In the mirror over the heads of Auntie
and Dr. Larry leading the church meetings? I was twelve, Sharon,
and couldn't take my eyes off you." Dirigible smiled and snorted
up his nose, "People notice, huh? Anybody in the church, when
I was twelve and you eleven, man, just look up from the flock,

man, and there we are, under the Kwan Kung over Auntie, and the golden Buddha over your uncle Larry, there we were in the mirror making faces."

"They said you liked to talk to me better than anybody, and you talk smart and very good."

"Talk! is that what they say I like to do with you? Is it a crime to get good grades in English? They want me to talk stupid to you?"

"They said when you're overexcited your talking just roll out words like lyrics to a song."

"Yeah, they call me *Dirigible the Mouth.*"

"Oh, you," Sharon said, and hit him solid on the arm with a little fist. A long time later outside of Chinatown adventuring for years, he'd feel how much he missed women talking to him that way, with the little pats and punches on the nonlethal spots of his body. "They do not! But they should call you Dirigible the Bad-mouth, the way you get people mad at you."

"Oh. Oh. I hear mixed emotions in the Movie about Me. Yours first, then mine. Seriously, you know, I'm quite a guy, you know? There is not another Chinese-American boy like my anywhere. Any where! Look around, you see another Chinese boy like me? NO! You don't even see any other Chinese boy at all! You know why? Because I am the only one!"

"Why don't you say Chinaman like you do?"

"You don't like me to."

"It's all right for tonight, isn't it?"

"Sure," Dirigible said, too quick, "Chinaman," and thought he had her.

Sharon giggled. "Chinaman," Dirigible said, and "CHINA-MAN!" he shouted.

"They say you should be an actor," Sharon said.

"I am an actor, didn't you know that?" kept Sharon laughing and, "I have to be an actor just to be near you, man. I'm afraid of you, man, you know? Because of them. You never know what shape they're in."

"Do you hate them?" she asked.

"Yes! No," Dirigible said. "No, I don't think I hate them. I don't like them. But they don't like me. They kicked me out of the church, said I'm going to die before legal smoking age. I should like them for that?"

"Are you lying to me?"

"Lying? What are we talking about?"

"They say you hate them."

"I dislike them a lot. You know what I mean? Honest."

"They still say you're going to die at eighteen, you know."

"We better hurry on and enjoy the few minutes we have left."

"Don't joke about them. They're not funny."

"Yeah, man, you don't know what or who you're talking to when you talk to me, man. I'm bad, man. I'm a bad fella. But I'm better than anyone you know. I know that, man. Sharon, I know that! And I love you, man. I do."

"They said you'd sound good to me."

"And they're right, huh? I sound good to you. Man, I sound good to myself. Boy! I love talking to you, man. With you around I could talk to myself all day and sound good all the time. Great stuff, and it's you, man, you know what I mean? And I'm going to kiss you right now. I can hardly wait. Right now."

"Not now," Sharon said. She turned her face. "I want you to stop talking for a minute, right now."

"I was only bragging . . . " Dirigible said, "But it's all true."

"You always are a bragger, you know that? Sometimes I like. Only sometimes. It's relaxing."

"Oh. Are you relaxed?"

"Uncle Larry said he talked to you."

"Yeah."

"He told me to ask you some question."

"Okay. Then we can talk about kissing you. If I'm not going to kiss you, at least I can talk about it."

"Please stop being funny."

"Then stop laughing, silly," he said. She stopped laughing.

"He said to ask you this question. He said he talked to you and asked you this question and to ask it to you so I wouldn't think he was lying. He said you wouldn't lie about your answer. He said it would be the same," Sharon said stiffly, suddenly Dr. Larry's Trojan horse, and she knew it. "Yes," Dirigible said.

"What," Sharon said. "Please don't interrupt. Sometimes you make me mad."

"The answer's yes. I know the question, all right. You want me to tell you how it was?"

"I said wait a minute, please. This is the question," she said slowly.

"The answer's yes."

"Please!"

"Yes."

"Do you, when a girl bends over, if she's wearing a blouse, look inside? Her blouse?" Sharon said. *Now I understand the Grandson's verse: "Give the enemy sweet sissies and women to infatuate him, and jades and silks to blind him with greed."* "He said to ask you," Sharon said. "It isn't important to me, you know."

"Yes, I look. So what. What do they expect if I'm going to die before I turn eighteen?"

They were upstairs in his rooms over the noodle factory. Her coat was off. Her blouse was wet and turned transparent. He was aware of the color of her bra, red through her wet blouse, was aware of her bent over looking at her legs and pulling stockings tight over her knees with the same detached awareness he had had when taking in the same sight from a moving train he had been riding for days. No direct relationship between his consciousness and his senses. He received everything in echoes. The rain, the noise, the bands, the shouting over the loudspeakers, the cold mud that had numbed his feet, the constant drone and vibration of his voice in his throat, the colors and sounds of the hysterically constant rain had done this to him, he realized. His nerves had taken to the noisy sounds of metallic jubilation joylessly dead to the narcotic and were quiet and soothed while he wanted to relax, stop moving, shut up, and go to sleep. His socks were wet, bloated about his feet. His wet clothes were like wet socks. His whole body was like spongy feet in bloated socks. He didn't take his clothes off, didn't even remove his overcoat or gloves because he was making tea, because he was talking now. He was making tea and talking with the desperation of fulfilling a promise, like a madman clumsily trying to make an action complete, a moment seem magic by encumbering himself, by not enjoying himself. "She was really beautiful then, you know, good old Mrs. Hasman. She was all smeary-eyed. She'd never been kissed in her life. Romantically, I mean. I knew that. Yessir, I knew that and I couldn't stand it the way she showed it to me. She tilted her head so. And looked smeary-eyed into my face and talked to me. She quoted me.

'Remember when you told me 'bout when you were a little boy?'
she said to me. 'About when you and your *ah-mah* used to go by
the place where they have the girlie show? And you told me how
you stare at the pictures of the woman with stars stuck on them
and tried to make like you wasn't doing that because your *ah-mah*
took you because of the old movies she liked. And you said there
were some shoe shop where these two old couple sat in the doorway in their blue-jean aprons and blue clothes with their windows
full of piles of shoes, you said. And you heard them once when you
snucked down there by yourself to look good at the pictures of the
naked women. Remember?' I said I did, because I did, and it really sounded bad. I was sorry, Mrs. Hasman, that I had ever spoken
one word to her at all. It really made me sick to my adolescence. I
told her I didn't mean to sound dirty, but as a little joke, you see,
and not mix it up with what her uncle had said. He's smart, that
Chinese King Farouk, in some ways. Smart like a catty woman.
She said, 'You said you heard them talking about their shoe business, how it was bad and soon they were going to be too old to do
anymore work. And you said you heard them say they wouldn't
have enough money to retire, you know, that when they got so old
they couldn't work, they wouldn't have any money because they
weren't making anything now. And he, the old man, you said, he
said to his wife that she couldn't love him because he was such a
mess making her come over here to this country and all...' Almost
my very own words, Mrs. Hasman. She had really listened to me,
you understand that. '... and made her work all the time and now
she would have to grow old with nothing to show for it all. He said,
she couldn't really love him anymore. And, you said she said that
she did love him all right. And there were tears in her eyes and she
kissed him with her wrinkled old lips on his old face and said love
was closing your eyes and saying I miss you and opening your eyes
and saying full of joy, you're as beautiful as when I last saw you,
and hello. And ah-Dirigible,' she said to me. I think she took my
hands, which seemed a strange thing for her to do then, I don't
know why. She said, 'I want you to remember that, because I
believe it. It's true.' That's what she said, Mrs. Hasman. And, of
course, it was goodbye, I suppose, she was saying underneath all
that. I couldn't kiss her then. No. Too icky. Not me. She'd made
me feel stinking rotten, reciting a little fairy tale I'd half made up,

true all that happened, but I meant it for her to hear, just once. Not to recite to me to move me without my own bullshit. I'm not like that. Don't fall for your own bullshit, says the sage. I wanted to go ahead, into lips and kisses, not backward. Ahead! It was very funny, you know. Me in my leather jacket and long hair with her, this delicate hothouse flower of that Buddhist church. She ended it there. Or they did. They kissed me off and kissed me goodbye through her lips. That was it. And that was our first and last date. That was the first time I'd seen her outside the church. Awww, enough of that," Dirigible said. "The tea's ready."

"Let me help you off with your coat," Mrs. Hasman said. "You're shivering."

"Hmmm," Dirigible said. "Good old Mrs. Hasman." She put her hand on his cheek and said his cheek was cold. He kissed her fingers. He sat with her on the couch, close to her, different than copping a feel from Sharon. "Your soul," she said, "it's like your whole soul has risen to the surface and is making your skin glow."

"Hmmm," Dirigible said and once again couldn't totally regret how dead and petrified Sharon was in his memory. She had died at eighteen, not him. She had cheated him out of the opportunity of forgetting her while she lived, and had left him a large fossil. A crowd of selves—the punk, the obnoxious adolescent fool, the lapsed Buddhist—mingled in the room, were him, watched him, all hating each other and competing for dominion over what the church, his mother, Mrs. Hasman, and various other creditors and probation officers, called his soul. How many times would Sharon help him, he wondered, sighing, gasping for fresh air out of the dense personality he had made of himself. He began, without making any sense of what had happened, of what he was doing to her. But he was not making love to a ghost he couldn't remember in anything but words. Sharon was pretty dead, all right, he thought, but she was real. His hands on Mrs. Hasman and her hands on him were real. The gaping sounds of the church with the doctor and his dying mother were real. Chinese New Year's and the parade and the rain were all real, and he had attitudes about them all. Soon a crowd of Chinese boys in sodden black silk sweatpants and white tennis shoes would come running down the street jumping in and out from under the glowing silk body of the world's longest dragon. Every year he saw them, different boys, sometimes a different dragon panting and padding down the street, the dragon's bamboo skeleton showing as a shadow through the colored spangled silk. This year the boys would be sweating through the wetness of the rain. Their tennis shoes would squeak. He found in this something to say. He would say something about being chilled from the rain, panting steam from mouths and sweating hot from running. Something like, "They're gonna catch cold," or "Strange how sweat and rain look alike on human skin," which would later sound very funny to Mrs. Hasman, Dirigible's mother, and the fat doctor. "I love you, you old Chinaman," Mrs. Hasman said.

Dirigible snorted, "Hmmm," and absently patted her breast.

"Don't laugh, it's not funny."

"Good old Mrs. Hasman."

"Hey! Wind Foh-errrrd car-errr, folks! Wind a Ford. Help build a church. The most noble thing to doooo. Help build a church. Wind a Ford for one dollah-errr, folks!"

A Chinese Lady Dies

MOUNT UP, BOYS! *It's time to ride. Another looney year's mooning high. Old West is a-gettin dim, boys. A Chinese lady dies, and song of the sixgun's nothin but a dull thud!* Now the process of living through the clamoring, metallic, operation of his body began in earnest. Awake. *El Chino is dark. His eyes slant and gleam like the flames of Zippo lighters deep in the dark under his sombrero. His droopy mustache don't look very Mexican or Indian, but there's nobody here with a question who a body is, or where a body comes from. Cuz o' custom on the Bravo and, of course, El Chino's most distinguishing feature is his astonishing coldblooded agility with a sixgun.* The clean-shaven face, washed and dried, cleanly, drily opaque for the time being, pinkish, brownish, yellow, and vaguely luminescent in the light, was grand. *Next thing everyone around El Chino learns fast is not to laugh at the way he has of failing every attempt at English. And the next, not to laugh at El Chino's munching and crunched failure at Spanish.* He looked closely at his skin in the mirror, touched his face with his fingers and rippled waves of color and essence moved through his face like sunlight stiffening petals and leaves. Wake up, skin. *Old West is a-gettin dim. Time to ride.* Pockmarked, lined, shadowed, full of character, like the face of a mudflat dried into a desert of potato chips. Dirigible's real face. He held it still with his fingertips closed on the joint of his jaw and felt a pulse through the flesh of the cheek into his fingers, pulsing like the body of a squab with its wings pinned in the grasp of his hand. Right about now she'll expect me to come carry her into the bathroom and put her on the toilet. The face was forced still, and looked at in the mirror by him. Even when he was alone, jeering crowds were storming the doors of his pores, sabotaging him, holding their breath in a clenched silence while Dirigible, in a fit of relaxation, felt cold pulses in his arms, dropping down his veins like women screaming down well shafts.

Nameless things he didn't like hid like chameleons on the walls.
No relief. High pressure, keep cool, iron-willed, muscular calm.
Intense inaction and spontaneous sweats. "Too bad," he thought,
feeling sorry for himself. He left himself alone. He wasn't inter-
ested. He had no belief, his mother said. She said things like that
now that everybody knew she was dying, without knowing how or
why, a mysterious paralysis echoing the paralysis of his father,
who had miraculously recovered and abandoned the family to
resume his Hollywood career as the Chinaman who dies. He was
more popular than ever now that he sounded just like a little boy
trying to mimic the voice of Peter Lorre reading Edgar Allen Poe.

Now that he knew she was dying, he knew he had never
wondered where he would be when her death caught up with him.
Out golfing? How old he would be, how much money in the bank,
how much hair would he have, how many marriages, children,
years in a jail when he got the news? Would he be there when she
breathed her last however it came out? He had never wondered.
Who would she die the mother of, the congressman of her dreams,
or the Chinese Richard Widmark, the first Chinese-American
flyweight boxing champion of the world?

*Frisco under the first full moon of the lunar New Year swollen
and bulged in the silvered headlights of a parked foreign car looks
like two sick towns afire in the sky-blue eyes of Henry Fonda in
closeup. El Chino mounts up.* Machines had character to his eye.
Their bulk and noise. Even when they were silent, machines with
their complex studded surfaces, their grease and cogs and levers,
suggested the magnificent noise he wasn't hearing. The way he
knew his face was on him, felt the heat of it from within and yet
did not see it as he had walked through Chinatown up and down
the streets—the streets barren and cluttered, cold as a woman's
face and hair sleeping on a pillow, the lightbulbs on the strings of
silk and paper lanterns turned off, leaving the tissue shells dull and
opaque. *The night of the first full moon is a night for lovers, and a
man has got to do what a man has got to do, gents. The town fathers
are fat and lighting up lanterns that are mechanical wonders and
class acts. The town shines like the moon tonight, boys. Every house
festooned with beautiful lights. The* Gum Sahn Paw *in China have
their hands between their legs tonight and wail for their husbands
taking their chances in the Pretty Country. Frisco's high on itself and*

spreads its legs to us tonight, and old grudges rise to howl at the moon. The alleys were cluttered with garbage cans from the restaurants. He was as alone as he could possibly be and didn't believe it; it wasn't profound. He couldn't be lonelier, and still he felt merely excellently ordinary.

The banners draped across Washington Street in front of the Buddhist church advertising the New Year's Bazaar and the neon signs were useless in the deserted morning. The grandstand in Portsmouth Square. Merry-go-rounds and tiny Ferris wheels were dead. *Let's be strangers riding into town. Like outlaws out of the pages of history, let's warn the populace, raid the capital, burn the city with the lights of its own celebration, slaughter the governor and his marshals and ministers who criticized my poetry so bad, I stopped writing poetry forever, as long as they live in luxurious corruption and successful greed. Mount up! Ask me if I have trouble with the language, will they?* Gay little flags off lamposts and from palm trees fluttered as irritating to his senses as twanging nasal hairs. He sensed his face then. The cold air was all his. He was alone with sleeping Chinatown, and walked on it, looked at it through all the paint and curios and carnival hoopla to the concrete and wood of it. Crowdless, silent. He scuffed through the exploded bodies of firecrackers and stared at two moth-eaten stuffed wildcats set in the display window of a fish market.

The wildcats were frozen in fierce expressions, looking into a pool which used to contain water and display fish. The inside of the window was dirty. Dead flies and moths spotted the dust at the bottom of the dry pool. He heard the voices of the crowd that wasn't shouting through all the streets after him. He saw the windows their voices weren't echoing off of. He saw all the space no one was occupying.

Standing there unseen, alone with pigeons and riderless wooden horses, watching everything, tensely doing nothing, nothing happening was pointless. His being there to see in dead grey warming morning, to ignore the signs and fluttering beckoning flags, was to make everyone this place and these things were for, dead. His eyes were the eyes of the weather. His face and the life coolly working through him were magnificent, almost completely satisfying. He felt himself kin to the idly creaking Ferris wheel and the dead merry-go-round, the fish in the display tanks swimming over each other's backs the way they were doing in shops around the corner. Together they were sublimely, magnificently, intimately peopleless. The spies had nothing to pry, the wise no stuff for plans.

An obsolete human being, like an obsolete machine, inherited the earth. For a moment no more anonymity, no more occupying his time with words and facial expressions and a few tears to pass the time, turning on emotion like a Christmas tree lighting up. Inorganically emotional. He worked. Now he worked. A machine, alone, being mechanically lonely, custom-made, one of a kind, musing nuts and bolts staring out of the window between the toilet and the tub, to a view of the Oakland hills and a patch of sky between houses and telephone poles. "You shouldn't hit me in the face," his mother said somewhere in a Bette Davis movie, on the toilet. Her playful, coy little voice sounded severely into his ears, punctured through membranes of silence into a narcissistic interior of spinning silk. No panic. No grief. No anger.

"I was trying to hit your shoulder," Dirigible said. "I missed."

"But that was my face, son!" his mother said. "You shouldn't hit people in the face!"

"I didn't mean to hit you in the face, Ma."

"Faces are what people look like. You just shouldn't hit them there. Even by accident. What're you doing hitting me anyway?"

"It's a long story," Dirigible said, already hoarse from not telling it. "I just felt like hitting you. Friendly like."

"You hit all your friends, I suppose."

"I sure do. All my friends."

"And they never sock you back, I suppose."

"You're my only friend, Ma."

"Good thing for you I should be black and blue all over to make you happy. I suppose when you don't hit me, you're in a bad mood, huh?"

"You'd rather I be in a bad mood?"

"You don't have to hit me to hurt me, you know," she said grinning. "You don't even have to be around to hurt your mother either."

"But it's better when I'm around, isn't it?" Dirigible said. "You can turn best profile and cry for me, and put your wrist over your face and flutter your other hand at me and say 'That's all right, son, that's all right . . . Just bury me in my jade and dress me in white and I'll be happy . . .' and I turn around and walk away and you have visions of me drowning my shame in drink and white women. Right? Now you're blushing, isn't that the movie about you? And I'll tell you, Ma. I'll tell you. It works! I'm not ashamed anymore. I may be drunk and all sexed up, but I'm not ashamed."

"You never know how much you loved someone until they've died," she said without conviction.

"I can hardly wait," Dirigible said.

"I wish you wouldn't talk like that, son. You know what Chinese New Year's means to me," she said with a coy expression on her face. *And El Chino leads an outlaw army of 108 different gangs toward Chinatown Frisco. Motorcycle gangs, Mexican Pachuco gangs in low riders and zoot suits, uneasy Chinatown gangs in jacked-up Detroit iron, Comancheros left over from the Old West, railroad gangs, mercenaries, the black sheep of every religion and philosophy. Commando gangs who sense a good man follow El Chino into Frisco to see the Chinatown lights that night of the first full moon of the new year. That's what Chinese New Year's means to me, boys! A big showoff explosion for show. Lovers. Broken hearts. And danger of burning cities lit by wishful thinking.* I've learned to bear grudges, Ma. If he said it aloud, she would only say, "No, you haven't," and that would be that. Gingerly and slowly, in the movie about her, with a faint smile on her face, as if rolling her cheek across something soft and furry for a charm, she exposed her cheek downward. She touched at her face with her fingertips and held her eyes still, touched her cheek, measured the merest tips of her fingers into the flesh and out again, feeling the cheek spring miraculously back into shape. "It still hurts. You always were clumsy. I keep telling you to get your eyes checked," she said, irritating him into participating in a chatty well-worn argument about his eyes, about his clumsiness, into seeing himself half-naked in the mirror, squinting at the muscles of a mummified boxer wearing glasses, while in some distant region, behind some motherly act of anger, she chuckled and tingled, displaying to the world all the tricks and acrobatics of her son's moods that made him a living thing in her eyes. As a cripple in a wheelchair, she played more and more at being an old woman. She played at being his mother, toyed with him like a child toying with her food. She enjoyed every loneliness of it, dabbling the sensations of an old woman just to experience feeling old in a world that mattered less and less the deeper she felt her death occupying her body. Her living coldbloodedly conscious of making herself up old with old-style cosmetics, of manufacturing the naive curiosity and wonder of a child dressing in her mother's clothes, and feeling great relief and sighs sprout from all her pores when people cringed and turned away from her was fascinating for Dirigible to witness.

She was taking every moment of her death seriously. He could see, could hear the rhythm of the realization of dying recurring in her with the changing tone of her breath twanging off the walls of her nostrils, flapping through her lips in subtle earthquakes. She had the air of a condemned convict, slowly, with excruciating deliberateness, tasting every bit of a last meal of exotic foods. He thought of her smacking her rouged lips and smiling wistfully, sparking her little eyes like an old woman suddenly attractive, innocent, full of ecstatic sensations, enjoying the beautiful symphonic boredom of going dead slowly, of dying minisculely, and wondering aloud at her latest lack of sensation. "I don't have the feeling of pissing, son. But I can hear it as plain as day. Isn't that strange?" she paused a moment, seemingly wondering frantic tendrils scouting through herself to finger and tickle the marvelous mechanism that set her to urinating, turning her urine on and off, smiling and sparkling her eyes all the while, all the while secretly grinning, on and off, Dirigible knew, purposely embarrassing him, making him cringe before the spectacle of a cadaver acting charming and sexy, then glowing all of a sudden, her voice wistful all of a sudden, and the sparks in her eyes, the tiny chips of light in her eyes, he saw, turning into a glaze of tears, as if her heart had just burst and she felt herself flooded with a new mood, breathlessly whispering with evangelical fervor, "Someday you'll thank me, son."

"Ma... Ma... Ma..." *La China dismounts and clears her mind with her bow and arrows warming up against her body. She spies El Chino signaling like crazy in the little window of the abode hoosegow on the other side of the valley, through her telescope. Schooled in Zen archery since she was three, she kneels, raises her bow and notches an arrow with a message tied around its shaft. She concentrates, stretches the bow, looks away, achieves perfect form,*

and lets go, all at perfect speed, in perfect proportion and balance.
She spies the window through her telescope and sees El Chino stag-
gering about the hoosegow with an arrow plunged into his shoulder.
"Aww Shit!" La China says, and kicks pine cones and throws rocks
at squirrels as she packs her things and mounts up. "Come on, Ma,
shit, and let's get out of here, okay?"

"For someone who's supposed to have gotten A's in all his
English courses, you'd think you'd think of a nicer way of saying
things like that to your mother."

"Yes, I would. But you have to see, I'm not myself all the time.
I'm real good at being the kind of son who just loves to come over
for Mommy's real home cooking. I am not myself as the son who
first wipes one parent's ass for a few years, then his other parent's
ass. Your shit often smells just like, but never as good as my own.
And I really don't like the smell of anybody else's but my own, in
my own time. Not even yours. Though there was a time, when
you were on your feet, if you had fluttered your lashes at me and
stuck your tongue in my mouth, there would be no stopping
me . . ."

"You know I don't like that," she said. He heard he was the
wrong movie again. "You always talk to me like that, son. And I
don't like it. Now what was I talking about?" Her voice trailed off,
not dying yet, another rehearsal of her death scene, leaving her a
little more old, a little more mother and playfully senile. The
whole inventory of her was comfortably familiar to Dirigible, old
hat, so much like the dying of the old women at the Eclipse Hotel,
where his mother had run the kitchen, and he ran room service in
a little starched jacket. This morning went back that far. The
mood of Oriental carpets and lace doilies and odd little birds the
old women kept for pets rose out of his mother to seep into him,
scent his presence about himself with mildewed memories of old
women looking flimsy inside flimsy dresses and overheated and
irritated in thick sweaters they didn't seem to have the strength to
remove, old ladies who faded into the pattern of the carpet after
standing a moment, leaning on their rosewood canes, stepping on
the elaborate curlicues of the carpet like stepping barefoot on shit,
and looking about to fall and frightened and about to wet their
pants—fell and wet their pants and went flat and dead like carbonation out of an open bottle of soda pop. One of them was on

the floor, knees bare, showing thighs with blue veins fat as healthy snakes wading out of the tops of her stocking, her bare elbows as angular as a stricken grasshopper's. What fold of skin could hide the mouth or become an eyelid in the crowd of all the flesh falling apart from the inside like a shocked angel food cake, like a suffocating insect? His mother later described herself as noticing she didn't know, as she had approached the dead woman. She would lock the door to the dining room and imagine herself deaf to the silence in the lobby, and sit at a table and quietly laugh aloud to herself, totaling up the dead's dining room tab, while looking lovingly into Dirigible's face. She would laugh at any click in the walls or sound from the kitchen, and heft Dirigible's wrists in her hands and clear her throat to say nothing. Then she would savor all the stillborn sensations she almost felt, fumbling about the dead woman as if she wanted something back. "You know for a long time after someone dies, I" — she smiled at him and crinkled the corners of her eyes and clapped his hands together to make him smile with her — "I get very sleepy for days after. All I want to do is go to sleep. And you do too, I wonder why?"

"I do?"

"Yes, you get restless and lazy like a nervous cat. And you go back and forth, like a clock pendulum and seem so angry inside." She would glance up from his face and seem to discover his hair was a rare and beautiful butterfly and smile and fix his hair a few strands at a time, talking all the while until her ghost came back to take the trembling from her fingers, until she was sleepy and suddenly bored with being with her son, and gently pushed him away from her like politely refusing an extra helping of fattening food, to leave Dirigible alone in the dining room to set her chair straight and turn out the lights, to go upstairs and put his white jacket and black bow tie on a hanger, say goodnight to his father after unfolding the man from his wheelchair and flattening him on his bed, to go to his room, and turn on his radio if he heard his mother weeping or praying.

His mother took him to every funeral. She gave him a ritual face to carry. Every funeral in every weather, in all colors, was sad and beautiful, she said. She knew all the favorite foods of the dead and stood by the graveside defying the relatives of the dead to touch on her secret knowledge. After each old lady died, she burned incense and paper ingots by meals she knew they would enjoy. The dishwasher and cook would burn parchment money, and Dirigible knew they kowtowed. She liked her customers. He learned his mother had an instinctive talent for attracting old people who were dying. She was a good cook. He felt her loving him throughout the hotel with a tender grimness, sorry perhaps that his destiny was to be her perfect mourner. Would she leave him all the costume jewelry and shiny trinkets, button collections and birdcages the old women left her? he wondered. He accompanied her movement toward death professionally, like a trusted chauffeur, like a good boy. Funny that she, like all the old women she had been pleasant comfort to, should feel her own death with such urgency; and yet she could, just like them, feel alive enough and loved simply by having someone to look at while she spoke. "What're you thinking, son? Why such a faraway look in your eyes?"

"Nothing," Dirigible answered.

"Don't frown so. Is it something I said?" she asked brightly.

"What?"

"Did I say something to make you frown like that?"

"I wasn't frowning. That's just the way my face hangs, that's all. Gravity."

"Were you thinking something scientific?"

"No, I wasn't thinking something scientific."

"Were you thinking about living in the country with Auntie Bea and Uncle Jackie?"

"You'll never know, Ma."

"What does that mean?"

"Nothing."

"You never know how much you loved somebody until they're dead."

"I can hardly wait."

"How do you know who I'm talking about, smartie?"

"Dying? Who are we all waiting for to die?"

"You?"

"Me?" he lied through his teeth.

"Me?"

"You?" he lied blinking his eyes.

"I was thinking about Uncle Jackie, when he died," she said, and proved something, he guessed from her tone. "It was just luck," she continued. "I always said so, just luck that you should be back just in time for his funeral," she trilled triumphant.

"Are you calling me a jinx?" Dirigible trilled back.

"No," she said. "Why should I do that?"

"Next thing you'll be saying, 'Too bad we weren't talking to each other when Grandma died,' then, 'Too bad you got mad and left the church just six years before Sharon died,' and so on and so forth and 'Too bad you short-changed Mrs. Jenkins after she left you a fifty-cent tip just before she had that stroke of hers.' I'll leave if you're afraid of me, Ma . . ."

"No, I don't want you to do that," she said. "It's just that things you do give me feelings." She managed a smile over her shuddering and was actually grinning; her eyes were thrilling, cold, ecstatic, gazing out of her gooseflesh. Dirigible saw it all. Shaving lather hissed and crackled on his cheeks and around his lips. A dirty fishsweat liquid drained from underneath the foam of his lips. First, the morning. A cool stainless-steel breeze against his bare chest and soapy face, pleasantly cooling the surfaces of his skin as if he had felt hot and bursting, his body one giant angry pustule now soothed in the cool. Nice day, he thought, believing in the effects of coolness and sunshine on his senses, feeling them spread inside him to nurse fevers throughout his body. He felt cool warily, superstitiously hopeful that the grey sunlight and breeze were more than cheap patent medicines. Then his mother on the toilet powders her face. Though he had brought her into the bathroom himself and sat her on the toilet, he stared at her without realizing who or what was so fascinating to his eyes like the piece of shit he had found himself staring at on the carpeted floor of his office. A turd occurred to him in mid-sentence as he sat at tea with a chubby redhead precariously balanced like a blindfolded tightrope walker in the middle of a sentence broken off by his finally connecting the odor he had been trying to talk out of his senses with the object on the floor. "A turd," he had said aloud. "There's no other word for it, a turd." Her girlish embarrassment, her laughing at him, all the jokes he had told, were no longer funny today.

"Jonah was here, I forgot. He's always leaving his shit lying around and going out of the room so it doesn't exist anymore."

"Johnny?" the soft redhead asked.

"My son, not my dog," he said, quietly livid, with nothing to tear apart with his hands. His mother occurred to him constantly, like that piece of harmlessly maddening shit, and she was nothing actual to be angry at. And crazy. His eye spun and desperately banged the edges of sight to look past the woman puttying her face, to look through her like a trick of light, look past the sky outside the window, seeing the slots of his eyelids open around blind eyes. *A Place in the Sun. We saw it together, Ma, holding hands.* "Things I do give you feelings," *Montgomery Clift say as me in the movie about me, Ma. Shelley Winters, the spongy petulant slob, and Elizabeth Taylor, impossibly young and beautiful, both play you, in the movie about me. I drown Shelley Winters in a lake, step through the other door, dry her off my conscience and ask for you to Liz me, Ma.* "You should have feelings about me. I'm your son. Look at me. Lay your bright little eyes on the mortal body of your own flesh and blood grown into manhood!"

"Ha! Manhood?"

"An infallible tin ear for corn for you? or from you? A little worn around the joints, you see. A little fungus in the blood perhaps. The sparkle gone out of the eyes. But you can still read my mind like an open book, can't you, Ma. Yes, you can, all right. I'm still your own little boy, aren't I? But grown older, that's all. I'm your old little boy. Yes, I am. Yes, I am. Take a good look with those mother's eyes of yours. You see I am, don't you, you little mother? I'll tell you something, Ma . . ."

"I don't understand you when you talk like that," she said and turned her face away. "I just won't listen."

"You won't listen," Dirigible said. *I drowned Shelley Winters to have at you with a clear conscience. I'm about to be strung up till dead and have a frog in my throat.* "She won't listen, everybody. Well, I'm not above talking to myself. I'm constantly surprised at what I have to say when no one is listening to me in the same room. Of course, I sometimes have the feeling that people right next to me are eavesdropping. But that's all right, I'm a simple man and don't really have much to say, and that's because my mother always hears me black. She finds me most alive around old things and dead people and mementos and memories of them. I have a terrible feeling what I've said is true. Perhaps that's why I'm not laughing. I don't think I'm being very amusing at all. In fact I'm so depressing I think I'll beat up my wife because she's so stupid she'd laugh at me not being amusing. She loves me so much she'd go hysterical with cleverly making me miserable, so I'm going downstairs and kick her in the head. That's a really good idea. Excuse me, I'm going downstairs to kick whatshername in the head."

"I'm not listening!" his mother said, raising her hand as he turned toward the door. "I won't listen! So you might as well shut up." He turned away from the door. She said, "Why are you so rude to me? Why is it I can't talk to you anymore." *Down off the gallows, Montgomery, shuck that tragedy and ride outlaw and righteous with us! El Chino says. Whaddaya say?* "Because you bother me," Dirigible said.

"So easy? Is that all? I bother you? Is that all?"

"All? Yes, that's all. It seems all you can do is bother me. A lot of things are bothering me these days. Plenty of things are bothering me right now and none of them are very serious and that bothers me. It just bugs me, and I don't like it. And I don't care."

"You artists are so suffering," his mother said smiling.

"And I don't suffer! No, sir. You'd like to think I do, but I don't. I don't care, and I don't suffer, and you'd better get that set in your mind, because everyone else has. I don't die either, like your stupid friends at the church waiting to bury you found out. Nothing happens to me and I do nothing except be bothered, and I'm working on that."

"You're jealous of the church, aren't you? You . . ." she said, taking time to not be fooled by the frankness of his gaze, taking time to find a squirm or a twitch belying his words. He blinked precisely as she spoke, "You think . . . I don't know what you think."

"True."

"You think I care more for the church than you. You hate Dr. Larry. You're jealous."

"Hate? Jealous? Mere words to me, Ma, simple literary catchalls that bore me. You're my mother, Ma. Is that all you can do? Bust a gut boring me?" he said and wasn't sad that it was so. All a part of the son's service to a dying mother, all a part of artificially aging her.

"You're waiting for me to die, aren't you, son? I really do bore you, don't I?"

"Don't bother me anymore with your theatrics for awhile, I really can't face them before my morning coffee and anchovies." The unresponsive silence after the sound of his voice lingered. Perhaps she was finally dead. "You really know how to hurt people, don't you," he finally heard.

"No," he said. "People just know how to be hurt by me, and that's too bad." He said, "Waiting for you to die?" and knew she had lifted her face. He knew the suggestion of a secret about to be told was rousing her ears to a magnificent effort of hearing, that behind the clear casings of her eyes and underneath the skin of her bare throat, her whole body was prepared to receive a kiss. First came the wailing priests in black tennis shoes and no socks down the broken pavement of Seventh Street. Wailing to themselves carrying incense burners, they were lost in the process of rambling down the middle of the street in the bright sunlight, as if they had never been here before, as if all at once all the owners of lost dogs had all wandered into the same strange section of town calling their dogs home. They were all thin and looked thinner because they were bald. They had knobby knees, knobby elbows, knobby Adam's apples vibrating and beating like tiny pregnancies in their throats as they wailed and moaned, and knobby heads. Then the brass band in black uniforms and red piping. Then the pallbearers and the coffin smothered with flowers, and a huge photograph of the dead. A huge face of her mother sweetly smiling, bobbing on top of her coffin. A huge photograph of Sharon squinting out of nowhere into people's faces, as the tiny cortege, quietly plodding under the cacophony of the brass band and the wailing of the priests, embarrassed people into stillness, embarrassed people on the sidewalks into shrinking away from the warm surfaces of their skins until they were mere remnants of themselves, until they were ivory. The sound of the dumb, predictable, monotonous footsteps of the mourners with their blank eyes, the unlistenable music and the shrill voices, was all very nice — all nice people making a sound like a vast fall of rain. The nice people in the orchestra pit provided an edgy impersonal sound to make his mother's isolation in a desert silence complete, as if she were absolutely alone, the last woman on earth, searching for a lover. She could see herself. Whoom and silence and whoom, the heartrending sound of the funeral drums, because

Dirigible had said, "Waiting for you to die?" Yes, he had. Then he said, "I don't wait. I could care less. Your death. What does it mean, Ma? I can see you die a million times a week on television, or in the *Reader's Digest*. I don't care to be concerned with your death because I don't care to perform when so many people do it better. Where's my payment for being sad? Where's my payoff for making a fool of myself dawdling around your grave? What can I say I've gotten for spending my time at some . . . some . . . what's a good word? Performing some unpleasant social obligation, not for my sake, but for appearance, as if my picture's going to be taken, as if it'll improve my trade in noodles and add to my importance, when it won't. When, if you look at me right now, I'm a nobody. I'm embarrassed with your condition. I mean, here I am a nobody, a meaningless part of the human economy, and I have a mind, but I really don't have anything to think about, I'm not particularly respected and don't have any self-respect, not that that's bad or good, it isn't anything, here I am nothing, not uncomfortably getting along with a mother who's dying. You see my point?"

"Yes," she said, lying in an effort to stop him.

"You dying should somehow make my living more important, or it should be ironic or paradoxical, you see? A president's mother dies and it's a wonderful thing. People say, 'Poor President of the United States of America, worrying about keeping the world free, his mother's died. What a load on that poor man's mind.' Say a stripper's mother dies, people say, 'Now I wonder what she feels like taking her clothes off in front of leering men, now that her mother's died, and she's no spring chicken anymore.' You see? Somehow, even though they don't change what they do afterwards, it's different because their mothers died. What they do has new meaning. You see?"

"Yes."

"Now you die and people say, 'Dirigible's mother's died. Who's he that he should have a mother?' You and I together become nothing more than some petty nuisance, like the telephone ringing in some middle of a comfortable dinner. They answer the phone, you're dead, and I'm your son, and all they see is that we've caused them to finish off cold food. You see what I mean? Now if I were really somebody . . ."

"You think I'm being impolite. You think I'm like one of those people that does something real sensational just to get their name in the papers."

"I don't think you're doing it on purpose," he said glibly. He didn't like hearing his ideas stated in simple matter-of-fact terms in her voice. It sounded as if she didn't care that he didn't care. He didn't care. He couldn't convince himself that he did, or bring himself to appear caring without feeling he was acting in a cheap drama that left him indifferent. But there were subtle degrees to not caring, he insisted. He didn't care only as a son couldn't.

Whoom and whirroom! was the sound of jet planes somewhere in the sky, pitifully similar to the sound of drums from her fondest memories. She was ashamed to remember. She was unfit to have such beautiful treasures and secrets of the dead, of herself. Something, a force less than supernatural, a makeshift spirit more mundane than the greatness of religion, of a god, something cheap that she was ashamed to own and couldn't surreptitiously pawn, perhaps her conscience, or just plain stupidity made her linger on the sound of the jet planes mingling with the echoes of her son's voice mocking the brilliance of livelier days, making her miserable, making her silent, so simplemindedly silent she didn't want to think about it. Jet planes! Vets. Ruptured ducks. Home from the war. Putty putty cement mixer. The men talked big, groped for words to make them sound like experts and prophets about jet planes, not really enjoying their conversations, she was sure, but mirthlessly killing time by turns with heaps of inanities, too lazy, too mired in their boredom after making the world free for democracy to notice her, almost screaming as she grappled with live turtles on one hand and suffocated in the steam coming from the boiling water on the other, helpless and insane in that moment all cooks seemed to arrive at sooner or later, when turtle soup defied logic. She wouldn't scream. She insisted the men see her. She appeared to scream, but didn't scream. They ignored her fingers, and the inhuman eyes of the turtles set right in their beaks, it seemed, and their dry thorny legs, and the necessity of watching her approach the cauldron of boiling water set precariously on the stove, on all that hot metal — they ignored all that steam and boiling water and the expanse of her bare arms and face. The men, the boys, the children all laughed at her. They didn't take her pain seriously, her cuts and scratches, her sweat and hair visibly curling into haywire on her head, no matter how real these were, no matter how severely she danced to show her discomfort. That's how meaningless jet planes were to her. "You don't care that I'm dying because I'm not famous enough? I see. All I am, son, is your mother." It took no imagination, no orchestra of footsteps, not even the edge of a memory, not so much as a thought of loneliness, after she had said the saddest thing she had ever heard. All she had to be was not speaking, near her only son. "I always bothered for you. You always used to pester me about my recipes, and you knew I never wrote things down, that I always just did things as I went along, and it was a bother to tell you. Really hard for me sometimes."

"You always talk about food when you're nervous, Ma."

"I'm talking about you. I always bothered for you. Now I see you can't be bothered with me when I need you."

"I can't stand people fishing for my feelings, Ma. It stops me cold. I'm sorry."

"Don't you have the time?"

"It's nine-thirty," Dirigible said, glancing at his wristwatch on the bathroom table. He realized he hadn't been quick. He had misinterpreted her question. He damned her quaint accent and the accents of all Chinese. They were both quiet. He felt her searching him like an old chest, and felt himself, his flesh and chemistry turning traitor, yielding to the search as her sighs and blinked-away tears found signs of life in him, found all her missing sensations being felt, trembling like lost sheep in his body. An echo of her in him she knew, as he watched her eyes till and rake him. It was a pity to have known each other for so long, so sad in their intense concentration with each other for so long to have somewhere lost count, somewhere failed to carry in addition, or count enough decimal places, until they were in constant error with each other. After consideration, he found he had no feeling for the sadness of the problem except the weary old words, except stifling monotony, which was just like her, just what she would have him think and feel sad about. An elaborate, ornate impotence, and an expression on her face as if she had dressed him in clothes she had made, and he was perfect, ornamental, her own "little gentleman," as she used to say. No use to know she was wrong and try to look like something different from what she saw, she would only say, "stop fidgeting," and chuckle too lovingly, and pull a cuff here, adjust a collar there, and move about him humming and tucking like a woman arranging flowers. "Yessir," he muttered to himself, "booze and white women can make a good man free."

"Well," she said, "anyway, Happy New Year, son," and grinned as best she could without going hysterical. Her face was done. As she spoke she grinned a safe grin. Layers of cosmetics as fragile and buttery as pie crust, sheared and shattered and crumbled. Unenthusiastically, he watched her gathering courage. "Ta tum!" she sang. "I'm ready to face the world now," she said. Without moving her face, she rolled the long sleeves of her black *cheongsam* down, the held her arms up. Dirigible picked her up in his arms and lifted her off the toilet, while she pulled her white pantaloons up under the skirt of the *cheongsam*. Her face smelled like a funeral parlor. He carried her downstairs to the living room and put her gently on the floor, where she kowtowed and clasped her hands and grunted as her body ached and sweat seeped through the secret formula of powders and rouges, recited the Diamond Sutra and made morning meditation. Dirigible saw no frenzy, no fervor, no guts, just calm calisthenics, nothing religious, no atmosphere of ritual.

"I wish you wouldn't watch me. It's embarrassing to me."

"I can see how it would be embarrassing to be caught doing something silly," he said with an edge of good nature. He didn't want to appear to take back what had gone on upstairs, but he didn't want to keep the bad taste of it either. Without betraying himself, he would cancel this morning out of his experiences. After a few smiles he would have nothing weighing on his mind.

"What do you want to talk like that for? You know you always liked to watch me. All the time," she said. "All the time sneaky too, pretending to read the paper in the bathroom while I sat on the pot. And at the oddest times telling me I had holes in my girdle? I know. You have a filthy sneaky dirty mind!" She smiled, her mouth opening slowly, exposing her teeth and dark tongue. "What kind of a son are you anyway? Certainly not Chinese."

I'm not Chinese, boys, they say I'm no good! "Whoa up there, Chinaman, what the fuck's goin on here?" *Confucius asks. I'm*

*havin me one identity crisis, Confucius. They hide their daughters
from me. Don't invite me in to supper.* "Identity crisis, my ass," Confucius says. "Don't you know there's no such thing, boy? Don't be a
sucker for Christian tragedy."

"Your son, Ma. I'm all yours."

"I don't like the way you say that."

"I don't like saying it at all, but it's true, isn't it? Isn't it, Ma?"

. Her mouth closed. She looked at the carpet and trembled and
touched her face with her hands, one at a time, groping blind for
the other through her hair, over her nose, about her mouth. *You're
smoking me, Ma. This your Helen Keller act? Are you crazy with
pain? Punch an elephant between the eyes? Kidney punch a black
bull in Madrid? Which movie about you is this? Lana Turner lus-
cious vulnerable and young? Loretta Young? I've seen this scene
with you, on a screen somewhere.* She hummed. She saw flecks of
her powder settling away from her face to the floor, the tiny tiny
grains drifting and wobbling, glinting in the sunlight, and was
shocked. Dirigible watched her act panic-stricken about her face,
as if she had undergone plastic surgery and the bandages were just
removed. She looked about her for a mirror and shook her head at
her hands covered with powder, shook her head at the door. "It's
Chinese New Year's," she said. "Today is Chinese New Year's!"

"You've been watching too many movies," Dirigible said, knowing she had meant her melodramatics sincerely, that in her every
muscle, movie star after movie star was sobbing and weeping,
streaming through her, feeling miserable for her the way she had
been miserable for them at their faces blasting off the screen. She
wept tearlessly, her eyes open, her tears forming a sort of gelatin
over the lenses. She wanted to feel her face with her hands, to correct the expression on her face, but didn't care. Everything about
her hung by a spiderweb. Everything she might say to her son to
make him sorry echoed in desolation, disintegrated into dreari-
ness. She felt echoes of pitiful shrieks twinkling in her eyes, felt
her head and face loom large in her mind, like a desolate screen in
some tiny theater, with half-lit cherubs and vine leaves carved in
the ceiling, half-lit rows of empty chairs and the cheeks of a few
sleeping men, as her sound repeatedly shattered the silence, tor-
mented the darkness with antique anguish. She knew what it was
like to be an old movie shown as a filler between strip shows; she

knew how uncaring and bored the derelicts were, going to sleep
with their eyes open at the sight of sad women wearing their
feminine suffering like warm quilts. She had been there. She had
taken Dirigible to the old Moulin Rouge theater, in an effort to escape from the cacophony of home and spend a few hours in that
dingy theater seeing movies she had seen before, discovering
what she felt like inside. "You know how important Chinese New
Year's is to me!" She saw him as she spoke, which was a mistake.
*"I feel like writing a poem on the shithouse wall, boys. Park your
ponies here. I have to answer the urge. I'll be right back." An odd
flight of late geese flies south overhead. La China shoots one down.
"Don't do that again," El Chino says. "Birds like us should take outlaws like them as kin."* These moments were always happening to
her, when she made the sad discovery of the limits of her insides,
realized the disappointment of being herself as, coming out of the
theater into the lobby cluttered with photos of women smiling
with stars pasted over their nipples, she breathed the sodden scent
of overused popcorn, and heard with absolute clarity the tires of
autos hissing down the rain-wetted streets, and saw through the
doors the night that had developed, the very night she had hidden
from in the theater with her son, hiding from the same sounds of
autos and loading trucks she had heard nevertheless through the
walls of the theater. Her eyes turned steely against the faces of the
men looking away from her as they ducked inside for the strip
show. Dirigible was groggy and complaining of hunger in Chinese
and seemed content to respond to the pressure of his mother's
arms, influencing rather than pulling him against her where he
loosened himself into a near sleep and she felt him relaxing and
heard his mind swirling in a confusing dazzle as he muttered, "I'm
not a airplane." He drooled on her shoulder. He was a big ten-year-
old boy drooling on her shoulder. "You're not an airplane," she
said, soothing him, vowing to protect him from airplanes. "Are
you an airplane?" she asked, patting his head gently, partially
awakening him. "I'm not an airplane," he said with his eyes opening, and realized who it was speaking, and laughed with his
mother. They would walk home without umbrellas in the drizzle,
and after a while stop asking who was cold.

She would begin to stop. Very slowly, like a wary animal, she
picked her steps and sniffed at the air, and followed the undula-

tions of Chinatown's darkness with her son to fondle bitter squash, and long string beans, and ginger out of the boxes set in front of the shops like pirate's treasure. At every shop the aproned clerks and owners with paper hats on stepped out into their doorways and welcomed her. They said she was pretty. They nodded to emphasize their words, and nodded again to reassure the first nod, and grinned and nodded as if they'd lost their minds, and chuckling and nodding and squinting, said she looked so young to have a son so nearly grown, and plucked the vegetable out of her hand and held it up like a jewel in the spicy murk, and nodded at it as if to include it in the conversation about youth and beauty, and said the vegetable was very fresh, but for her they had fresher vegetables, for her they had the freshest grown by Chinese farmers who grow their vegetables as if they're growing orchids. Such care! Such freshness! They couldn't stand to talk about it any longer. They had to go fetch some right away, if not for her to buy, then for themselves to marvel at, they were so overcome. And they would be away into their stores, bumping pails of snails and sacks of rice with their ankles and knocking dangling lightbulbs out of the way as they rounded a corner into mystery. She would dally with her son over a sack of peanuts and wonder who enjoyed these clandestine excursions more, she or Dirigible. Did he enjoy being in the company of his mother, being treated this way, more than she enjoyed being with him? It was a lovely question to ask herself, and it made her all the more happy.

Then home to the restaurant, closed for the day, instead of going back to her mother's house from which they had fled a few hours earlier. "We don't want Daddy to know you didn't go to Chinese school today, do we," Ma said and closed the doors between the big kitchen and the hall and stairway. They ate at the kitchen table next to the cold empty steam table. She treated him to cold-pack cheddar cheese from the naval commander's pot, and matzoth from the Jewish lady's package, and giggled nicely with him, not talking to him about her mother and sisters and brothers-in-law who mocked and scolded her gangly ten-year-old boy. She giggled alone with her son because she wasn't at the house of Sixth Street, talking herself into crying in front of all of them calling her son evil. "Isn't this nice?"

"You're a good cooker, all right."

"Why the long face?"

"Because I think this is bad."

"Why do you think that? I'm your mommy, and I say it isn't bad, so there we are."

"What about Daddy?"

"I bet you and Daddy have secrets from me, don't you?"

"No."

"Well, one day isn't very important. You can stay down here and study till it's time for bed."

"What about them at the church?"

"What about them?" she asked. She chuckled and gave him another spoonful of cheese from the commander's pot and caressed his cheek. "Anyway, between you and me, Dr. Larry has a crush on me and won't get mad at you if I ask him not to, all right? You worry so much! It's a wonder, you'll be an old man soon," she said. Dirigible would sigh and go upstairs blankminded to his room, disturbed by something his mother was incompetent to help him understand. At least since those days he had been sorry for her. He felt he must have, as he climbed the grey stairs running his fingers along the waxy yellow wall, been very sorry for his mother, been pretending his innocence, been knowing all the while that as he faked and bluffed his way through childhood with her, he was tending and pleasing her for his own ends, like a gigolo. He must have known, he was sure, during those evenings he spent with her drawing drawings that made her proud of him, while she knitted and they both listened to the radio, that it was an imaginary paradise. He had known it, and he had been a child consciously and cunningly, like a full-grown midget playing a role, and was now embarrassed at all the happiness his mother recalled from his childhood. He knew how miserable she felt on the floor. He had the tenor of her very soul in the palm of his hand. He knew the chemistry she meant to set working in him as she had thrown at him, "You know what Chinese New Year's means to me!" and was sorry that only tired, embarrassed groans wound through him, as he if had heard her tell an old joke.

She leaned over cautiously into a crouch and rested, poising herself, displaying herself as a pitiful, inwardly suffering heroine about to crawl someplace, when Dirigible said, "Aww, Ma!" *El*

Chino smacks his lips, grinds his ink, wets his brush, and slops his poem in seconds on the wall:

> *Hear the wild goose cry*
> *For a mate shout out of the sky*
> *Reeds for a nest in winter*
> *And the line flies on.*
> *Frisco, light your lights tonight.*
> *Here comes a timely rain*
> *of tigers and dragons to collect*
> *Kingdoms rise and fall*
> *Nations come and go.*

And there he was, after knocking her down onto her side with his knee, just for the finality of the action, toppling her over, hearing his wailing voice trailing away, a note she had struck out of him, and blushing, her own, ultimately satisfied adolescent son, bending over his mother on her side, who was still poised and tensed for crawling, like a mechanical toy tipped over. She had made him something for her eyes and ears to behold. It served her right. It served her right. His skin was repulsive to himself as he put it against her, his repulsive skin against hers as he picked her up because she didn't belong on the floor and it was the least he could do to show her nothing for her efforts. Meantime he picked her up like an expensive vase he had broken and had to hide and was helpless against sounding like a pleading little boy (much to her delight) as he carried her into the kitchen where Pete, Hyacinth, Barbara, and the children all smiled and lit up at the sight of him, as if he could make them all happy. "Ta-tum-mmmm!" Ma said. "This is my son, everybody! *Goong Hai Fot Choy!* Happy New Year! Tonight is the night of the first full moon! *Goong Hai Fot Choy!*" They all knew what Chinese New Year's meant to her.

The Sons of Chan

THIS CHARLIE CHAN'S NUMBERED SON REMEMBERS. He does. Oh, darlin, you know he does! I forget nothing. I remember Chinatown, my Chinatown. Being in Chinatown some skinny greasing the daggers of my hair down, singing flamenco clapping kid. Just a little kid far from any Charlie Chan.

I lived in a hotel, above the kitchens. A neon arrow hissed and throbbed by the window. On and off. A red electric arrow. At night I lump on the bed, holding onto a bare wire coming out of the back of the radio to make the radio receive. My body, skin, blood, and bone mysteriously brought the signal in. My body is the radio's antenna. When I touch bare metal with my free hand or my foot or any bare skin against any bare metal, I'm grounded out and God zaps me a little smooch.

But I used to hold on. Going through puberty I let the radio's electricity into me to feed and fatten up, flash crazy from pole to pole in my flesh to bring the Lone Ranger in out of the sky for me to hear, and Terry and the Pirates, and O. Henry's Robin Hood of the Old West, the Cisco Kid. None of the Mexicans I knew wore spurs in those days, but they walked like they did. Long-legged and strutting like a high Tom rooster passin in review down the pecking order, done up in the finest grease and silk, making all them hens pass out.

Meantime Charlie Chan, my movie father, God's gift to Chinamans, was taking shape out in the void and was on his way after me from Earl Derr Biggers tanning in Hawaii.

Like all white men who go to Hawaii, Earl Derr Biggers went nuts on the islands.

Here was a racist's mind-boggling wetdream paradise. The Christ-crazy hogcallers of the China mission had carried on here. Civilizing the heathen. Cut them off at the tongue, the nuts, the mind, the memory, put shoes on their feet, mush in their mouths, white on their minds, perfumed flowers round the necks of the men, ukuleles in their hands and set them loose dragging cellophane grass around their asses. This was Chinatown on a large scale. This Hawaii was Hillbilly Heaven, where every colored boy and girl danced to the whiteman's crazy tune, sang his songs, talked his language, did his work, believed in his God, which not even the whiteman believed in that much.

So here, Earl Derr Biggers, the reincarnation of an antebellum southern cracker overseer sitting on the verandah, sippin his mint julep, listening to the happy darkies choppin cotton in the fields making racial harmony, was fixed in Hawaii, sitting on the lanai, sippin' his mai tai, whooping his ears out to hear the Kanakas harmonizing on a hit of the period as they chopped sugar. "Sing song, sing song, so Hop Toy/Allee same like China Boy,/But he sellee girl with joy/Pity poor Ming Toy!" And Earl Derr Biggers read about a Chinese detective named Chang Apana. He'd never heard of an "Oriental detective" before. A vision came to him. God kicked Earl Derr Biggers in the head and commanded him to give us Chinamans a son, in almost His image. And Charlie Chan was born. And, in a sense, so was I.

When Charlie Chan first flickered to life in 1926 with the Springer and Barris hit "Hong Kong Dream Girl," the book was closed on my case. I would be born. I would endure self-administered electroshock therapy through puberty to get my radio fix, and late in life take to a white man badly disguised as a Chinaman. He would show me face-to-face what we looked like to whites, just how far whites had seen into our faces before they couldn't see any more. He was Charlie Chan. I took him for my father in one of my early movies. For seven years till after the Spanish gypsy dwarves had stomped through Chinatown and left us popping flamenco through our adolescence, strutting out a highstep to be men by, I had a white man for a father.

One hand on the wire from the radio and the other holding on crazy to the metal window frame, I fought electricity like a man, to the death, and would sometimes be found crying like that, crying and rolling on the ground, refusing to let go and turn it off. Gene Autry singing loud out of the radio, well tuned in and out of rhythm with the flash and throb of the red neon arrow on and off over me. Then one day I could hold on and never cry. I was blood brother to electricity and sensitive to thunder and lightning going off.

I'd lie there jiggling electricity like Frankenstein's spareparts patchwork monster being raised from the dead jiggled electricity, and stare at pictures of the Shanghai Low's Chinatown fan dancer showing everything but nipple and the El Rey Theater's Tempest Storm half naked in newspaper ads. Tempest Storm stayed in our hotel. I ran room service for her.

I grew up, graduated from college, embarked on a career, and every year of it was a miracle of her still young and naked, dancing the biggest tits alive through the El Rey, the Gayety, the Bryan Engal circuit, the Boston in Scully Square, through the years of Hollywood's Charlie Chan Chinese High, through my marriages, the return of Charlie Chan to the screen with me as Chan's Number Six Son, to irreversible balding and I am old, wearing a toupee and all my dreams are gone dead of old age. And there's Tempest Storm, still redheaded, still young and naked, dancing the biggest tits alive, waiting for me in a big Las Vegas casino.

Since the time she stayed in our hotel and I ran her room service and fell in love with her out of fright of the sight of her, my mother had grown old, lost her looks and figure, gotten thicker glasses and died in an auto wreck, a president had been assassinated, an ex-president died in a hospital, there was a romance between a movie actor and a president's daughter, Russia was the first in space, America was first on the moon. I'd become a father and a divorce, had a daughter by an elderly ex-nun and returned to California to play yellow bit parts. Tempest Storm was still perfect. I could show her what had become of me. I had never forgotten her. I was sexy now.

It wasn't every boy that could grow up to this. Others who'd chosen Ava Gardner, Betty Gable, Marilyn Monroe, Jayne Mansfield had grown up devoted to hags, grotesques, and suicides. Mine was worth showing who I was. That hey pop geewhiz poppin high eyebrow messing up slang screechy talkin Number Six son is only in the movies, Miss Storm. My voice has changed. I've lost my innocence, and all of my dreams but you are gone. I'm a man now. And I'm on my way. I will ghost write your autobiography. I will win the Nobel prize for this.

I am writing this report to my government down, way down on Thunderbird wine. Cold indoors. I look out the window into the slimy snotlight of a rainy day in the city, writing on wine, on pot, on antihistamines, dead drunk, the elbows come down on the table, on the counter, come down on every tabletop, bartop, countertop my elbows ever banged on, ever! And they are many. Many. Many. We will talk astrology. She will remember me. She will remark at the strangeness of a burn scar on the head of my prick, boost it gently with her fingertips and examine it closely. I will sigh. I will no longer be a busboy. I will become brave. I will tell the world my pop ain't no Chinaman. I will be a hero of my people. And it will be over. This living nightmare of being Charlie Chan's Number One Son.

"Who are you?"
"We call ourselves the Sons of Chan."
"You are not my sons. Keye Luke, Victor Sen Yung, and Benson Fong are my sons. Why do you call yourselves my sons?"
"We have forsaken our Chinaman fathers for white."

My life as a Hollywood specimen Chinaman began early.

I played the part of abandoned and orphaned Chinese babies, crying my heart out in smoking ruins, and became known in the industry for my wail being sent out over the sound of exploding Japanese bombs to jerk out tears. Such an angry, pitiful wail it still is on the after-midnight TV picking up ghosts. I see a China Shanghai night breaking apart with Japanese bombs falling from biplanes putt putt in the sky. Whistle. Crash of light. A flash of the Chinese running invisible in the dark and flames. Deep cellos fiddling gloom on gloom. Bodies of the dead are silhouetted by the rumpling flames. Then my wail. And there I am, singed, covered with soot, all my hair burned off to a little tuft that stands up on end on the top of my head. The flames of a burning derailed locomotive profile me. I'm crying. I'm tearing myself apart inside, crying. Spittle spray blasts out of my mouth on each sob. The flap of the flames muffles the bomb explosions and the biplanes' putt putt and is the loud low sound echoing cellos on the scene. My wail is the high sound. It fills the wide shot. It echoes off the exposed and bent iron girders, reaching for the sky. The U.S. Army Air Corps tuned the whistles of their bombs to my wail. I recognize myself by how the sound of my wail makes me feel, not the sight of me as a baby beating my heels on hot rubble.

That's me, I say aloud to myself, every time, and I shudder. I wear a toupee now and play the parts of hairy men much younger than me. Years of this have given me a simpleminded sense of irony and superiority. In the pop universe, you grow terrified growing old and retire when nothing can make you look young a minute longer and take up dark glasses, fatty foods, booze, and making commercials for savings and loan outfits in your own suit. Out of all showbiz I love the Negro bluesmen and the country'n'western cattle-calling balladeers most. They grow old and raunchy, falling behind, out of fashion, right before your eyes, on every album cover and guest shot and song they sing, and begin to haunt and hound you until you trust them. And then they're classics. And the singers, bald and spotted, wrinkled, white hairs thick as cat whiskers sticking out of their knuckles, clapping off their words with false teeth. And legendary they grow old nobly, with only a little shame. All but one of the Charlie Chans has died and been forgotten without a legend. His death is mine. "Who are you?" "I am your Number One Son." Late at night, after a hard day's shooting *Charlie Chan in Detroit* for TV or checking out my restaurant chain, with a whiskey in my hand and the tv on, I see myself as a baby wailing in the rubble of Shanghai. And something they did to me to make me cry so in the movies has never left. For whenever I hear myself crying on the late show, I feel things. I feel I must find the last surviving Charlie Chan of the movies and kill him. I will use what I learned being his Number One Son against him. Gee, pop, have I got a surprise for you!

In the twenties when Charlie Chan came into being, the Chinese in American pop culture was a sex joke. America was laughing off her fears of Chinese reproduction in America in energetic song and dance. Since the 1900s America had moved hard and fast in news and entertainment, storytelling, joking, legislating, and singing in the streets to exterminate the Chinese here, to shut off the flow of women, strand the cheap-labor males, guarantee an end to Chinese population. By 1923 the laws made America proof against Chinese women and Chinese reproduction. No Chinese woman could enter the country legally. No American-born Chinaman woman could marry a man from China without fear of losing her American citizenship and immediate deportation.

Our men began to die. They died fast and heavy through the forties. I heard them go. With the national average of around thirty Chinamans for every yellow woman, and most of those copped by Cameron House, the Salvation Army, and other members of the lunatic fringe in the name of the whiteman's god, that was a lot of death. A lot of loneliness. A lot of grief. A lot of walkin in the streets in year-round rain-or-shine funerals. I was a celebrity giving elegies. I ate big dinners. Did you know these streets were once stalked over by a mighty race of womenless and restless men? They say they were yellow and looked like us! They say they took to burning their papers, letters, diaries, journals, bills, everything with their names on them and threw the ashes into the sea, hoping at the wharf that that much of themselves would reach hospitable ground. The headline will read: CHARLIE CHAN MURDERED BY NUMBER ONE SON. I'll burn it up. I'll throw the ashes into the sea after the old Chinaman names. I'm on my way now. I'm getting mad.

I smell bread baking now, but am cold and dry. The steam inside the smell of baking bread isn't here. I'm breathing air off the night desert after a rain. I'm hungry. It's fine being hungry in Las Vegas. Tempest Storm is naked in this town. I'm going to look at her tits.

The alley was a vision of home. No one brought me out here to beat me up for trying to talk to Tempest Storm. I came here clean and upright in my lightweight polyester knits on my way back to the Aloha Outrigger Inn where they had beds bugged with Magic Fingers and nailed plastic plates of different colors and sizes to the walls in artistic arrangements for decor. I'd been to the Big Casino where she was dancing, called downstairs to her in her dressing room, and heard her down there sounding old and brittle as I found myself staring at a man with his hands growing out of his body at his shoulders. Instead of armpits he had palms. His hands looked like little cupid wings hiding in the little sleeves of his short-sleeved shirt. He was playing roulette. His hair was combed in great greasy waves. Beautiful bareshouldered women stood on either side of him at the roulette table. They held his hands when the wheel spun. I wondered if he lit his own cigarettes, if his palms were ticklish, if he buttoned his own shirts, unzipped his own fly in public johns, combed his own hair. I wondered what he could do with those hands and couldn't keep my eyes off him as I talked at last to Tempest Storm and did not recognize her voice. Maybe he had a specially made comb.

I was going to ask her first off, to set the tone, make things easy, open her up, I was going to ask if she believed in astrology maybe just a little bit, ha ha ha, make her smile, see if she kept her belly in by holding her breath through life. Make her smile, maybe laugh, and see if her belly moved out, and if it didn't, I had it figured now was the time to lean back at the smile, as if her smile walloped me, and pass my grabeyes around the room for clues. It would be in her dressing room that I'd be with her after all these years away from her hotel room, bringing her dinner on a tray. I'd pick up the colors of the place, flock wallpaper, a folding screen. Maybe she'd be changing in front of me after asking me to keep my eyes closed. I'd offer to close my eyes to her. "I ran your room service when I was ten years old, Miss Storm," I said. "Now I'm way over thirty years old, a man, and want to talk with you."

"What?" she said from inside her dressing room, and I told her what she had meant to me and the Chinamans in the kitchen who had cooked her food with surgical precision, licked her dirty plates and dishes off with their tongues, saved the napkins with her lipstick on them, and how I thought the charming story of a has-been over-thirtyish Chinese-American actor meeting his well-preserved childhood sex symbol would make me a few extra dollars. "Oh," she said and told me to call the Big Casino's publicist, Marcel Cassarole, in the morning. I hung up and on turning to leave saw a four-foot-eight-inch-tall hunchback in black leather walk by. A woman on each side of him held his hands. No thugs in tuxedoes took me out to the alley and beat me because I'd gotten too close to Tempest Storm.

The alley was a vision of home. A narrow street of oily wet brick built and gleaming like an uncoiling outstretched lizard tongue, red and black under my feet. I walked inside. The buildings were oily wet brick. All the whitewash washed and worn away years ago. Rain had pooled in the concavities. They shone silvery milk in the dark, like bits of antique mirrors aflash, as I walked sinking into the shadows.

She didn't want to kiss me at first and kept her eyes open, and muscled away. She screamed bloody murder into my head through my kiss. My brain and eyes and tongue and stomach absorbed the noise of her scream, filtered it down to a squeak that leaked a multiple-toned snooze out of my pores. Then she stopped screaming and settled into blowing cool and easy into my head. Drool in our mouths welled up higher and higher up the sides of our tongues and sloshed over our teeth and sealed lower lips to flood each other's mouths. I heard stardust hissing through the long corridors of my ears. My inner head lit up with a sound like gas escaping, or a faroff river. Both her hands came creepily across the side of my face up the back of my head, the back of my neck to run fingers through my hair and press me to her face. She looked like she was playing my head like a harmonica.

Our mouths were connected by an ocean of overflowed drool. Our teeth, gums, and lower lips disappeared like Atlantis as our spit had become one. Her tongue splashed through the caverned sea into me like a whale.

I am a movie star. As a movie star of cheapie movies hungering around the world, a known scavenger, tourist-class jetsetter in permanent press, I am quite often called on by my government to perform underhanded tasks and act shady in foreign countries, Chinatown and Hawaii. My government has me trade in secrets. Voice down and slurping deep, like a shovel plunging into rich gritty earth, diggin deep, I talk chasing down for the heart of women I kiss to keep America free. Down voice, down. Lurking along the bottom of a midnight alley's scummy shadows, I talk up a moist hypnotic darkly into her ear. My other self comes alive secreted in back alleys and dark doorways, waiting, like a molecule of aspirin out to jump the next soldiering particle of headache that drifts by. I made my American medicine. A genius of violence and intrigue by night, and a meek Chinese-American actor playing Charlie Chan's comic lovably asshole son by day.

I learned around the world white women in the dark find a Chinaman's kiss rare. But there are national secrets I have available that no one has asked for because they are so well kept. No one but the keepers know they are there to be had. Is it true that there are no cats in Chinatown? Is it true that Chinese restaurants all over America have closed on Wednesdays for night choir practice every Wednesday like clockwork for a century, and that white Christian missionaries had chanted up a hereditary crackpot reflex into our genes to turn off the flames every Wednesday, leave the chairs upside down on the tables, lock the doors, and go sing the magic spells of the whiteman's religion in the whiteman's church? Whites in the church doorway watched every Wednesday and laughed at us trying to be magicians of white magic. No one but one in the know could ask the truth of these secrets. Yet she asked for them and I was here to find out why she asked for them all of a sudden. Suddenly the secret Chickencoop Chinaman was in town and on the case, when a moment before I was just Charlie Chan's son come to Las Vegas to hustle up a little nostalgia and a few extra bucks interviewing the superstar of strip, Tempest Storm.

I'm walking slowly. Listen. Winter is so quiet. I can hear my heartbeat above the call of a far-off bird. Above the sound of my footsteps breaking through the hard frozen crust of snow that's grown all over the ground, in the night, like a scab . . . I hear my heartbeat. All over the earth. I hear nothing but me. That far-off bird could be songs in my bone. Berserk flashes of brain. My heart sounds farther away, deeper in the night from me than the bird that might be songs in my bone. I'm not happy, not without songs, though I'm not a known singer, not famous for whistling, singing along, popping fingers. But I sometimes strut like a black Spaniard. And people who know me know that music makes me smile.

My footsteps breaking through the snow sound like girls biting into crisp apples. I swallow back the juice gushing out of the flesh of the apple around the chomp of the teeth and walk on, stepping into the sound of girls biting into crisp apples. One girl biting into a crisp apple. Lily up on bennies, again and again, bit into an apple, crunch crunch, my bone song that might be a far bird and beyond . . . my heart. She spit out every bite, said she wasn't hungry on bennies and bit and spat again. So many women and dark corners. *Charlie Chan in Istanbul, Charlie Chan in San Fransico Nights, Charlie Chan in Zurich.* One wasn't home when I wanted her. The mother of my child and not home after I'd walked through the cold volcanic glassy black of winter to lose, to give myself up and lose to her. Not in her apartment. Barbara wasn't home, not Lily. Lily would always be home. She was home now driving me crazy. Her father was the last surviving Charlie Chan. I had to keep Lily close.

I went away and threw knives at the kitchen door because Barbara wasn't home. The miracle of birth. Birth was a miracle to me then. I wanted to be part of it and out of this stupid phase I was in, of me staring into paint jobs on the walls, seeing up whirlies, and getting caught staring into the circles flexing away from the plop of a stone through the water of something, a puddle, a pond, dishwater, looking for something in everything I see, really looking. Looking for meanings and significance and breaking out in sudden chills and itches, and fighting back farts and a crazy intense thundering weariness I come to with my eyes thrown open most cold-bloodedly on my cat, and come conscious in the echo of having meticulously plotted the foolproof murder of my cat.

The government had secretly taught me to flow in several foreign languages. Over the phone no one suspected I was a Chinaman. I lived to be in over a hundred movies and television commercials. Yes, there are killings in my past. The first one came because I kept stepping in the shade for my government until I had killed someone. Looked in his face, felt for his pulse with my own fingertips, seen up close for myself he was dead, killed someone. Until then, I hadn't been living. I like blood on my hands. I am Charlie Chan's son.

I listened to the radio alone with the lights out. The lights were always out when I took off my socks. In the dark I was severely conscious of the smell of my feet. I was young. I laughed away everything. I liked hearing me laugh. That was when the restaurant chain with the neon caricatures of me lit up at night on exotic slopjoints all over Los Angeles began to pay off and I could cash-buy my Cadillacs. I liked the feel of it. I liked the physiology of my laughter. I liked to be naked, snug under the covers with a naked girl, holding her in my arms and laugh and feel her laugh. My laughter then was rich, dark and glowing like fig newtons were when I was very small, like the first time I came throbbing gobs of jizz twenty miles deep into a woman. I laughed. No, that wasn't my laughter at all, but her's, Janet's, in Las Vegas. She laughed,

kicked at something awful, a madness, a demon. Sucked drool
fizzing through her teeth and said, "Janet," and wouldn't look at
me or stop laughing. I'd only asked her name. She told me too
much walking up and down the front of a restaurant bar, picketing. She'd been in Las Vegas seven years. Fifty years old. Her age
didn't show in her walk, her laugh, her skin, her eyes. When she
was nineteen she was "young, no know nawting," and was in love
with a boy who "treat me nice" and fooled her. He promised to
marry her, went off to war, never came back. She waited or was
evacuated to another part of China, where she waited, and he
never came back. Or he told her to forget it. I'm not sure how I understood her. We couldn't talk to each other in any language we
knew. Only in the way she said her name was she much older than
me. "No calling 'Janet' nawting," she said and put fingers on my
lips when I'd spoken her name. "Chinese!" she said. She wanted
to hear her real name. I was the first Chinese she'd seen in seven
years. She'd been singing a Chinese song to herself when a car
stopped out of the night and out stepped a Chinaman. I was sent
to make a silly dream come true. To be a Chinese calling her by
her Chinese name. It took me fifteen minutes whispering it back
and forth in an alley to get to saying it right. We were like witches
chanting up a spook to haunt her body. I will pay back. I will be a
hero of my people.
  "Who are you?"
  "Geewhiz, pop. You know me, I'm your Number One Son."
  "You are not my Number One Son. Keye Luke is my Number
One Son."
  "We are all your Number One Son."
  "Who are 'we'?"
  "We are the Secret Sons of Charlie Chan hunting our father
down, the society of assassins known as the Midnight Friends of
Justice, known for the holiness of the death we bring, for ours is a
happy holy war to the last Charlie Chan."
  "And when the last Charlie Chan is gone?"
  "We will be heroes of our people. There will be no more Char-
lie Chan. The buffalo will return. We shall return to Chinatown,
legendary."
  "And how will you be known?"
  "By our war cry, 'Gee, Pop, have I got a surprise for you!'"

I knew Pop was in Las Vegas. I could smell him on the rainy night air. But first, for my government, I had to meet a Chinese who'd spent all his life in France. He would be the only Chinese in the Denny's eating with his fork in his left hand.

Tempest Storm , the stripper, had given me the brush when I called to interview her in her dressing room. On my way back from the Big Casino I passed a Chinese girl walking a sandwich-board picket sign up and down the front of the restaurant. She could become the very first and most authentic Chinese girl I'd ever fucked, I thought, and turned the Chevy around and stopped. I was going to make this Las Vegas happen to me memorable.

She was from the North, from near Shanghai. A country girl. She still looked so young, though it might have been the dark midnight hour. A farmer's daughter from the North who'd moved to Shanghai when Japan invaded China. She'd been there. A woman I was hustling had been alive in a time that was ancient history to me, and my teeth began to chatter. Though it might have been the midnight cold of Las Vegas after a rain.

And I am old — over thirty — and am drooling over putting my hands out of my pockets on a woman old enough to be my young mother. I remember my young mother. I remember when my mother was my age. A woman of thirty.

Janet was fifty years old. She spoke some Shanghainese. Though I'd never heard Shanghainese before, she tried it on me. I didn't understand a word. She made it weird music. Strange bonechilling little shrieks and batflight swished through her clenched teeth. I knew a few words of Mandarin, the Chinese national language. *Gawk yer* or *goowaw yer*. Strange sounds from Chinese school. The Saturday sessions of the Chinese school under the Oakland headquarters of the Chinese Nationalist Party was our weekly dose of Mandarin. She spoke Mandarin. The Chinese national anthem and a few words of a lesson I remembered only as sounds were all I had left of the lessons. I made the meaningless sounds as best as I could remember them and watched her face. We laughed. Neither of us knew what I'd tried to say and we laughed, turned at the end of her picket site and walked back.

I kissed her in the alley. She was the oldest woman I'd ever kissed mouth to mouth with. Traffic was light. She spoke no Cantonese.

She knew a few words. She'd been here in Vegas seven years, married to an American soldier fourteen years ago. "No ejukayshung, no know nutting. I work anyting. Shoeshine shoes. Everyting." She says she has to work. She longs for home. Thinks about the betrayal of her love in 1947. Two sisters still on the mainland. Married to a lush. Hates America. Wants to go back to China, the mainland, but can't. She's been homeless so many places. Formosa. Tokyo. Hokkaido. Kyoto. She says "needle" for "need." "Universe" for "university." Hates American food. "Yeeh. Steak. One meat! No good. Chinese no like." She wrote her Chinese name for me and apologized about her writing. She hadn't written Chinese in so long and her hand is bad. Even I can see her hand is bad. She can't write her own name in her own language anymore.

She refuses to become an American citizen. She has beautiful dreams. She kept clasping her hands together and biting her nails, swinging her hips and shoulders round and round giggling, like a young girl. I told her I was from San Francisco. She looked to San Francisco as Heaven for the Chinese, said something about a "fish place" and something "so nice," and "Chinese food." "I never been in China in so long. Never go back now. Old. Maybe dead here. Then maybe ghost fly back to China," she said. "I hate dey talk English. Hah-low! How var you. Tonk you. Yis. Yis. Tonk you. Now dem say , 'How var you.' I say, 'Okay. Okay.'" She laughed, said, "Everybody say she so hoppy, say I hoppy laugh all time. I laugh because I happy all the time thought. Thought all the time China." Her husband liked booze. She liked tea. She talked and I hated her husband. With no language common between us, she managed to tell me all that. This is the story of my fascination with older women.

I'm the kind of guy who laughs and when I'm eating and laugh, snork up food. I've sniffed up and sneezed hamburger, olive pits, water, and a hot cherry from cherries jubilee. Always into the right nasal chambers. Perhaps that is scientifically significant. I'm the kind of guy who gets airsick, goes to the airborne flying john, crams his head in the stainless steel toilet, and vomits. And in a long spasm pistoning up puke, I realize I haven't locked the door as the plane descends for a landing and I come sliding out of the john feet first, gushering vomit, and I helplessly look up into the eyes of the passengers watching me slide down the aisle. I see what's in their eyes. I remember their faces. I will see them again.

I have a saving grace. I love flamenco guitar. I appreciate good flamenco. I will grow old and corrupt happily, get fat and power- ful, outwhite the whites, transcend the curse of being the kind of guy who gets drafted, stationed in Alaska, and runs out of the showers back to the barracks, racing against stiffening into icicles. Fast barefoot through a soundless cold faster than flash-freezing to jump up and down on a bare wooden floor to get the blood going. For the heat, in front of an antique railroad station pot-bel- lied stove. And my prick drops out of the bathrobe. In a state of uncontrollable hysteria my cock is out and whangs its head into a sizzling kiss on the lip of the iron stove. I know I'm a clod and people don't want to be my friend. I make people laugh dirty on me, and nobody wants to be the friend of an obscene joke. But still I have feelings. I'm hurt. I want revenge. I remember their faces. I made myself better than them and treated them like scum, and for all the rest of my life, for years, decades, wars, revolutions, movements, great periods, I have never been crossed, never been hurt again, and know I am inhuman and love it. Only in my love for Flamenco do I show any human feeling. After I am dead my children will speculate with the world's fan magazines on a Spanish gypsy in my past and feel even sorrier for their mother. For I will be a famous and powerful man who has been on the outs with their mother most of their lives. I will die without having seen them but once since my twenty-seventh birthday, when they drove away. I am Charlie Chan's son. I must pay.

The story of the Spanish gypsy girl in my past might explain something to them. Why, for instance, one night, a few years before my death, when I was dining with the king of Norway after having received the Nobel prize for Outwhiting the Whites, I found myself listening to a flamenco guitarist, a live human, gypsy flamenco guitarist who played flamenco Muzak. A toneless, un- melodic saddening sound of flamenco gone bloodless and zombie on me in the middle of the grandest dinner of my life. I, who cherished the memory of the world's greatest living flamenco guitarist taking the hand of a pudgy, snotty, filthy-rich Chinese- American Hollywood star into his hands and calling me "Maestro," and the "Buleria por Fiesta" he played for me in San

Francisco. I was listening to the ruination of this wonderful music and finding it irresistible to keep from singing to "Fandango de Huelva." A beautiful rough ugly song full of teeth and hair, sweat, religious gore, and a lingering grieving anger. I'd never been good enough to sing it. I sung it now, knew it was fake, and couldn't stop. They still say a Spanish gypsy girl, perhaps the one I met in *Charlie Chan in Barcelona.*

Yet there are women who love me. They laugh when I sneeze multi-colored gobs of glacéd fruits from Christmas fruitcake and make me think I am funny, that I did it on purpose to make them laugh. And it always ends up I've treated them like shit.

She missed China. I kept my hands in my pockets and walked up and down with her in front of the restaurant she was picketing. "Can I read your sign?" I asked. Then she stopped giggling and before I recognized the language, she had clearly asked about the Chinaman known as Iron Moonhunter and if it was true that flamenco from the bars around Chinatown popped in our Chinatown souls and left us walking high Spanish ass. All Chinaman secrets no one had ever asked before. Was there an old Chinatown joke among ancient Chinamen that a Chinaman invented the game of golf one day, sweeping off the sidewalk the eggs a *lo fan* had left in front of his hand laundry? She knew enough to laugh.

My hungry upbringing breathing rotten plaster and piss on piss made me take her on as a special event. Don't show her no fear. Treat her like a killer on the loose. Treat her like a bomb. Treat her like a trembling fuzzy virgin with your hands on her, not yet shouting through the thin walls. She was so much older than me.

She was the first Chinese girl ever to get naked for me to fuck, as I knew she would be when she came to my room with plastic plates and saucers nailed to the walls. Over my bed a Tv tray and two saucers were nailed up in a symmetrical arrangement. Jimmy Stewart was on TV packing in baseball to fly silver bombers in *Strategic Air Command.* I knew I'd fuck her. And I fucked her. She didn't know I was Charlie Chan's Number One Son. I didn't think to tell her till it was over. I pulled it out. It came out painfully, sounding like a drumstick being twisted off a turkey. She kept her legs spread and jizzem and jellyfish came out of her twat and pooled in the dimples of the naugahyde couch. I did it without ya,

Pop. Nothing proverbial about it. She lay back on the naugahyde for me after a few minutes of saying things we didn't understand. And I fucked her.

Her husband was dead. She took me to her place in the car he'd shot himself in. The insides smelled like Lysol.

Candles burned. Men's boots were piled high on the living room floor. Men's shoes were in another pile. The hallway was lined with shopping bags full of men's ties, socks, shorts, undershirts, sport shirts, and pipes. The full bags leaned neatly against the wall. Her husband had shot himself six days ago. I was glad I'd never met him, and after fucking his Chinese wife, and looking around the room, was really sorry he was dead. The Goodwill was coming to take him away in shopping bags and cardboard boxes. The woman who had separated him into piles and brutally and tidily packed him up to be passed out among the handicapped had groaned at the sight of my cock, almost fainted. Pulling it out of my fly, it struggled in her hand, like a salamander being pulled out of the dark, head first. Her palm, with her fortune on it, was wrapped around my prick and she groaned to see it, and spoke Chinese to it. My meat did funny things to her voice. My prick and her were into a private conversation.

She smelled like Egyptian mummies, like the insides of old refrigerators, like an old dirty, dug up, grown over kitchen that hasn't been used for a thousand years. Nothing dead in her smell. She wasn't death. A Son of Chan cannot die. She was old living things. We had to have screwed a million years ago and stayed wallowing in it to smell like this. I was fucking a living fossil, a being with a pre-electric mind. There was a whiff of the prehistoric swamp in the smell of our hot fuck that frightened me in midstroke, going into her.

She was very dry all over. Like a mummy. More supple than a mummy but dry. Her skin was like toast. If I could get into her soft dry pouches and bags, crawl around inside with a nose for old times, Egyptian old days and China of the dynasties, I'd smell, I'm sure, the ghost of wines that had been spilled at pagan orgies and find bones and the hum of laughter at old jokes. Even the insides of her mouth were dry. My spittle rose up behind my teeth and flooded a desert on the other side. My tongue came down in her mouth like a dead brontosaurus thumping on a dried-up pond.

She even speaks the ancient languages of ghosts. I am a killer. Yes, there are killings in my past. There are reasons secrets are kept at all costs. There are secrets so well kept they cannot be asked about by accident. I had to fuck her. I am Charlie Chan's Son. I shall not want.

Gee whiz, Pop. Have I got a surprise for you.

At the roadside Denny's you were fingering your ring. A dead giveaway. Your fork was in your left hand. You had chopsticks in your right. You were the European Chinaman I was supposed to meet for my government. You really believed you were a European Chinaman. For you had crummily disguised yourself as a white man over your crummy Chinese disguise and looked awful. You were both Charlie Chan and Colonel Sanders licking chicken. "Gee whiz, Pop," I said, "everybody knows you're not white anyway. You look awful." And you will ask, "Who are you?" And I remembered they talked about the millions of starving children in China to make white kids eat their vegetables. No one talked about the Chinese in America, so I starved. And I heard about you, Pop.

We will talk awhile. We will recall the old songs, the taste of old wines, and those forty-seven Charlie Chan features, one by one, through the fine days at Fox and Republic, the gifts, the dinners, then I will kill you, Pop. Even as the smoke still empties from the muzzle of my .45, I will begin to miss you a little and nurse a fondness. But there will be no regrets. I have given myself to killing you. You will die. It will be a legendary death. I will be the hero of my people.

I was on my bed getting my body buzzed by the Magic Fingers and writing this report to my government, cool and crisp as lettuce in my air-conditioned room. I was in the dark TV late show light of *Strategic Air Command,* flashing up Jimmy Stewart playing a baseball hero recalled to active duty. "Sorry, sir," the M.P. at the gate said, "We can't allow a civilian onto the base without identification." I'd never been in a city where there were no mosquitoes in the night after rain. The cars ran outside down the highway sizzling to Vegas like hamburgers. "I'm not a civilian. I wish I were," Stewart said.

"Are you Dutch Holland, the ballplayer?"

"Yes, I am. I was a ballplayer."

"I've been reading about you in the papers. You don't look much like your picture, captain. Gotta be careful about phonies. We once let a phony onto the base with a picture of an orangutan."

"No orangutans allowed," muttered Stewart.

Chinaman folk tell their young that the white people of town give themselves away on the nightrays. They show themselves off raw in the TV late show movies they lap up out of the dark. You can read a *lo fan*'s soul in what he chooses to fall asleep to, make after-midnight love on the couch to, come home drunk to. We have learned to live undercover in large numbers in towns that fill their night air with old World War Two black-and-white anti-Jap war movies, gloomy recreations of Pearl Harbor under heavy thickening music and Charlie Chan reruns. We act differently in zones dense with monster movies and tinny nasal musicals than in John Wayne festival zones. A glance at the daily TV listings told me Las Vegas was Air Force movies about big bombers, *12 o'clock High*, *The Dam Busters*, *The War Lovers*, *Bombers B-52*, life stories of bandleaders, and war-torn China road-of-life movies. I could see myself crying as a baby often if I stayed in Las Vegas and watched all-night television. I should have known we'd meet here, Pop. The electric substance of the night air, the first Chinese fuck in my whole life, Tempest Storm, Marcel Cassarole . . . I knew it all. I was alert, Pop, a killer, and completely off-guard.

I didn't account for your having bammed Chan on the screen once too often and been long gone, bammed off to another planet where you really were Chinese, and really were the one and only Charlie Chan, father of eleven children, husband of one wife, Lieutenant of Detectives, Honolulu Police Department, on his wily, creeping way home to Hawaii. And you had a Chinese cunning and wisdom all your own. You muttered in an unknown Chinese language. You were the most beautiful, lasting, and wonderful invention of the four-thousand-year-old Chinese culture you'd gone crazy to create. I didn't know what you were doing Pop, but the night air full of bombers and little baby me crying in the rubble of bombed-out backlot Chinas all over L.A., that ancient Chinese girl, a living fossil of a young Chinese girl making love to me made sense. I should have known you expected me.

I was watching *Strategic Air Command*, when the door opened to the night outside. The darkness after a rain. And she stood there silhouetted by deep blue moonlight, stars, and headlights of cars running down the Vegas-bound lane of the highway, late at night. She'd followed me in an air-conditioned white Cadillac car, parked, taken off her bra and panties, changed into a miniskirt and put a pink ribbon on her hair just to see me. I felt like crying. I was tired. Do you hear that, Pop? I wanted to stop awhile. But I couldn't while you lived. Instead of stopping I got mad. I went to sleep angry.

Now I go to sleep on the verge of tears. I think of suicide like pretty girls think of flowers. And I think of pretty girls. My first daughter was a pretty girl when I last saw her, when she and my son and my first white wife drove off. I think of suicide, flowers, and pretty girls, just like you did, Pop. You were crazy just like me. That's why we were fated to meet in Vegas. That's why you surprised me. Parts of me stopped, broke down while I ran on after you, kept on going without slowing, on after your ass, Pop.

"'You are either a liar or an idiot. I will give you the benefit of a doubt and assume you are not a . . .' Which would you say, Honorable Son?"

"What is this?"

"A Son of Chan can answer the question correctly."

"No speakee duh Englishee."

"You are truly a Son of Chan."

Parts of me stopped. My pecker stopped. It had stopped for me. It comes alive with the bats I feel in every horror show, and Halloween, or when I'm asleep, or driving in my car in races. Sometimes when I go to a peekshow fuck and suck, stand behind a curtain in a booth and drop quarters to watch a skinny blonde suck and lick a dick in closeup, lap up come, I feel my pecker move in my pants and I know I am a man, and am disgusted at how I find out. Then in the daylight, on the street, it dies. But that night, when I thought of the girl I loved at that time, nothing happened. I must have been afraid of her, whoever she was. It ended up I'd treated her like shit. It always ended that way. I didn't like fear. Then Janet smiled at me. Ancient. Classic. Chinese. Her small breasts wobbled and throbbed inside her blouse like giant maniac oysters in a monster movie. Back to the old days of black and white when I lived in a room over the kitchens, was hysterical starving skin and bones, soaking up whistling volts, bringing the radio signal in with my will, and looked at the newspaper theater section for tit. If I could teach that boy a lesson. She breathed the smell of cold milk into my mouth. My pecker rose like a cobra. I wound my watch.

I think I'm tired. I'm so tired my thoughts come to me as hearsay rumors of bats and strange birds and the swimming of dark Chinatown fish. I have to womanize! I have to womanize! I am too much for them. I am too much for friendships. I have no needs. No wants. I come from the flaming names. From Chinamen who were too many for women. Too much get a move on for friendships. We each of us have our war songs to protect us. I sang mine often. Charlie Chan is my father. I am Charlie Chan's Number One Son. I am given to Charlie Chan's death. Then the Sons will be free. Not much of a song without the guitar and voice I wrote it in. But I wasn't a known singer and could sing it unnoticed and keep it secret.

If I cried now, I don't think I'd ever stop. That would scare me. And I think of shouting sometimes. The old dry woman lay down her cold superb flesh on me. And her breasts came down and spread like pancake batter on my chest. Her hair came down onto my face like the feet of thousands of parachuting insects. I was mad. And I go on low. Run in a crouch, remembering the teaching of my masters, step on the gas and sing bass with the boom-chuck boom-chuck guitar of my song out of the radio and think of crying, think of tears, run on, on the low-grade energy of sleep and dream of sobbing like a child banging down the road into Las Vegas, Tempest Storm, and my first Chinese fuck.

I sat on the couch after she left the room naked. The naugahyde didn't soak up the come she'd drained. I sat in it, got it all over my hands, wiped it on my shirt, blushed hot, and smelled like fish. I wiped the ooze up with used tissues I found in the wastebasket. It was as if I were in a movie with you, Pop, looking for clues. Then I was asleep in her arms, between black satin sheets. Her husband had been emptied out of the closets and drawers. She'd vacuumed the floors. But my trained grabeyes could make out he wasn't all gone. There were toenail clippings worked deep into the carpet pile, and hairs in odd places. There was a smell.

I woke up looking deep into the eyes of Janet's twelve-year-old daughter, standing at the door. She was naked, beginning breasts, on the verge of taking shape and getting fuzzy. She stared at me cruelly. I did not flinch, though she was totally unexpected. I have been in haunted houses with Charlie Chan. I have had snakes come at me out of the dark. She'd brought nothing for me. No juice or toast. Just walked in naked to wait for me to open up my eyes into hers. I looked in and knew she wouldn't kill me.

She was half ancient Chinese woman trapped inside a petrified teenage girl deflowered by a soldier who never came back to Shanghai and half white American, blonde, well-manicured, keno-dealing, Las Vegas lush. She was the only person in the world who could talk with her mother. And she told me what Janet said in strange, correct, slow, rockcrushing old lady English teacher English. "My mother wants to know if you think China will take over the world," she said. I was too old to remember one word long after the other. I'd done nothing wrong. I didn't go to school anymore, except in nightmares that wake me up in sweats. And I'm not in school anymore when I wake up. "What time is it?" I asked.

"What's the connection between Tempest Storm and your interest in Chinese?" the naked girl asked for her mother. Janet's arms were around me. Her hands were on my chest. Veins, arteries, and ligaments bumped up their backs and valves through the backs of her hands, like plumbing and drainpipe on the back of a house. "I have no interest in Chinese," I said. "Tell your mother I have to call up Marcel Cassarole at the Big Casino."

"Why do you refuse to answer our questions? Don't you trust us?"

"I don't have time to explain," I said, closed my eyes, and in this strange room with these strange naked people, out of my sight, I once again, as I did every morning in Vegas, ran down the little I knew about Tempest Storm. She'd been married to Herb Jeffries, a black singer famous for hitting it big with "Flamingo," had a kid by him and recently divorced him. She once said she was giving up stripping for serious acting. She toured with *Born Yesterday*. Her trademarks were her full-length mink coat and her big boobs. Plaster impressions were made of her boobs in the fifties. I had a note to be careful with the name of another stripper, Virginia

"Ding Dong" Belle around Tempest Storm. "Stormy Weather" was her theme. I didn't know her real name or the sex of her child. I didn't know her age. This was me as ready to meet her as I could be. With this I'd try to make her friendly and remember me up enough from Oakland for me to tell her what I really know of her, what I did to her pictures in the paper, what Chinamans in the kitchen did with her dirty dishes and napkins when I brought them downstairs.

I opened my eyes and saw nothing but the girl's eyes staring into my head, as if my eyes were binocular lenses. Her eyes were like shotglasses half full of whiskey. Her nipples were swollen and large, shaped like rubber baby bottle nipples. Like her mother's nipples. Her mother's were darker. Tougher. My stomach growled.

The last time I'd seen a naked twelve-year-old girl like this, I'd been a twelve-year-old boy. We lay on my bed over the kitchens and listened to my radio together, got zapped and did not scream. My cousin from Chinatown Frisco across the Bay smelled of sweet baby powder in her armpits and between her legs. "Wow! *Gum dai guh!*" she said, looking at my prick grow in her hand, "So big," in Chinese. My twelve-year-old cousin was the first girl to ever talk Chinese to my prick. "I attend what is Chinese in you," Janet's girl said and left me with a memory of deep kiddie eyes and a strange threat to attend what was Chinese in me. A little girl being good. A China doll of song hallucinating miracles from home out of me. A tourist looking into me like a Chinatown curio shop. "You are the first Chinese man I have ever been close to," she said. A zombie. Your blood was in their veins, Pop. I said, "Tell your mother I don't care if China takes over the world."

"Don't you dream of China in Chinese?"

"No."

"My mother says I do," the girl said. "She says I sleep on dreams dreamed by the dead." I didn't like being naked up against Janet anymore. But I had to keep away from the girl. The girl talked too old. Waking up like this into her eyes out of a deep roaring dream wasn't doing me any good. I sniffed her food cooking. I tried to guess the time. "Can you see the Chinese in me?" she asked. Her hair was soft as white ashes.

"Listen, little girl, your mother's Chinese, not me. That's why I came home with her," I said and remembered the car full of Lysol I'd ridden in. It'd kept in the pungent air, something like a corpse keeping fresh in gas.

"She told me you'd come someday."

"I'm way over thirty years old and everyone all my life kept telling me about Chinese women . . ." Janet moaned into my back every time I spoke, making alien music of my sounds. "And I was doing only what had been expected of me a long time ago. Catchin up with lies. What do you mean she told you I'd come someday?" Janet's hum and growl invaded my chest and faked pneumonia in my lungs. I breathed her voice out of my mouth. Her lips were wet on my back, getting wetter in response to some code of tones in my voice only she knew.

"You're my Chinese daddy," the girl said and stroked my face. My need to kill you, Pop, bulged all my muscles up hard. I was holy with the power to kill you and looked for you round the room. Mother and daughter smiled at each other. The girl climbed in bed with Janet and me. Cool air slurped me as she lifted the blankets. They both put their arms around me. Janet's nipples were tough as pencil erasers stubbing the flat of my back. Her daughter's soft and cold like curds of cottage cheese. When I was married and had children, nothing like this ever happened to me.

I had dreamed of wooden stairs, dark walls, old paint. I was breathing cooking grease in my sleep. The smell of pork sausages that had been fried minutes ago. I woke up sniffing and hungry. Then the last trace of the dream was gone. I wasn't among friends. I had a hardon in my hand like a microphone. I felt it picking up sounds and translating them into electricity. "I want you to know something," I said, and mother and daughter cooed. Pictures had been taken off the walls. They'd left the wooden clothes hangers hanging in the closet. The wire hangers were in a snarled pile in the corner against a full-length mirror. "I want you to listen to me," I said.

"Now I will be your Chinese daughter."

"Not mine," I said, and was Number One Son again, playing dumb in a Charlie Chan movie, Pop. This was the ancient Earl Derr Biggers mumbo jumbo formula gurgling me up goofy. They were the witches of your bad magic, Pop, making sweet greeting-card poetry of me, talking me apart into two half-men. Half and half. Ping! Chow mien. Pong! Spaghetti. Ping! East. Pong! West. She was two half-girls. She talked to me one half at a time. I was afraid to tell her her white father was dead and let her run her psalm of the legendary Chinese father her mom had dreamed up crazy in Las Vegas to blow the monsters away.

"You are Chinese aren't you?"

"No," I said. "I am Charlie Chan's Number One Son." I hated you for these ghouls stroking my skin with their hands. Through her daughter, Janet remarked on the strangeness of a scar on the head of my prick, giving me up my secrets before I'd ever gotten close to Tempest Storm. And I felt my luck go. I hated them being kind the only way they knew how, flattering me with the China they found all over me as I got out of bed and moved. They oohed all over the so American haps coming from me as I sung my war song to save me, protect me, aim me to kill you, Pop. "I am no one's Chinese daddy. I am no one's white daddy. I come from a China no Chinese from China comes from. A China beyond the Pacific, beyond Asia, beyond any kind of East. Beyond anything known. Beyond belief. Uncharted. Unknown. Unexplored. And under your nose," I said and stepped out into Las Vegas sweating under dead daylight. It was Wednesday. All the Chinese restaurants were closed.

The daylight was a cement slab laying on Las Vegas, hardening up thunder. Sulky, touchy. Holding back lightning. Pocket combs crackled all over town. Showgirls walked in the gloom sounding like their hair was a house afire or Rice Krispies. Cars drove with their headlights on. The electricity of a thousand old radio shows loud with the voices of dead stars shuddered in my antenna bone from pole to pole, like ancestors, put my blood and me on like clothing, kept me company, and were anxious to ride as I searched for Marcel Cassarole round the daylight neon. These mean clouds had come for me from the Sierra Nevada.

Marcel Cassarole was in a booth at Denny's sitting on royal blue naugahyde. He wore a white suit; his hair, mustache, and goatee were all the same white as the suit. He ate with his fork in his left hand and chopsticks in his right, schizophrenically working over a plate of French fries. Cassarole was everybody I had looked for. So I looked at him.

A fiery horse with the speed of light, a cloud of dust and a hearty
HI YO SILVER. *I know many things for I walk by night. I have seen the*
men and women who have dared step into the shadows. Listen! . . .
while traveling in the Orient I learned the mysterious power to cloud
men's minds.

I was so old and stuffy, so long with my grudge run to the end
of the chase after you, Pop, I didn't think of you growing old too.
Gee whiz, you looked awful. Senile old Charlie Chan looking like
Colonel Sanders the finger-lickin chicken king rotting fast. We'd
all become pitiful. We were two old men. I could have killed you
for my government, for faking yourself up a European Chinese
running a pass. White people never did have the eyes to see
through fake. I never could understand that, never really believed
it. But looking at you then, a whiteman in yellowface and tape
faking Chinese eyes under the lard and cornstarch whiteman's
disguise that had gone rancid and smelly on your skin, attracting
flies and clogging your pores, one hand with a fork full of French
fries racing the hand with the chopsticks full of French fries to
your mouth, making no one wonder, I knew I could lie to my
government. I could tell them you were, indeed, the European
Chinese they wanted, and they would believe me, just as they always had, in our movies. But the man I was in the movies, Pop,
was given to your death. I could become a hero of my people. "Hi,
Pop. Tempest Storm, the stripper at the Big Casino won't talk to
me unless I get your permission," I said.

"I say, hello. How are you? How are you? Fine? Fine. I am fine.
I am Marcel Cassarole, me. I am so happy to be meeting you," you
said. You had learned to use first person pronouns as part of your
whiteman act and blabbed wild with "I," "me," and "we" talking
strange like no one had ever heard Charlie Chan talk.

But you still walked in the fetal position, still fingered your ring
and wrinkled your nose and bucked out your teeth when you
spoke. I hadn't seen it live in a long time. I hadn't seen you live,
closeup, and in color since that last day I saw you in Honolulu. I
was sorry we never shot a Chan in color, Pop, and could have
hugged you. Feelings like this I could only have for my father. I
was back with you at last, showing you what had become of me,
asking you for a favor and full of violining emotion for you. I like
looking at you. Tears in my eyes. We'll talk awhile, recall the old

songs, the taste of old wines. I'll hold my .45 steady in my hand, ask, for the sake of leaving no questions unasked, what you think of NBC-TV and Universal Studios saying, back in 1971, they couldn't find a yellow to play the new Charlie Chan and got white Ross Martin to carry on, in your name, Pop, amen. And I will kill you and go on gunning to the last Charlie Chan.

"I would want to be knowing to me, why you wish to see Miss Storm, I think, I might know for my forming in me my decision as I see fit, please?"

"Pop!" I said, "I have learned around the world white women in the dark find a Chinaman's kiss rare." Tempest Storm should have been the first to know when I was ten years old running her room service. Maybe she'll kiss me, Pop. Maybe she'll kiss me in her dressing room and make me well all the way back."

"I am Marcel Cassarole. How are you? I am fine. I am in consideration of your requisition at this very moment, even eating as is my habit. You may noticing from me, my European-style speaking which suits my name also. I am Marcel Cassarole."

"Don't you know me, Pop?" I said. "Drop it! I know you're Charlie Chan."

The cloud was over me, waiting full of storm. It mountained up spellbinding lumps of thunder, my thunder, flexing my lightning and lay face down on Las Vegas, making the town hot and sweaty and strangely gone dark in the daytime. It looked like that early morning darkness scummy with light before sunrise all day long. Gamblers stayed in their hotel rooms with their dark glasses on and watched the clouds gnash and gnarl. Their fingertips itched. Their palms were sweaty. Downstairs the heart had gone out of the cards and slot machines. And from the Sierra Nevada, from Chinamans clanging iron in the river canyons, came the power of the moment. And the moment, Pop, was mine.

No one spoke a word. Not a dog barked. Engines all over the world gasped. All the birds were out of the sky clawing to hold telephone wires, power lines, and TV antennas. The birds knew to stay out of the sky when the Chickencoop Chinaman's about to close a case. And every Chinaman not even knowing why, felt the heart skip a beat inside them and turned suddenly like they'd seen a shadow pass, and looked in the direction of Las Vegas, pitching me my strength on invisible rays. Children, do you feel the power!

Put down them dishes a minute, come on, children, get your head out of that washin machine a minute and look hard toward Las Vegas just a second, right now. This message was written into your blood a long time ago in the screams of your fathers in the Sierra Nevada where the wind has suddenly stopped, and the trees are full of birds. Not a wing flaps. And the trains have died, children. There's not a wheel turning and trainmen scratch their heads and look down the track into the distance. Every yellow dentist and seamstress with so much as the shadow of a drop of blood from the granite-face stone sixties not even knowing why, does turn toward Las Vegas to let the Chinamans of the Sierra Nevada see. Nothing can hurt me. Moments like this are hard to make. They are the rarest kind. Especially for a Chinaman. All over the continent and very heavy on Las Vegas it's suddenly hush hush. And cats and dogs everywhere snap their heads round to face the direction of Las Vegas and perk up their ears. "Gee whiz, Pop, have I got a surprise for you," they don't know why, passes word for word through the mind of every Chinaman kind, in my voice. Some actually say it aloud, sounding like me. And the ghosts of all the Sierra Nevada Chinamans rise to watch. It's just like it was told to me in Chinatown. Just like it. I do feel the power. My flesh throbs from the beat of every radio show I'd ever heard inside out pole to pole blasting again. I used to think of this moment coming when I was a kid standing in the rain with his pants pockets full of balled up soggy sandwiches with coins and paperslips imbedded in the bread. "Who are you?" you asked, and this was the moment. The neon had never looked so pale in Las Vegas. Every parking meter in America jammed. I spoke. "We call ourselves the Sons of Chan."

"You are not my sons. Keye Luke, Victor Sen Yung and Benson Fong are my sons. Why do you call yourselves my sons?"

"We have forsaken our Chinaman fathers for white."

"Who are you?"

"Gee-whiz Pop, you know me. I'm your Number One Son."

"You are not my Number One Son. Keye Luke is my Number One Son. He is a blind Chinese priest on TV."

"We are all your Number One Son."

"Who are WE."

"We are the Secret Sons of Charlie Chan hunting our father down."

Then you laughed. Charlie Chan had never laughed before.
This was Charlie Chan's first laugh. A fake laugh. A part of your
whiteman act. We'd never had any laughs together, Pop, did you
know that? The Sierra Nevada shook. Birds were rattled off the
branches of trees. They didn't open their wings to fly. They fell on
the ground. The air was full of ghosts laying track of Vegas. The
Iron Moonhunter was mounting steam, working up pressure to
run down the spirit rails, come pick me up, and leave you dead.
But you laughed, a fake Chinaman faking white. You never knew
what a Chinaman calls a whiteman. I know Chinamen like you.
You always laughed at me. A bunch of hisses and poppin spit behind your grin. You always giggled. Everything I ever tried, you
giggled at in public in forty-four black-and-white talkies around
the world. And I only tried to please you, Pop. Only talking to me
in private did you slip a few of them rare first-person personal
pronouns out. You never dared say "I," "me," or "we" to the *lo fan.*
There were blondes and brunettes in those movies with me. You
made them laugh at me. Charlie Chan's Number One Son
remembers. He does. Oh, darlin, you know he does.

"Who are you?" Charlie Chan asked.

"I am your Number Two Son."

"You are not my Number Two Son. Victor Sen Yung is my
Number Two Son. He is a Chinese cook making people laugh on
TV."

"We are all your Number Two Son."

"Who are WE?"

"We are the society of assassins known as the Midnight Friends
of Justice, known for the holiness of the death we bring," I said.
And you laughed again.

"But what of your fascination with older women?" you asked.

"Whaddaya know about Janet?"

"I know her Chinese name," you said, "in Shanghainese, Mandarin, and Cantonese. She doesn't like to be called 'Janet' does
she?" You grinned your Charlie Chan chop suey grin at me and
laughed Charlie Chan's Halloween whiteman's laugh. I'd never
heard my father laugh. I thought of tickling your ribs. I thought
of teaching you to laugh. If only you'd seen me as a kid in Oakland
learning to be fast and flashy with my tongue running the You
Mama Alphabet, learning how to talk people down till they're

doing nothing but being laughed at. They'd surround us and clap together and stomp a foot down together, clap and stomp all together all around us and sing "Ayy!" And you have to be fast, gotta pop a fast nasty or get hit. "You Mama wear Army boots."

"Bee!"

"You Mama bites on dong."

"See!"

"You Mama comes fishy on the shoeshine boy's tongue." I think you'd have laughed at hearing how we got our English on. Sometimes late at night, waiting for a call in an out-of-the-way phonebooth or running my lines for the morning's shoot I'm caught sweaty in the memory of how hard I played the Alphabet. I don't remember the losers' names. Only their faces. And I laugh at that boy trophy-casing the losers' faces. I laugh at him now. This was my moment, Pop. I could have anything I wanted. I wanted to be a good son. I wanted to have the sound of my father's pure laughter to remember before I killed him. But you were trying to hurt me, Pop. "But you don't know how to call her anything but 'Janet' do you, son?" you said.

"Pop."

"But when I mentioned *older women*, I was still talking about Tempest Storm. I thought you wanted to talk to her."

"Gosh, Pop," I said, "that would be swell! But, heck. My government wants me to snuff ya out for passing yourself off for Chinese. And my people just want me to kill Charlie Chan. And a fella just don't know what to do, you know, Pop. This is my biggest case, Pop. And I'm in a jam!"

"Now, tell me, son. Who are you?"

"I am your Number Three Son."

"You are not my Number Three Son. Benson Fong is my Number Three Son. He owns a chain of sweet'n'sour joints in Los Angeles and gets killed on TV."

"We are all your Number Three Son."

"Who are WE?"

"WE are know as the Midnight Friends of Justice, known for the holiness of the death we bring, for ours is a happy holy war to the last Charlie Chan."

"And when the last Chan is gone?"

"All will be quiet. We will be heroes of our people. There will be no more Charlie Chan. No more numbered sons. We will have names of our own. Everyone will hear them."

"What will your name be?"

"I will be Charlie Chan of the movies. And Charlie Chan will be like the real me. And Charlie Chan's Numbered Sons will be like you, Pop. Then Charlie Chan will laugh. And everyone will hear." All the words were said, just like I'd been told a thousand times before, they'd be said. I'd been told I would touch you now, that I'd take your head in my hands like a basketball or touch your hands and you'd fry. From Chinaman hand to Chinaman hand, pole to pole all them forty-four Charlie Chan features would bam fast black-and-white movies sizzling in your nerves till you burst hot grease from your insides, like an overcooked sausage, shit and piss your pants, die and be charred smoking rubble. I'd been told to expect a smell like burnt meatloaf. And all the Chinese restaurants would open up on Wednesdays from now on with sweet'n'sour meatloaf as the Wednesday special. All I had to do, Pop, was touch you. I didn't need no .45. Charlie Chan had made Chinamans the chosen people.

But maybe because I was Number One Son way over thirty and balding and you'd never said a word, Number Two Son laughed at all my life and you'd never listened to me without your buck-toothed Chinky grin, Number Three Son who'd never won a fist fight but had to fight, no matter what they said about my father being a lovable fairy being true, and maybe because I felt the lows of every minute I'd ever lived feeling me up sadly now, like good-bye kisses brushing off a doomed one, and because in the murmur of my radio spooks singing all the old songs round my bones, cracking all the old jokes, I got sad and weepy over the abandoned, ignored, picture-perfect Chinaman child I'd always been and hated myself hating that kid, and because I couldn't help it, I sat down without a damn for anybody, nothing but selfish for once in my life and wanted you to listen to me, take me for serious, do what I wanted right now, without setting me wailing immersed in the sound of singing bombs, without slicking me over with any of that Confucious Says crap from the cocktail napkins. I'd never spoken anything but the sacred words of somebody's spiritual ritual to you, never gotten out of the motion of somebody's magic plot.

Even now I seem a creature out of an old hit tune that had America singing the miseries of womanless Chinamans when you first came to light up the silver screen. And I don't not like the song enough to give it up. Maestro, if you please!... *Hong Kong Dream Girl." Here in fair America he sings a lonesome song/While his little China maiden/ Waits for little China boy in far away Hong Kong/ He cries and sighs "it won't be long."* No, sir, Pop. It won't be long. *My little Hong Kong Dream Girl/ In every dream you seem, girl/ Two almond eyes are smiling/ And my poor heart is whirling like a big sail round my pigtail/ I dream of you till dawning/ But early in the morning/ Oriental dream is gone/ China boy is so forlorn/ Hong Kong Dream Girl good bye.* Even now I catch myself humming that tune and getting an urge to step out dancing. But I don't dance. I leave the music echoing hollow in me, haunting me to run a rage after your blood, not because I was my people's killer priest and the high rites were over. But because I had children who laughed at me for being the Son of Charlie Chan and ran away from home. Things like that I don't forget. Me first. All for Number One. "Listen, Pop. I wanta see Tempest Storm's boobs up close in good light," I said and betrayed my government. And my people too. They let Las Vegas go. They let me go. The birds let go of the wires and flew. I didn't have a people anymore. Just you and me, Pop.

In the liverlit high indoor twilight of the Big Casino's showroom saloon, old men in metallic suits gleamed like iced fish. And old women in furs dusty with old face powders and topped with metallic hair whispered and showed their teeth. The light was a dark bloody slime in the air shot through with mirrorshine. Tobacco smoke rose from the cocktail tables and turned violet in the light and waved like long hair, caught in the suction of the air conditioners. The sweaty oily skins of people shone like sheets of cobweb, like unfolded bits of used waxed paper in the candlelight of the tables. Teeth flashed like fireflies. There was a mood in this room, a living breathing quiet that blotted up noise. The sound of chips and money falling, of slot machines rolling in the casino just through an open arch wasn't thunder anymore. The laughter that roared from the floor of this room didn't resonate. A trumpet sputtered up a shrill squeaky note that got loud then flopped to a stop. It spat another, different quivering sound seeking shape. And the

band plodded and thumped after the trumpet laying heavy feet
under the high-sheen honky-tonk squeal into the opening of
"Stormy Weather." "And now, it's star time at the Big Casino!" a
woman's voice said out of the livercolored air. "Ladies and
gentlemen, Miss Tempest Storm!"

"I have to go backstage," my father said. "You just look at her
beautiful body and don't worry about her dancing. Because she
can't dance. She couldn't find her ass with her hands if she had a
road map," he said and did his imitation whiteman's laugh,
slapped me on the back, then shuffled off, tripped on the pile carpet, bumped into tables, edging his way out, and loosed an absent-
minded, "'scuse please," out of my sight.

"She's in great shape for a woman her age," I heard at the next
table. "Oooh, I'm going to have trouble tonight . . .!" She moved,
throwing herself out of joint, strutting in her high heels to no
rhythm at all but still like something that had known how to dance
once, like a rusty robot with broken gears, cranking through the
motions, like an old arthritic dog struggling to lift a leg to piss. She
had the moves of a calcified hardened-up angry old woman. But
long fine legs without a trace of varicose veins were fair in the
bright light, solid. The shadows of flexing muscles weren't stark,
didn't open up ravines and canyons on the insides of her thighs or
between her shinbones and the flexing bulge of her calf. The
rounds of her ass didn't change color as she shifted her weight hard
from foot to foot. As the strength in her muscles ran up and down
her legs, stiffening up one side of her ass then the other, she didn't
show up flaws, dimples, holes and stretch marks like other white
women I'd seen naked whose legs changed color when they
walked, dumping one buttock and hardening up the other, the
hard one full of holes like a side of moon and the relaxed one
wrinkled and sagging like an old toy balloon that's lost air. She took
off her clothes with all her strength, as if they weighed a thousand
pounds. Her long, sequined gloves had swallowed her arms up to
the elbow, like feeding boa constrictors. Her gown was nailed to
her body and had to be violently wrecked. She smiled all the time.
The strain showed in the formation of deep ruts and gorges as the
muscles of her chest and back rose like a circus tent up her neck,
under the dazzle of a huge necklace. Her belly was flat and plated
like the belly of an athlete, the belly of Tarzan. The lights dimmed

each time she wrestled off a piece of clothing, pink to navy bean to red, to green to deep sea blue that made everyone's eyes look plumping out like poached eggs at her tits coming out, into the beam of dim purple rays deepening on her body, showing her veins and arteries up through her skin, revealing the darkness around her eyes, the continents of makeup built onto her face, the coldness of her big round breasts. She stood in the eyestrain of a crowd that drooled and stared into a grisly purple glow just a shade from total darkness at Tempest Storm's shimmering ghostly flesh. She stretched her arms out and wobbled her breasts and grinned. She looked like a vampire, plump and dark with blood that was already dying in her. Then the lights were all the way out, and she was gone. The glitter of the diamonds round her neck and between her legs lingered as presences in my eyes a while, interfering with everything I saw and were strangely disembodied from the immediate memory of her. They could have been the flash of running water dazzling me, and she something I might have seen deep under. I didn't feel I'd ever seen her before. Seeing just what everyone else had seen of her wasn't good enough for me. She'd had no effect at all, made no connection good or bad with the memories of the redheaded woman in opaque white bra and panties who I remembered let a ten-year-old Chinaman boy into her hotel room. There'd been nothing familiar or unfamiliar about the sight of her. I wanted to be known. I had a right to be remembered. I phoned down to her dressing room and told her I had talked with Marcel Cassarole. She said she'd never heard of him. "But you told me to call him up. He's the publicist . . ."

"No, Herman Miller is." I heard nothing familiar in the sound of her voice. It was any old tired white woman's voice. No one special.

"I ran your room service . . ."

"I'm sorry," she said.

"Remember Oakland? I mean, I've been in Vegas a week trying to get up the nerve to see you, then I phoned you and it's been twenty years and you said see Marcel Cassarole, and I saw Marcel Cassarole like you said and now . . ."

"Who's Marcel Cassarole?"

"What's going on, Miss Storm?"

"I'm tired and have to rest up before the next show. I'm sorry," she said as if she hadn't heard a word I'd said and hung up. My biceps were in the grip of two thugs in tuxedos. They held my arms like apes holding bananas. Their fingers went all the way around and squeezed. I felt their knuckles grind in my armpits. They were big men. One hung the phone up for me as my arms went dead and bloodless on me, no feeling in the fingers, no strength to hold the phone anymore and I dropped it.

"Marcel Cassarole?" I asked.

"Never heard of him."

They carried me out to the parking lot. They didn't beat me. They opened their hands and let me walk. I remember their faces. And I'm still in a Charlie Chan movie, walking a step at a time not too fast away from the men I feel watching me, and slowly heard less and less of their laughter that burst louder out of them when I flexed my shoulders. I didn't run. I didn't turn around or rub the soreness of my arms or cry or plot revenge. I concentrated on getting to my car. I remembered their faces and sighed, then stamped my foot. My deepest feelings, no matter what, only moved me to do things people had seen me do before in the movies, as if there was nothing else I could do. I couldn't think of any minute of my life that hadn't been silly and drove back to Janet's place because it was easy and she and her daughter wanted me. Like everyone else in the world they couldn't understand what I thought of them or didn't care. And I didn't care that I found them disgusting. I liked them wanting me and was ready to take them awhile, and stood a long time in the empty apartment, listening to my heavy breathing echo through the dark barren rooms and bounce off the walls before I realized the place was completely empty. No piles of boots and shoes. No shopping bags in the hallway. No furniture. No pictures on any of the walls. Nobody lived here anymore. They'd even pulled out the nails and removed the lightbulbs. But the white Cadillac was still parked in front. That's why I'd been so slow. I must have thought they would come back for the car. I don't think I could leave a car like that behind if it were mine. It would be like leaving food you'd paid for uneaten. I went back to my car without having said a word or called a name out loud, and sat behind the wheel wondering if perhaps they were asleep in one of the dark rooms. I hadn't walked through the whole apartment.

I hadn't made much noise going the few steps inside to where I'd stood. I didn't go back up, or get out of my car to look inside the Cadillac for clues.

The cloud had broken and come down rain drizzle and fog all at once all over town. The weather held a strange light, a lilac violet wino's muscatel glow hanging in the fog broken by an occasional scattershot of rain. On the way out of town toward the desert highway to California, I snapped the sight of what might have been Janet and her daughter with a couple of suitcases on the curb, squinting against the wet, with no umbrellas, trying to thumb a ride, and kept on going. The further I drove on, the more sure I was that I'd seen them and that they were going to San Francisco and purposely left them back there now. I drove home alone. I didn't get into Tempest Storm's dressing room. I didn't kiss her. I didn't kill Charlie Chan. I have nothing but failure to report from Las Vegas. Charlie Chan's Number One Son remembers a lot of failure. I am a legendary failure in America. I am a loved one, the chosen of the Charlie Chan chosen people. Pop, I will find you. I will be a hero of my people. Gee whiz, Pop, have I got a surprise for you.

Afterword

THE MOST POPULAR BOOK IN CHINA is the autobiography of a white woman born and raised in a French hand laundry in south China. The meek, sycophantic nature of the French of her childhood clashed with the aggressive, individualistic nature of the un-revolutionized Chinese, who embraced her as one of themselves.

A female raised a French Catholic, she is, by the terms of her thousand-year-old religion, the meekest of the meek, the mildest of the mild, basking in the grace of God. She is forbidden by French culture to speak of herself except in the third person, and must limit her use of the first-person pronoun "I" to quoting the exact words spoken by card-carrying Judeo-Christian white men.

She cunningly transcends the religious ban on female first-person expression by writing of herself in metaphor. "Once upon a time, in a once-upon-a-time China, there lived a once-upon-a-time little French girl in a little French hand laundry, in the little Frenchtown on the edge of the mighty port city of Canton," the book opens. Very quickly this unusual autobiography of a Christian convert in China becomes a poetic evocation of a heroine of French feminism. She wrote a book about her imagined French ancestor Joan of Arc.

The old French people of Frenchtown on the edge of Canton didn't like the book. They didn't have Smith Mei-jing's grasp of the Chinese language, the Chinese who loved her book said. The people of old Frenchtown said her book falsified history. They are conservative and old-fashioned and don't appreciate good writing, the Chinese who loved the book said.

The picture of Joan of Arc as a man forced to dress and act like a girl and castrated after ceremonial incestuous relations with his father to satisfy the perverse sexual lusts of her parents was not historically accurate and was so inaccurate as to demonstrate that the woman had gone mad, the French people of Frenchtown on the edge of the port city said. The French girl is writing not history, but art, the Chinese who loved the book said, and continued: She is writing a work of imagination authenticated by her personal experience.

The French people of Frenchtown said, her own experience is an insane, paranoid distortion of basic knowledge common to all French. She mangles what no sane Frenchman could get wrong without going mad: Joan of Arc! the people of Frenchtown protested.

And the Chinese who loved the book said, her personal experience was authentically French and her unique understanding of both the French and the Chinese views of life brings the Chinese the closest, most human understanding of the French ever produced in the Chinese language. Her book gives the Chinese insights into the French mind and the French character, not French books, the Chinese who loved the book said, and declared Smith Mei-jing the hope of French literature written in Chinese.

She violates French history, culture, and language, heaps contempt on her ancestry, and depends on the ignorance of her Chinese readers for her Chinese literary success, the old people of Frenchtown said, and waved old books over their heads.

Sour grapes, the Chinese who loved the book said. She's not writing history or about history, therefore the accuracy of any of her history is irrelevant to the question of her artistry, authenticity, or psychological reality, her Chinese admirers said.

The French autobiographer's name is Smith Mei-jing, her autobiography, *The Unmanly Warrior.* The Chinese *Children's Digest* version of the book has been translated into English with the hope that it will be adopted as an aid in teaching American fourth and fifth graders a little about France, French culture, and the relevance of Joan of Arc in the world of personal experience.

Unmanly Warrior
BY SMITH MEI-JING

Once upon a time, in a once-upon-a-time China, there lived a once-upon-a-time little French girl in a little French hand laundry, in the little Frenchtown on the edge of the mighty port city of Canton. A lone little while girl in the splendor and civilization of China. Am I so alien to my vague Europe? My far France?

The French are a distant people. She dreams about my French self. How strange it is to be French in China. Surely the grandest place in the world to be born. In France they burned women. They held a lottery, and each year more and more women were burned.

Joan of Arc was the last woman to be burned by my ancestors. Surely Joan imagined herself Chinese, in China where woman warriors abound in the heroic tradition from ancient times. And she thought herself born again someday in me. Poor Joan of Arc. Born a son to a family that craved a daughter. They dressed their boy as a girl. They forced him into homosexual relationships with the surrounding court society, while young and naked virgins pranced through the deer park singing Vivaldi with ribald discretion.

Joan of Arc grew up a strong and muscular boy. Yet his parents dressed him in gowns and wigs and powdered him and admonished him to seduce princelings and influential priests at the crown balls. Joan took to bright lipstick and shiny satin masks and riding rescue, snatching women from the flames of the lottery.

Soon Joan mounted an army of masked women fed up with the silliness of court life that threatened to topple France, determined to make it a nation ruled by women rescued from the flames of French male bigotry.

The Church would not be denied its divine right to burn women, and mounted a Catholic army of the church militant and all-male aristocracy to destroy Joan's army, capture the female general, and burn her in a public place at rush hour.

Men who formed around Joan called themselves the Nazi party and named Joan their leader. No one knew Joan of Arc was actually a six-foot-four, 225-pound man. At the head of his army, Joan was free of the homosexual affairs forced on him by his social-climbing parents. The inevitable happened. Fighting side by side with the sexiest and fiercest women of France, in battle after battle from Hastings to Waterloo, Joan fell in love with one of them. She fell in love with a militant lesbian of an aberrant Christian sect. The young girl warrior was at first seduced by the lovely Joan she had admired and defended and come to love, fighting side by side in the clang and gallop of battle as women.

The first kiss that night they kissed made them sigh. Their ton-

gues touched and they shivered. The night the young militant lesbian grabbed Joan's naked male member vibrating at full tumescence, her mind snapped. A yelp squirted out of her throat. Her
hand clenched in a death grip around Joan's throbbing hardon.
She chanted Hail Mary's and tried to face west, but had lost all
sense of direction. Joan's member shrank out of the grasp of the
only girl Joan of Arc ever loved. If Joan had only known the
Chinese were using compasses at this time, she might have turned
her dead comrade-in-arms' and lover's face to the west. Joan became the elected ruler of the new Franco-Germany created by a
Nazi referendum, and became the first leader of a European
democracy. She pitted her army of freed women, excommuni-
cated nuns, and fed-up ladies of the court against the armies of
the Roman Church.

Joan's parents betrayed her just as she was making advances on
the body of a young lapsed nun who had confessed to years of
desiring intimate contact with a male organ at full tumescence.
The Christian concept of original sin made no sense to Joan of
Arc. She would not accept its intimidating, bullying claim to prior
ownership of himself. Yet the odd notion had a strange grip on the
bodily functions and thought processes, and the perversions
about the mother we Europeans who have been more or less
Christian since possibly the death of Jesus Christ all share. Christ
lived about the time the Han was peaking. Five generations later,
the Three Kingdoms period came on China and the mandate of
heaven was renewed almost daily, for 150 years. By then Chris-
tianity was in its first Dark Age.

Women in the Nazi party wanting more power in the structure
betrayed Joan to his parents, who betrayed him to the church
militant of Rome. They captured him, castrated him in public, in
the middle of Paris, then dressed him in underwear from
Frederick's of Hollywood, and high fashion from Oscar de la
Renta, Gucci shoes, and coochie-coos. Priests of the pope painted
his face. They put false eyelashes on his eyelids, wigged him,
pierced his ears, gave him a nose job, and cut half-moons under
his breasts and slipped in bags of silicon to give him the breast of
a woman. They painted his nails, stockinged his legs. He bled from
the nose job. He bled out of his nose and mouth. He bled from the
half-moons cut under his breasts. He bled from the groin, where

he had been castrated. The faithful of the church chanted and rocked their censers back and forth, back and forth. The army of women had abandoned Joan when there was no doubt about Joan of Arc being a man. The women set the torch to the faggots surrounding Joan's body, and they burned him.

I identify with me, Joan of Arc tells me. He might have been a great-great-grandfather. How could he stand to read the scrawly, wormy, patsy writing of the French? Their first-person pronoun looks like a child's earring. Where are the solid weapons of the Chinese "I" I wonder, and pity the people confined to communicate with each other with an unarmed, uninhabited, passive first-person pronoun to assert themselves with, Joan would think if he were in China now.

Joan suffered for the lack of a proud "I." Humiliated, he defended the honor and equality of French women, and they betrayed him. His parents betrayed him to better their positions in court society. The rituals and traditions of the Roman Church demanded he be burned as a woman. After they realized they had burned a man — no matter that they had burned him as a woman, they had *burned a man* — they ended the burning of women. Thus Joan of Arc lived and died the daughter her parents had always wanted.

How lucky I am to be in China where civilization is whole and healthy. If only my own parents had been more adaptable and not brought all this misery to me. They make me feel so foreign. Their superstitions for every occasion have me dizzy. I like to think Joan of Arc would not have put up with this fanatical fear of life outside the small precinct of the white ghetto. Luckily the Chinese comfort and understand me. They treat me as a human being. The French do not. I come home at night and avoid my parents hunched over their Webster's Dictionary playing Scrabble again, and climb into bed and say, as I say every night, Good night to my ancestor. "You're a good man, Joan of Arc."